"To what do I owe the honor of this visit, Chief Tanner?"

Facing Jeff Rowan was more difficult than Catherine had expected. The old-timers who had worked with her in homicide years ago said she was one of the best interrogators they'd ever met, able to coax a shy pervert into confessing his misdeeds or stare down a serial killer until he spilled his guts. Those skills didn't apply here. She wasn't the one in control.

"I'm not here in an official capacity, Mr. Rowan. I have a personal matter I'd like to discuss with you," Catherine said.

"If you need my help, you must be really desperate," he said. "But let me assure you, anything you tell me is confidential and will remain that way."

"Detective Rowan, I've done you a terrible injustice. I'm sorry."

"You were right the first time. It's Mr. Rowan now. It's also a bit late to be apologizing. Besides, it doesn't matter."

His hostility disheartened her, but what could she expect? Being a cop had been his life and she'd stolen it from him.

Dear Reader,

Writing a continuity series with other authors is a challenge and pleasure, and this WOMEN IN BLUE series is no exception. If you've read the preceding five books (I sure hope you have), you know that the women in those books all attended the Houston Police Academy together. One of their instructors and their greatest inspiration was Catherine Tanner, who has since become a police chief. This last book is her story.

Catherine has endured very trying times in the past year. Her husband, a man of color and the editor of the *Houston Sentinel*, died suddenly last year under suspicious circumstances. Her daughter has renounced the married life and joined a convent. The police department is rife with corruption, and now she's learned that the raw materials for weapons of mass destruction may have gone missing from her city.

Jeff Rowan was a good cop until Catherine fired him for racial profiling. All he wants is the job he loves and his good name back. In the meantime, he's doing quite well as a private investigator. Imagine his surprise when the very person who destroyed his career comes to him for help.

I hope you enjoy the exciting adventures Catherine and Jeff share and the love they develop in the face of what seem to be impossible odds.

I enjoy hearing from readers. You can e-mail me at kncasper@kncasper.com or write me at P.O. Box 61511, San Angelo, TX 76906. Please also visit my Web site at www.kncasper.com.

Sincerely,

K.N. *Casper*

A Mother's Vow
K.N. Casper

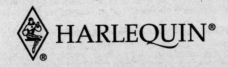

HARLEQUIN®

TORONTO • NEW YORK • LONDON
AMSTERDAM • PARIS • SYDNEY • HAMBURG
STOCKHOLM • ATHENS • TOKYO • MILAN • MADRID
PRAGUE • WARSAW • BUDAPEST • AUCKLAND

ISBN 0-373-71260-X

A MOTHER'S VOW

Copyright © 2005 by Kenneth Casper.

www.eHarlequin.com

Printed in U.S.A.

To my partners in crime and punishment, the authors
of the other five books of WOMEN IN BLUE:
Kay David, Sherry Lewis, Linda Style, Anna Adams and
Roz Denny Fox. It's been a privilege and an inspiration
collaborating with you. Ah, the joys of email, and of
course the telephone, in those dark moments of panic.
Thanks, too, to our editors, Paula Eykelhof, Laura Shin,
Zilla Soriano and Kathleen Scheibling, who brought us
all together and kept us on track.

Books by K.N. Casper

HARLEQUIN SUPERROMANCE
  806—A MAN CALLED JESSE
  839—HER BROTHER'S KEEPER
  884—THE TEXAN
  915—THE MAJOR COMES TO TEXAS
  951—THE FIRST FAMILY OF TEXAS
  978—THE MILLIONAIRE HORSEMAN
1006—THE FIRST DAUGHTER
1022—GIDEON'S BABY
1041—A MOTHER TO HIS CHILDREN
1100—FIRST LOVE, SECOND CHANCE
1134—JACKSON'S GIRLS
1161—THE WOMAN IN THE NEWS
1213—THE TOY BOX

Don't miss any of our special offers. Write to us at the
following address for information on our newest releases.

Harlequin Reader Service
U.S.: 3010 Walden Ave., P.O. Box 1325, Buffalo, NY 14269
Canadian: P.O. Box 609, Fort Erie, Ont. L2A 5X3

CHAPTER ONE

"MOTHER, I THINK this man was murdered."

Catherine Tanner's head snapped up from the police reports she'd been reviewing. She had been only half listening to her daughter's rambling on about her preparations to teach the second grade in the coming school year.

"What are you talking about, dear? Who?"

Kelsey held up that morning's *Houston Sentinel* and pointed to an obituary. "This man, William Summers. I think he may have been murdered."

"William Summers," Catherine muttered, as she took the newspaper. "Is the name supposed to mean something to me?" She scanned the death notice. The sixty-seven-year-old retired teamster had died after languishing in a coma for the past year, following a fall from his roof.

"He's the man who told Dad about the missing uranium."

Evoking the memory of Jordan had a predictable effect. Catherine felt herself pulling in, withdrawing from the conversation.

"What missing uranium?" She felt like the straight

man in a very bad knock-knock joke, parroting everything her daughter said.

"We were having lunch at the deli around the corner from his office when this man came over and asked Dad if he was the editor of the *Sentinel*. When Dad said he was, the guy told him the numbers in that day's newspaper article were wrong. There should have been sixty barrels of yellowcake in the warehouse on the waterfront that the Superfund was cleaning up, not forty."

Yellowcake. The first step in enriching uranium for nuclear reactors—or weapons. Its potential, especially in the wrong hands, made it a commodity that needed very careful guarding and tracking.

"How did Summers know that?" Catherine asked.

"He said he was the warehouse foreman when the place closed in '77 and the last one out the door. He insisted there had been sixty barrels of uranium stored there."

As the man in charge of the city's largest newspaper, Jordan was meticulous about ensuring the accuracy of his information.

"What was your father's reaction?"

"He asked him if he had any proof. Summers claimed he did, so Dad jotted his name, address and telephone number in his pad, thanked him and said he'd be in touch."

Catherine glanced at the picture on her desk, the one taken two years ago when the mayor swore her in as police chief of the country's fourth largest city. The unmistakable pride in the smile on Jordan's face as he stood behind her threatened now to bring fresh tears. She blinked them ruthlessly back, ashamed of her momentary inability to cope with the loss of the man she had loved so deeply.

"Why haven't you ever mentioned this before?"

Kelsey screwed up her mouth. "Because Dad died right after that and I had other things on my mind." She rushed on to add, "Besides, you know I rarely get to read the newspaper anymore. I wouldn't even have thought of it now if I hadn't noticed the obit on your desk and recognized the name."

Catherine cleared her throat. "I still don't understand why you think this man Summers was murdered?"

Kelsey snorted. "Well, let's see. In front of a bunch of people he blows the whistle on a cache of uranium missing from an abandoned warehouse, claims he can prove it, and that very night he falls off his roof. The timing doesn't strike you as a bit strange?"

"But that was a year ago—" Catherine picked up the newspaper and scanned the article again "—and he only died yesterday."

"Without ever regaining consciousness."

"A year-long murder. It's a stretch, Kel."

"Aren't you the one who's always telling me coincidences are in themselves suspect?"

"I'm a cop," Catherine reminded her daughter. "It's my job to be suspicious. But if I investigated every coincidence, I wouldn't have time for anything else." She stood up. "Let's get out of here before someone comes charging in with a reason for me to stay. We haven't had lunch together in ages—"

"Mother, it's only been two weeks."

"Ages," Catherine repeated with a smile, eager to escape the happy dark eyes of Jordan Tanner. Her daughter was all she had left. She snatched her leather shoulder bag from the coat tree by the door and stepped into the crowded, noisy outer office.

"Annette," she said to her administrative assistant, "we're going to lunch. I have my cell phone if you need me, but try not to call unless it's absolutely necessary."

The thirty-something brunette nodded. "Got it, Chief. I won't buzz you unless City Hall is burning down."

"Call the fire department instead," Kelsey said with a wink.

Annette chuckled. "Enjoy your time together."

"In the mood for Chinese?" Catherine asked, as they entered the elevator. She pressed the button for the sixth floor where they could cross over to the high-rise parking garage. "Mei Lu told me about a new place in Chinatown that specializes in Sechuan and Hunan." Lieutenant Mei Lu Ling, who worked in white-collar crime, was one of her protégées from the police academy. "You like spicy."

"Love it."

They took Catherine's black Lexus, which, though a personal vehicle, was fitted with a police radio. She kept it at a very low volume, soft enough not to be a distraction to their conversation, loud enough for her to passively monitor what was going on in her city.

The restaurant on the outskirts of Chinatown was little more than a storefront operation with plain square tables and straight-back wooden chairs.

After being seated by an elderly man with nicotine-stained fingers, a waitress came to their table and greeted them. The large, plastic-coated menus listed a typical variety of choices ranging from hot-and-sour soup to kumquats.

"I'll try the Kung Pao chicken." Kelsey handed the menu to the waitress.

"Crispy duck for me." Catherine didn't share her daughter's or late husband's taste for hot spices.

"Don't you think it's a little extraordinary," Kelsey said, as if their previous conversation hadn't been interrupted, "that the very day Summers hands Dad a blockbuster of a story, he falls off his roof?"

Catherine watched the waitress pour their green tea. She picked up the small handle-less cup and blew over the steaming contents before answering. "It could have been just what it appeared to be, Kel, an accident."

"Yeah, right, Mom. The warehouse is owned by the Rialto Corporation. Doesn't that tell you something?" She removed her chopsticks from their paper wrap and split them apart. "Then the next day Dad mysteriously drops dead."

"Whoa." Catherine's heart did a jolt. "Are you suggesting a connection between your father's death and Summers's?"

Their meals arrived and for a moment the sight and smells of the hot, fragrant food distracted both of them.

"I don't know." Kelsey sampled her spicy chicken and nodded approval. "But the idea's been bothering me for a long time."

Catherine had had her own doubts from the beginning. She'd grilled the cops who had responded to the 911 call, as well as the medics who had tried to resuscitate her husband on the jogging path in Memorial Park. Even questioned the medical examiner who'd signed the autopsy report. She finally backed off when word began to circulate that she was so distraught by her husband's death that it was interfering with her job.

Then six weeks ago, Abby Carlton, another of her former students at the police academy, came to her with a disturbing story she'd recently heard from a homeless drunk by the name of Harvey Stuckey. Catherine had had it looked into, but it turned out to be more delusion than fact. Doubts, however, continued to linger.

She sighed. She'd expected to grow old with Jordan, imagined the two of them sitting in rockers on the front porch in their golden years watching their grandchildren play.

The first glitch in the plan had come when their only child informed them the day after graduating from Rice University that she was joining the School Sisters of Our Lady to become a nun. Glitch? More like a thunderbolt knocking them both off their feet.

"Denial is one of the steps of grieving, Kel," Catherine said now. "It's natural for us to see villains behind misfortunes. But you above all should know we can't second-guess the will of God."

"I'm not second-guessing God," Kelsey snapped, then sucked in her breath when she realized she'd raised her voice. She brushed back her short gray veil in a nervous gesture. "I'm just not sure if Dad's death was the Lord's will or someone else's."

Neither am I, Catherine thought. *Neither am I.*

AFTER DROPPING Kelsey off at the convent, Catherine sat in the car for a minute rubbing the bridge of her nose, her mind rerunning their conversation at lunch. She had a meeting with the Civilian Review Council at one-thirty. That left her just enough time to make a quick stop at home.

She went directly to her bedroom. Even after all these months the scent of her late husband still lingered in his closet. The initial sense of contentment and feeling safe was immediately followed by a sharp stab of loss and loneliness. She reached into a box on the floor and removed the small notepad she had given him as a Christmas present fifteen years ago.

Sitting down on the bed, she brushed her hand over the fine calfskin cover, soft and shiny now from years of handling. His hands had held this object, only minutes before he died. The warmth of the smooth leather against her fingers stirred a connection. She bit her lips. Her throat burned and a sob threatened.

Steeling herself, she opened the pad. She'd only glanced at it when it arrived from the athletic club, along with the rest of the things from Jordan's locker. As she flipped pages, the sight of his handwriting brought fresh tears that blurred her vision. Brushing them away, she read the last entry: William Summers, an address and phone number.

If Kelsey was correct, if the teamster's fall and subsequent death were the direct result of his telling Jordan about missing talcum-fine uranium powder called yellowcake, Jordan's death the next day may not have been an accident, either.

"THIS ISN'T THE FIRST TIME Fontanero has been accused of running a protection racket," said Dieter Walsh, chairman of the Civilian Review Council.

"And he's always been cleared," Paul Radke, Catherine's deputy chief and the head of the Internal Affairs, reminded him.

"Where there's smoke there must be fire," Walsh countered.

"In other words," Radke retorted, "if you make accusations often enough, they must be true." He took a breath. He was a big, imposing man who didn't often lose his temper. "I refuse to railroad a cop with nothing more than a bunch of unproven allegations."

The CRC reviewed all internal investigation recommendations before they went to the police chief's desk. By then, Radke would have mediated any disagreements between IA and the council, so Catherine could be given a consensus report. Today was different. The IA team chief had recommended dropping the charges against Fontanero for lack of evidence, while the CRC, led by Walsh, just as adamantly refused to concur.

The final decision was Catherine's. If she accepted the IA suggestion and the CRC decided to go public, she'd face more press allegations of a police cover-up. If she sided with the CRC, her own people would perceive her as caving in to political pressure.

She'd long suspected Sergeant Fontanero was dirty. His name cropped up too regularly on a host of complaints, but none of the allegations against the twenty-year veteran ever stuck. In Catherine's mind, that meant he was either the unluckiest guy on the force—or the luckiest.

"I understand your concern, Dieter," Radke said. "But we've run sting operations against him twice in the last year and a half. We came up with zip both times."

"Because he gets tipped off. He needs to be kept under surveillance for at least three more months," Walsh persisted.

Radke threw up his hands. "We don't have the manpower for this witch hunt. We have complaints of soliciting sexual favors by—"

"They're probably bogus," Walsh admitted.

A group of prostitutes claimed officers had arrested them only after they'd refused to service them for free. The charge wasn't uncommon, but it was difficult to substantiate, a typical case of *he said, she said.*

"Then there are the allegations of police harassment and planting evidence by those truckers who were found carrying narcotics," Radke went on.

Catherine held up her hand. She'd heard enough. This discussion was going nowhere.

"Fontanero has been officially notified he's the subject of an investigation," she noted, "so right now the chances of a successful sting against him are extremely small, unless he's stupid—" she offered a thin smile "—and that's one thing he's never been accused of. I'm closing this case."

She could feel Walsh's temper mounting.

"That doesn't mean we do nothing." She turned to Radke. "If Fontanero isn't on the take, someone is out to get him, in which case, we owe it to one of our own to look out for him. Let's find out who's behind this campaign to smear him. Also make sure Fontanero and his family are protected." A subtle way of keeping Fontanero under surveillance without officially admitting it.

"You all right with this, Dieter?" she asked.

"It'll have to do, I guess."

In spite of her Solomon-like compromise, Catherine had no illusions that she'd solved the problem. She'd already dismissed more than a dozen bad cops from the force during her tenure, but there were more.

Radke presented three more cases for which the recommendations were unanimous. The charges against one cop were dropped, another received a written reprimand for excessive use of force, and a third, who admitted to taking a bribe, was allowed to resign in lieu of termination.

Finally they came to new business. A suspect in a vehicular homicide had accused Detective Allan Clemson of planting evidence at the scene of a crime while suppressing exculpatory information that would have exonerated him. IA's preliminary findings were that the allegations appeared to have substance. The DA had dropped the charges against the suspect, and the chief of homicide had Clemson on suspension with pay pending further inquiry.

This case was particularly distressing to Catherine. She'd worked with Clemson years ago when she first came to homicide, respected him as an honest cop and learned a lot from him. More recently she'd entrusted him with a very personal matter. Now she had to wonder if her trust had been misplaced. Was he a cop who had simply gone sour, or was he part of the network of corruption that was plaguing her administration?

CHAPTER TWO

"OFFICER PAGER IS here to see you, Chief," Annette announced over the intercom an hour later.

Derek Pager was poster-handsome, standing tall and straight in the doorway. His uniform shirt was precisely tailored to his athletic frame, his pants sharply creased.

He took three steps forward and saluted.

She returned the courtesy. "What can I do for you?"

Catherine had an open-door policy, allowing any member of the department to come to her directly with problems. Doing so could be tricky, however, since it meant bypassing supervisors. Pager, a rookie, wouldn't make the decision lightly. What could possibly be so important that he would break protocol?

"Ma'am, I just ran into a guy in the parking lot. Almost literally, as a matter of fact. His name is Harvey Stuckey."

Catherine pressed her lips together as unpleasant emotions twisted inside her. "Close the door." When he had, she motioned him to one of the visitor chairs across from her. "What about him?"

"He wanted to know why no one was doing anything about Mr. Tanner's death. He said Officer Carlton promised him someone would be looking into it, but he hasn't seen anything in the papers. I tried to tell him there was nothing to look into, that Mr. Tanner died of a heart attack."

Catherine had heard all this before. From Abby Carlton herself. Six weeks ago. Just before she resigned.

"Ma'am, he insists it wasn't a heart attack. He says he saw Mr. Tanner running in the park that day, saw him drinking from a Gatorade bottle, then collapse in violent convulsions."

Her temples throbbed. She didn't want to think about Jordan suffering. Alone.

"I asked him if he was sure," Derek went on, "because heart attack victims don't normally have convulsions, but he was adamant that's what he saw. Claims he wanted to help but didn't know how, so he ran off and called 911."

This version coincided with Abby's, but it contradicted Detective Clemson's later report that Stuckey kept changing his tune and getting details all mixed up. Where was the truth?

"Was anyone with you when Stuckey told you all this?" she asked.

"No, ma'am. I'd just dropped my partner off in front of the building so he could get started on our shift report while I parked. Nobody was around."

"Have you told him or anyone else about it?"

He shook his head. "I thought I ought to bring it directly to you."

"Yes. You did the right thing."

"Ma'am—" he hesitated "—if what he says is true,

that Mr. Tanner had convulsions, perhaps it wasn't a heart attack after all. Maybe he died of something else." He worked his jaw as though he wasn't sure if he dare make his next statement. "He could have been poisoned."

She'd never believed…never wanted to believe that Jordan had just dropped dead. He'd been forty-seven years old. In perfect health. The angry part of grief clamped around her heart. She couldn't fight the will of God, but by God she could find murderers.

"Let's not jump to conclusions," she said, straining to sound objective and professional, even as her stomach churned. "According to the medical examiner, Jordan was badly dehydrated. It's my understanding that heatstroke can cause convulsions leading to a heart attack."

She'd asked questions, lots of them. The answers were all the same. Jordan had suffered a myocardial infarction while running in Memorial Park and had died before medical treatment could reach him.

"Officer Carlton told me about Stuckey, and I had him and his story checked out," she said, not mentioning that it was by Allan Clemson, who'd just been relieved of duty. "It's true the person who called in the 911 was a man, but we have no way of verifying it was Stuckey. Also, in his second interview, which he apparently doesn't remember, he changed his story several times. He's not a reliable witness, Derek, even if he was there."

The young cop nodded, but his assent was wary. "What reason would he have for lying?"

"After you've been in police work as long as I have," she said with a faint smile, "you'll learn that people say and take credit for all sorts of unlikely things. They'll swear they saw and heard things that couldn't possibly have happened, tell you what they think you want to know, even confess to crimes they didn't commit. Sometimes it's to protect friends and loved ones. Sometimes it's to get attention. For a few it's a matter of compulsive behavior."

Derek sat motionless, waiting for her to continue.

"Stuckey's an alcoholic. That brings in a whole new set of problems. Confusion, delusions, mistaken identity."

"Are you saying you're not going to pursue this any further?"

"Of course I will, but in my own way. Meanwhile I'd appreciate it if you'd keep this information to yourself."

"Yes, ma'am."

"Thank you for coming and telling me about this," she said in a tone that signaled the meeting was over.

He rose from the seat and moved to the door with no great haste. He had his hand on the knob when he spun around and blurted out, "How is she?"

Catherine's heart stirred. No question who he was referring to.

"She's fine," Catherine said. "I had lunch with her today." She would have liked to add that Kelsey had asked about him, too, but nothing would be gained by the lie. "She'll be teaching second grade this fall. She's really excited about it."

He nodded, but Catherine could see it wasn't Kelsey's teaching career he was interested in.

"About Mr. Tanner—" he prompted.

"I'll take care of it from here. Thank you."

He wasn't pleased, but this time when he turned around, he opened the door and went out.

Catherine closed her eyes and slumped against the back of her seat. Tears threatened, but she blinked them away. Over the past year she had been accused of obsessing over Jordan's death, and maybe it was true, but how could she not? He and Kelsey had been the center of her life. Now he was gone and Kelsey had all but abandoned her.

Still, she thought she'd come to terms with both issues—until today. First Kelsey suggested her father had been murdered. Then Clemson, the cop she'd counted on to look into the circumstances of his death, turned out to be dishonest, if not corrupt. Now Derek had renewed her doubts.

After referring to her Rolodex, Catherine dialed a number in North Carolina. On the fifth ring, just when she was about to hang up, someone answered.

"Hello?" The voice was breathless, but Catherine recognized it immediately.

"Abby, have I caught you coming or going?"

A split second elapsed. "Catherine? Is that you?" She laughed. "It's so good to hear from you. As to whether I'm coming or going, I haven't made up my mind yet. Thomas has a couple of days off, so we're trying to build a deck. Emphasis on *trying*."

"Sounds like fun."

"Fun, yes. But the sounds coming from Thomas...I don't think I've ever heard him use such descriptive language before. I suspect some of his allusions are anatomically impossible, still, they're interesting."

"*You* sound happy."

"I am, Catherine. Happier than I ever thought I could be. But hey, it's a weekday afternoon. That means you're at work—unless you're sick."

"I'm fine, and yes, I'm at work. I wanted to talk to you again about Harvey Stuckey."

"Is he all right?"

"As far as I know, but I need to recheck some facts."

"Shoot."

"He told you he had seen Jordan drinking from a Gatorade bottle while he was running, that he then collapsed and went into convulsions."

"That's what he said. Have you learned more?"

"Not really. I asked Allan Clemson to look into the matter privately for me. He talked to Stuckey but had a hard time getting straight answers. Stuckey kept changing his story. He also seemed to get the incident mixed up with a 911 call in the same area a couple of days earlier. In that instance, medics were dispatched to help a middle-aged man who was having an epileptic seizure. That guy survived."

Abby made no comment, making Catherine wonder if she had been aware Clemson was dirty.

"He also checked with the coroner's office. They assured him the autopsy had been very meticulously performed and carefully and accurately documented."

"They would, wouldn't they?"

Catherine was a bit taken aback by the anger she heard.

"Abby, how sure are you that this guy Stuckey was telling you the truth?"

"Talk to him yourself, Catherine. Listen to his story

firsthand. Look into his eyes. Guilt has already half killed him for not being able to save Jordan or not coming forward sooner."

She took a breath. "I believe him, Catherine. Otherwise I wouldn't have passed the information on to you. I know how much you loved Jordan and how hard his death has been for you and Kelsey. I would never do anything to add to your pain, unless I was sure it would help in some way."

Catherine sensed the younger woman wanted to say something more, so she held back a response.

"As for Clemson," Abby went on, "word is that he's burned out and having a problem with Brother Bourbon. He probably didn't even search for Stuckey."

Catherine tugged her fingers through her hair. Another disappointment.

"Thank you, Abby, for your candor. Now go back to Thomas and your deck and have fun."

"You'll keep me posted on what happens?"

"I promise." Catherine hung up.

Maybe she was obsessed, but letting matters rest wasn't an option, not if she was to find any rest for herself.

Obviously she couldn't trust the experienced people on the force to probe into the deaths of Jordan and Summers, and she didn't have the time to play detective on her own. That left only one alternative—hire someone else to do it.

Her stomach, already jittery, began to ache. She knew exactly who that person should be. The question was whether he would forgive her enough to accept the job.

Jeff Rowan juggled a paper cup of hot coffee and a bag containing a cinnamon streusel with one hand while he unlocked his office door with the other. Inside, he strode purposefully to the security-control panel and poked in the code to disarm the system.

The headquarters of Rowan, Inc. was small, compact and uncluttered, the way he liked it. He set out his continental breakfast, tapped in his password on the terminal, sipped the steaming hot latte. As his programs loaded, he watched the second, smaller monitor that afforded him surveillance of the strip mall outside his door.

A woman was crossing the parking lot. A mere glance was enough for him to recognize her. Tall, slender and well-dressed. She paused, studied the discreet gold-lettered inscription on the reflective glass window beside his door, set her jaw and entered.

Even with the bright sunlight behind her, casting her features in gray shadow, he could feel her eyes focusing on him. He climbed to his feet.

"Come in." He circled the corner of the desk.

She let the tinted glass door swing closed behind her. Though she was at least ten feet from him, he caught her scent—or thought he did—a subtle, elusive, effervescent trace of flowers or incense.

"To what do I owe the honor of this visit, Chief Tanner? I hope I haven't broken any city ordinances." He could tell by the quick flash of discomfort in her blue eyes that she caught his words' sarcastic edge.

"I'm not here in an official capacity, Mr. Rowan."

He swung his arm and motioned her to take the visitor's chair in front of his desk.

"Sit down. Please. I'm sorry I don't have coffee to offer you, but since I can't compete with Starbucks, I don't try. I do have cold soft drinks or juice, if you'd like."

"Nothing, thanks." She planted herself in the leather-upholstered chair and tugged at the hem of her blue skirt as she crossed her legs. Nice legs, he couldn't help noticing. Long and shapely. Annoyed by the distraction, he resumed his seat. She was trying very hard to conceal her nervousness, but he'd observed too many clients in that spot not to recognize the symptoms.

She scanned the long, narrow room with an appraising glance. He tried to see it through her eyes. The decor was Spartan. Beige-painted walls. Minimal furniture. All of it quality.

"You've done well."

He said nothing, though he couldn't deny a rush of pride that she approved. Not that he should care what she thought. Two minutes earlier, before she'd arrived, he wouldn't have imagined he could. The modest success he had achieved was his own, no one else's. In a way she'd been its cause, but he wasn't about to give her any credit for it.

She lowered her gaze, joined her fingers, before addressing him again. The old-timers who had worked with her in homicide years ago said she was one of the best interrogators they'd ever met, able to coax a shy pervert to confess his misdeeds or stare down a serial killer into spilling his guts. Those skills didn't apply here. She wasn't the one in control.

"I have a personal matter I'd like to discuss with you."

"I'm honored that you would seek my advice."

"That's the second time you've referred to me honoring you."

"What do you expect me to say?" he asked. "That I'm pleased to see you?"

"No," she muttered. "Under the circumstances, I don't imagine you are."

CHAPTER THREE

LAST YEAR THERE had been a series of convenience store holdups that resulted in two killings. The three culprits had left no finger- or footprints to help identify them. None of the bystanders had possessed the presence of mind to get license-plate numbers. The bad guys had all worn masks and gloves and had spoken very little, so those present couldn't state whether they were white, black, Hispanic or Asian, or even if they had accents. Only that they were probably all male.

Jeff had been in charge of the homicide investigations and had interviewed witnesses. Two women described a smell from the men who'd held knives to their throats. Someone else noted that all the hoodlums wore a particular brand of running shoe with the laces tied in an unusual manner.

Based on these scant details—the scent of a particular hair product being the primary one—Jeff hypothesized that the perpetrators were black and members of a street gang. A reporter from one of the local television stations got wind of the story and Jeff found himself crucified on the evening news as a racist cop. Catherine researched the matter and concluded Jeff's assessment was reasonable. It later proved to be true.

Before she could publicly defend him, however, another story broke which purported to demonstrate a pattern of racial prejudice in Rowan's record of arrests. In ten of his last twelve cases he'd pinned the blame on black suspects, even though the evidence against them was tenuous.

That wouldn't have been so bad if seven of the ten blacks he arrested hadn't later been released, either by the District Attorney's office for lack of sufficient evidence, or because the state failed to prove its case in court. In six of those seven cases, the evidence in police custody mysteriously disappeared or was found to have been tampered with. His accusers proclaimed it had never existed, that it had been manufactured or was planted.

Jeff was placed on indefinite suspension and Internal Affairs was called in. He and his fellow officers were questioned at length regarding their methods and rationale in handling cases. The unanimous recommendation by IA and the Civilian Review Council was that he be terminated. Which was what Catherine had done.

Facing Jeff Rowan now was more difficult than she had expected. She'd interviewed bereaved parents, gone toe-to-toe with brutal killers, faced down angry mobs and ambitious politicians, but the vibes she was getting from this man unsettled her in a way she didn't understand. He had reason to despise her, but that didn't explain her reaction to him, her impulse to get up and walk out.

"If you need my help, you must be really desperate," he said. "But let me assure you anything you tell me is confidential and will remain that way."

He put the plastic top back on his nearly full coffee

cup, pushed aside the piece of pastry, then, clasping the arms of his chair, rocked back. Waiting.

"Detective Rowan, I've done you a terrible injustice. I'm sorry."

"You were right the first time," he said. "It's *Mr.* Rowan now. It's also a bit late to be apologizing. Besides, it doesn't matter."

"It matters. To both of us."

His hostility disheartened her, but what could she expect? Being a cop had been his life and she'd stolen it from him. She met his eyes. "I made a series of mistakes last year. Firing you was just one of them."

"It's nice to know you didn't single me out for special treatment."

She studied him, his even features, his cleft chin. He had thick brown hair, neatly trimmed, and hazel-green eyes. She knew from reviewing his records that he was divorced. No children. And he was six years her junior, which made him thirty-nine. Despite the calorie-rich pastry and frothy coffee sitting on the edge of his desk, he appeared quite fit. Deep chest. Broad shoulders. His short-sleeved white shirt exposed thick biceps and sinewy forearms. He probably pumped iron three times a week in a gym somewhere.

"I wish I could rectify some of those errors of judgment," she said.

He raised his eyebrows. "So you're not here to tell me my appeal has been adjudicated and you're offering to take me back on the force?" When she didn't respond, he chuckled. "I guess not." Their eyes met, locked. "Now, why are you here?"

"Do you read the obituaries?"

"They're sometimes the first clue to the whereabouts of missing persons," he said.

"Then you know two days ago a man by the name of William Summers passed away after being in a coma for over a year."

"Didn't the paper also mention that he'd fallen off his roof?"

"Correct. And the day after Summers's accident my husband died while out running in Memorial Park."

Jeff Rowan knew Jordan Tanner only by reputation. The elder son of a prominent and very wealthy African-American family. Catherine's marriage to a man of color had no doubt been a titillating scandal twenty-five years ago and difficult socially. Such unions were more accepted these days and didn't raise the eyebrows or rouse the rancor they once had, but heads still turned at the sight of an attractive blonde on the arm of a black man.

Jordan had taken over as editor of the *Houston Sentinel,* the city's largest newspaper, some ten years ago. From Jeff's perspective, Jordan had been fair and honest in dealing with issues and personalities. He had clear, consistent standards of right and wrong and didn't hesitate to voice them. Jeff admired those qualities.

"He suffered a heart attack, as I recall. I'm sorry."

She nodded, and he could see sadness wash over her features.

"You're implying a relationship between the two events," he said. "Why?"

"The day Summers had his fall, he approached my husband in a restaurant and told him sixty, not forty, barrels of yellowcake had been left behind in the Rialto warehouse the Superfund was getting ready to clean up."

"What's this yellowcake?"

"Uranium ore reduced to powder form."

"How did Summers know how much of it there was?"

"He claimed to be the last person out of the building when it was abandoned in the late seventies. My husband was a thorough and meticulous man, Mr. Rowan. He didn't often get his facts wrong." She retrieved the bag she'd placed on the floor beside the chair and removed a worn, leather-covered notebook. Thumbing to the last entry, she handed it across the desk to Jeff.

"He jotted down Summers's address and telephone number," she explained, "and promised to look into the matter further, but—"

"But he died before he got a chance."

She nodded.

Jeff memorized the information and returned the pad. "You think the two events are related."

"I don't put much faith in coincidences."

He could attest to that.

"I don't like coincidences, either," he said, "but that still doesn't answer my question. Why are you here?"

"I checked the accident report this afternoon. The first officer on the scene after Summers took his fall was Eddie Fontanero."

She'd aimed her arrow true. Fontanero was the person who had leaked the "racist" story to the press. Over the years, Jeff had had several run-ins with the patrolman, whom he considered a bigot with a chip on his shoulder, but who, because he was Hispanic, got away with attitudes and statements his Anglo counterparts, like Jeff, could not.

Fontanero had been promoted to sergeant at a time when preference was given to ethnic minorities. He'd had a reputation as a lousy cop then, and as far as Jeff was concerned, he still was, but the officer knew how to play the game. He ingratiated himself with the right people on his beat, got attaboys for rescuing little girls' tree-climbing kittens and little boys' lost puppies and knew how to smile into the camera. As a result, politics and politicians saved his butt on more serious matters. That he had succeeded in getting Jeff thrown off the force was only one example. Giving Eddie his comeuppance by proving he had screwed up on a call and perhaps helped cover up a felony, was enticing.

"I've moved on," Jeff said.

Catherine's tight smile congratulated him for taking the high road, while telling him she didn't believe it. She was right, of course. He hadn't forgotten Fontanero's role in ruining his career, nor was he magnanimous enough to forgive.

"I need someone to probe the death of Summers," she continued, "as well as his contention that twenty barrels of yellowcake were missing from the warehouse. I also want you to look into Jordan's death."

She had a whole department at her disposal, but Jeff appreciated her predicament. According to his friends on the force she'd already asked so many questions she had developed a reputation for being fixated on the loss of her husband. She couldn't afford to spend more police resources checking out yet another false lead without becoming a laughingstock and compromising her authority.

The problem went even deeper than that, though. If she was correct about this missing yellowcake, she was dealing with more than simple theft. There could be only one group of people interested in black-market uranium. Terrorists. Under those circumstances she couldn't afford to have leaks from her department putting them on the alert.

"You seriously think your husband might have been murdered?"

The desolation he'd glimpsed earlier returned to her eyes. "I don't know. I have new unsubstantiated information from an unreliable source that suggests his death didn't happen the way it was reported."

"What information? What source?"

"Do you remember Abby Carlton? She worked in the crime intervention unit—"

"I heard she quit to follow that Delta Force guy she was involved with."

"They're married now, living in North Carolina. Just before she left six weeks ago, she dropped by my office to say goodbye and to pass on something she'd just heard from a drunk she had been trying to rehabilitate. He claimed he was the one who called 911."

"He didn't identify himself on the phone?"

She shook her head. "The call, like so many, was anonymous. Anyway, this guy, Harvey Stuckey, told Abby he'd been in Memorial Park the day Jordan died and had seen him running and drinking from a Gatorade bottle. A little while later, at a spot where the path doubles back, he saw Jordan again, except this time he was staggering, then he collapsed. He said Jordan went into convulsions. The guy ran to call 911. When he got back Jordan was dead and the bottle was gone."

"That happened last year and he didn't tell anyone about it until six weeks ago? Why did he wait so long to come forward?"

"He's homeless. Abby picked him up in a bar fight and tried to get him help. It was in the course of one of their conversations, that he blurted this information out. She wanted him to come in and make an official statement, but of course he wouldn't."

"Abby believed him?"

Catherine nodded. "I asked Allan Clemson to track him down for me. The story Stuckey apparently told this time didn't match his earlier version."

Jeff knew Clemson. He'd been a good cop once, but maybe he'd seen too many corpses, too many battered and abused women and children, watched too many sleazebags and perverts with slick lawyers walk out the courthouse door. Cops tried to compartmentalize, but sometimes it didn't work. Sometimes the only way to cope with the ghosts who inhabited those hidden compartments was to drown them with alcohol, or give in to the cynicism that perpetually peeked around the corner and beckoned. Jeff wasn't sure what had happened to Clemson, but he knew he wasn't the cop he'd once been.

"But you're still not convinced," he said.

"I'm not even sure he talked to the man."

Catherine gazed off into space before returning her

focus on him. "I loved my husband, Jeff." So she was addressing him by his first name now. "Losing him was the greatest tragedy of my life. I can accept his death if it was from natural causes. I can and will move on. But I have to know the truth. If Jordan was murdered, I want the person who stole him from me brought to justice."

Her eyes stayed on him, intense and determined. He didn't doubt her resolve or the anguish he read in their depths.

"People would say my feelings about Fontanero constitute a conflict of interest," he said. "That it will taint my objectivity, turn my investigation into a vendetta. Maybe in this case an accusation of prejudice would be valid."

She shook her head. "You're not a racist, and since you do have a vested interest in the outcome of this investigation, I'm confident you'll be extra careful in drawing any conclusions or making any accusations."

She was manipulating him. The question was whether she was lying in order to set him up for another fall. If so, she was the best liar he'd ever run across, and he'd dealt with quite a few.

"I didn't trust my instincts when I fired you," she said. "I took the easy way out and accepted the recommendation of IA and the CRC. There isn't any excuse for what I did. My only defense is a selfish one, that I'd just lost my husband and our daughter had rejected the kind of life we'd envisioned for her. I'm not proud of that, nor is any of it justification for what I did to you."

The strange part was that somewhere inside him Jeff had understood that at the time. It didn't make him any happier, didn't mitigate the humiliation of being disgraced in the eyes of his peers. Perhaps because he recognized she was hurting so much in her private life, he hadn't pursued legal action against her personally when he had sued the Houston Police Department, though his lawyer had insisted he had a good chance of winning. Instead he'd convinced himself all he wanted was to clear his name and get on with his life. But an ugly anger was still shifting inside him, as if he had fled a fight or left a job unfinished.

He couldn't imagine what good would come from taking this case. Constant reminders of the injustice she'd done to him wouldn't help.

"Whatever your fees are," she said, "I'll pay double. Knowing the truth is important to me."

He'd be crazy to take on this job, insane to make himself vulnerable to this woman who'd already admitted shafting him. What did he care if her old man had been murdered? He didn't owe Jordan Tanner or his widow a damn thing.

On the other hand, there was that little matter of twenty barrels of uranium, which, in the wrong hands, could wreak the kind of havoc that would make 9/11 seem like a footnote in history.

"I sometimes give clients discounts, but I don't double fees," he heard himself say.

"Then you'll take the job?" She sounded so hopeful, so relieved, he didn't have the heart to turn her down, or maybe he didn't want to.

"I'll think about it. No promises."

CHAPTER FOUR

JEFF SAT for several minutes, contemplating his visitor. She'd changed his life last year when she'd thrown him off the force. Now she wanted him to help her.

Why should he? There wasn't much she could do for him in return. She couldn't reinstate him. That was in the hands of the board of review. His appeal had been pending for months, thanks to the interminable dickering of lawyers and bureaucrats.

He'd loved being a cop. But what he wanted more than anything was to get his good name back.

His coffee was cold. He poured it into a ceramic mug and zapped it in his small microwave, broke off a piece of the pastry and popped it in his mouth. He still wasn't sure why she'd chosen him for the job, but he found himself fascinated by it, by her.

Not all his old friends had abandoned him. He picked up the phone and called Maurice Blalock, a member of the city planning commission.

"I was wondering how the cleanup was going down on channel row," he said.

"A new client, huh." Blalock chuckled. "Okay, I won't ask who it is, because you wouldn't tell me anyway. What do you want to know?"

"Just general information. How's it progressing? I haven't seen much in the papers or on TV lately."

"Because there isn't much to tell. Nothing particularly exciting about asbestos abatement and carting off rotten lumber."

"How about toxic waste removal?"

"Yeah, the Environmental Protection Agency has had fun with that. Leaky drums all over the place."

"Heard they found uranium stored there, too."

"Yep, forty barrels of it. Is that what you're interested in? The yellowcake?"

"Just curious. I didn't even know we had any of that stuff around here."

"Goes back to the late seventies."

"What are they planning to do with the real estate now?"

"Ah, now I'm beginning to see where you're heading. Somebody wants in on the action, huh? Well, I'm afraid they're too late. There's a consortium already formed to redevelop the area. A loading facility for shipping containers."

Jeff decided he might as well reinforce Blalock's mistake. "Who's in it?"

"Rialto is the prime contractor." Blalock named half a dozen other large companies involved in construction, import, export and shipping.

"Didn't Buster Rialto own some of the warehouses that were torn down?"

"Yep. He uses the logic that since the Superfund spent most of its money cleaning up his facilities, it gives him the right to be the controlling shareholder.

Doesn't pass the giggle test for me, but I guess his financial largesse struck the funny bone of enough members of city council, because it approved the contract. Of course, you didn't hear that from me."

"Any proof?"

Blalock's chuckle was his only response.

"Thanks," Jeff said. "Give my best to Elsie."

"You need to stop by one of these days. She always enjoys seeing you, and I'd welcome the male company."

Jeff laughed. Blalock had six daughters. And his mother-in-law lived with them.

"You're on. I'll give you a call."

After hanging up, Jeff turned to his computer and called up the *Houston Sentinel* Web site. He began with the obituary of William Summers published two days earlier, then found the brief news item the previous year that reported his fall. Except for a short announcement the next day that he was in a coma, his condition critical, there was no follow-up on the story.

Jeff sat back and stared at the screen, his mind trying to sort through possibilities. Could William Summers have been shoved off his roof simply because he'd told the editor of the city's major newspaper that there was more uranium in a warehouse than had been reported? And could Jordan Tanner have been murdered because a guy in a delicatessen said he'd gotten a number wrong?

THE SOUND OF THE DOORBELL had Catherine checking the clock on the kitchen wall. Seven-forty-five. Jeff had called about half an hour ago and asked to come over.

She took that as a good sign, but he wasn't due for another fifteen minutes.

Pressing the start button on the coffeemaker, she went to the front door. The person she saw through the glass panel wasn't Jeff.

Frowning, she swung the door wide.

"Derek, what brings you here?" Under other circumstances she would have been delighted to see him, but his showing up unannounced right now was inconvenient. And after his visit to her office yesterday, she had an inkling of why he was here.

"Mrs....er...Chief, I'd like to talk to you about something."

"Come in."

He stepped inside. She closed the door behind him, but didn't invite him into the living room or offer a cup of the coffee they could smell brewing.

"What can I do for you?" she asked.

"About what Stuckey said...I'd like to help."

"I appreciate that, Derek, but there's nothing you can do. If I need your assistance, I'll let you know." She regretted sounding cold and ungrateful, but he was a rookie still in his probationary period. She made a move to open the door for him, but he didn't budge.

"Mrs. Tanner, your husband was the closest I've ever had to a father. If what Stuckey said is true, if Mr. Tanner met with foul play... If he was...murdered, I want to help catch the guy who did it."

Catherine was touched by the young man's emotion and the sincerity of it.

"He thought very highly of you, too, Derek. He was

looking forward to the day when he'd be able to call you son." She stopped. No use going down that path. "I'm very grateful for your bringing Stuckey's information to me directly and your discretion in keeping it to yourself. I assure you I'm pursuing it, but in my own way."

He nodded. "Yes, ma'am. But I'd still like to help. I need to do something."

"I have an experienced investigator looking into the matter. I can assure you, Derek, if there's anything behind Stuckey's rant, we'll get to the bottom of it."

The way the young man lowered his head and worked his lips indicated he wasn't satisfied with her response, but she knew he was disciplined enough not to question it.

The clock struck eight.

"Derek, I don't mean to be impolite, but I have a meeting scheduled—"

The doorbell chimed. Too late.

JEFF STOOD on the step and noted the well-tended flower beds bordering the path and driveway. Catherine's house, a block from Memorial Park, was unlike the others in the upscale neighborhood. Instead of antebellum Greek revival, Victorian or Tudor, the single-story structure was long and angular, reminiscent of the prairie style of Frank Lloyd Wright. An espalier covered a blank wall to his right. A tinted plate-glass window balanced it on the left.

Class, he thought, and a lot of money.

The door opened. He spun around to face it.

Gorgeous was the first word that came to mind.

"Right on time," she said, yet there was an uneasiness in her blue eyes that suggested his arrival had taken her by surprise.

The Houston Chief of Police was wearing baggy jeans and a pale-blue blouse with small ruffles at the collar and short sleeves. Her shoulder-length blond hair was tied back with a matching ribbon, exposing small gold studs in her ears. Her complexion was peaches and cream. Her eyes a soft, expressive blue. And her mouth…could make a man wet his lips and stare.

Then Jeff spied the lanky black man standing behind her. The guy didn't appear to be much over twenty. He shifted to the side to get a better perspective on Jeff.

"You're—" his forehead wrinkled "—the detective who was dismissed last year for—"

"Jeff Rowan," Catherine said, cutting him off, "this is Derek Pager, a new officer on the force." She stood aside for Jeff to enter. "He was just leaving."

"He's the guy you've got investigating Mr. Tanner's death?" Pager asked her.

Catherine stared in shock at the rookie's impertinence. Pager had the good sense to look away. "I'm sorry. I was out of line. It's just that—"

"Mind telling me what's going on here?" Jeff stepped out of the oppressive humidity into the square, high-ceilinged foyer. Her cheeks hollowed, Catherine closed the door behind him.

"Earlier today Officer Pager ran into the witness I told you about," she said, "the one who alleges he saw Jordan drink from a Gatorade bottle and die of convulsions."

"If Mr. Tanner was murdered," the young cop said forcefully, "I want to help find the killer."

"Has the chief asked for your assistance?"

He shifted his eyes.

"It's not your call," Jeff told him.

"Hear me out. Please," Derek implored. "I can do some of your legwork. I'll find Stuckey so you can talk to him yourself."

"How long have you been on the force?" Jeff asked.

"Seven months."

"I've been tracking people down for more than fifteen years."

"Then I can learn from you."

Jeff glanced at Catherine and thought he saw her lips twitch.

"And I'm an expert with computers," Derek added.

"Good for you," Jeff said. "I'm no slouch with them myself."

"But you're not authorized to use the department's files and database. You may be clever enough to hack into the system, *Mr.* Rowan, but if you do, you'll be breaking the law. Anything you find won't be admissible in court. Whereas I have legal access."

Jeff shook his head. "Passing official police information on to me would violate department regulations. Not only will it end your career, but you could find yourself doing time in a federal prison. Trust me, you don't want to go there."

"I won't have to if the chief details me to work with you on special assignment."

Catherine did indeed have the power to protect him.

The kid was not only gutsy, he was smart. Jeff had to give him that.

She shut her eyes and shook her head. "It's out of the question, Derek. I appreciate the offer, but I can't let you get involved." She opened the door for him. "Thank you for coming."

Taking a deep breath, he crossed the threshold, then spun around to face them both.

"I'm not going to quit," he said, his tone firm and just short of defiant.

Catherine closed the door behind him, turned and led Jeff through the living room, which was large and open, its ceiling crisscrossed with dark beams. Beyond the grand piano was an immense window that looked out on a colorful garden, lush and dense as a rain forest.

As they were walking through the dining room to the kitchen, he said, "I don't know too many rookies who would have the nerve to come to the home of the chief of police and challenge her. What made him think he had the right—"

"We're old friends. He and my daughter went to college together. They were practically engaged."

"What happened?"

She poured two mugs of coffee. "I wish I knew. They seemed perfectly happy with each other, then one day she announced she was becoming a nun."

"Just like that." He snapped his fingers.

She nodded unhappily. "Just like that."

The coffee was first rate. "How did he explain it?"

"He couldn't. In fact, he seemed as baffled by her decision as Jordan and I were."

She looked so fragile and vulnerable as she curled her hands around her mug and leaned against the counter, it made him want to fold her in his arms and comfort her. The urge astonished him. There were so many reasons for him not to sympathize with this woman. But they were logical. What he was feeling had nothing to do with his brain.

"I understand you not wanting to use Derek," she said. "He's smart and energetic, but he's also young and inexperienced. There is someone else who can help you, though. Did you know Risa Taylor?"

"Not personally. She was accused last year of shooting her partner but was eventually cleared."

Catherine nodded. "She knows the streets, has a lot of contacts. I'll ask her to beat the bushes for Stuckey and report to me directly if she finds him."

Jeff would have preferred her reporting to him, but under the circumstances this was probably a better plan. The fewer people who knew he was involved the better.

He leaned against the adjacent counter and crossed his legs at the ankles.

"I did some checking this afternoon," he said. "You were right. Clemson's partner told me he never made a serious effort to track down Stuckey. He apparently made up the report he gave you, except for the part about talking to the M.E.'s office. That only took a telephone call."

"He used to be a good cop. What happened?"

He shrugged. "He started to fall apart a couple of years ago after he went through a messy divorce. It wasn't his first. He seemed to bounce back from it well enough, but his partner told me he saw him with Fontanero a few weeks ago. At a bar."

"Fontanero again," Catherine said.

"He keeps turning up like a bent coin."

She flashed a smile. "So you are going to take on this case?"

Let her think it was because of Fontanero. He nodded. "Yeah, I'll take it on."

CHAPTER FIVE

THE NEXT MORNING Jeff put the finishing touches on a report concerning the mysterious disappearance of inventory from a computer warehouse. The elderly man who had started out selling electrical equipment over forty years ago wouldn't be pleased to learn his grandson was stealing from him, or that he was doing so to feed a drug habit. Jeff suspected the old guy, like many of his clients, already knew the truth; he just wanted independent confirmation, while hoping he was wrong.

Jeff signed the cover letter he'd just printed out and wondered if the story would have a happy ending. He entered a note in his computer scheduling program to call in six months for a progress report.

Glancing at the surveillance monitor, he saw a street kid approaching. The black teenager wore a nylon skull cap and a pair of gold earrings, a shiny gray shirt that hung down to his elbows and mid-thigh and a pair of faded baggy gray pants that dragged under his scuffed running shoes. A silver chain dangled from his neck. Looking around, the teenager moved to Jeff's door, then pushed his way in with a hostile shove.

Jeff rose from his chair, not sure what to expect but

prepared for the physical confrontation the dude's attitude implied. The guy stared at him until the door closed behind him.

"Don't recognize me, huh?"

The voice did it. "Pager?"

Derek smiled, showing even white teeth. "The same."

Jeff relaxed his tensed muscles and laughed. "Man, you got me."

"I brought some information I thought you might find useful."

"I told you I don't need or want your help."

"Maybe you ought to see what I've got before you reject it."

Jeff made no move to take the manila envelope Pager produced from under his shirt. With a shrug, the rookie let it fall onto the desk. Cocky, he plopped into the visitor's chair and extended his long legs. After a good two minutes of silence, he broke the stalemate.

"I'm sorry you don't want my help," he said, "but I can live with it. I'm more concerned that you're willing to cheat your client." Pager pulled his feet under him, rose and started for the door, then turned back. "I know what some people on the force say about you, and I admit I was surprised when you showed up at Chief Tanner's house. But she hired you, so there must be a reason."

Jeff wasn't sure he liked the tone or the vague innuendo that he and Catherine might share a relationship beyond the purely professional. Or was a secret wish causing him to make too much of an innocent remark. In other circumstances he might find her attractive. No, he corrected himself. He did find her attractive. In other circumstances he might do something about it, but not under these.

"She fired you last year for racial profiling," Pager said. "So tell me, are you a racist?"

Strange, no one had ever asked him that question before. Not the people who accused him of prejudice or the people who seemed to think it was perfectly natural to discriminate. Even Catherine hadn't asked it. In spite of the rookie's insolence, Jeff realized he liked the brash young man.

"Because, if you are, I can live with that, too," Pager continued. "You wouldn't be the first bigot I've had to deal with. I'm not interested in redeeming you or making you like me. All I want is to help Mrs. Tanner find out if her husband was murdered, and if he was, to catch the son of a bitch responsible."

Yesterday, after leaving Catherine's house, Jeff had done a preliminary background check on Pager. One of eight children of a single mom, he'd earned both athletic and scholastic scholarships to Rice University, where he'd broken several school records in track and field while majoring in electrical engineering. He'd also graduated *summa cum laude*.

Instead of moving on to the computer world where his credentials could have reaped him big bucks, however, he'd joined the Houston Police Department, finishing the academy at the top of his class. On the force he had a reputation for being polite and quiet, a bit intense, but he could also handle himself physically and had never backed down from a fight. Those qualities had earned him respect, but they'd also gained him a few enemies.

Jeff chuckled to himself and shook his head. "And your long-term goals?"

"To be the best man I can."

Not the best *cop,* but the best *man.* An interesting choice of words, yet Jeff wasn't completely surprised by it.

"For the record," he said, "I am not a racist. My objection to bringing you in on this job is essentially defensive. You're an unknown quantity. I can control what I do, but I can't control what you do. That makes me vulnerable, which is why I work alone."

"Then you have a problem," Pager said with a smile. "Jordan Tanner meant a lot to me, Mr. Rowan. I can't ignore doubts about his death just because it's inconvenient for you. I'll try to stay out of your way, but I can't promise that my investigation won't collide with yours."

"Chief Tanner isn't going to appreciate your meddling in her private affairs."

"She'll get over it when I help her find her husband's killer." He started to turn for the door again, but once more stopped. "That folder, by the way, is yours. A gift. Do with it what you like."

"Wait," Jeff said, unable to resist reaching for it. "What is it?"

Pager's smile resembled a smirk. "Jordan Tanner's last editorial. In it he corrects his previous misinformation and demands a full investigation into the twenty missing barrels of yellowcake, pointing out that it would be worth a great deal to terrorists. He also calls whoever sold it a traitor to his country and a threat to world peace."

"I don't remember ever seeing that editorial, and I read the paper every day."

"It was never published. Someone deleted it from his computer files after he died."

It was difficult keeping his face neutral. "How did you get it?"

"I told you I was good with computers. Some people say I'm a genius." Pager's expression was one of amusement now. "Deleting a file doesn't erase it. It only strips it of its title. I admit to being lucky with this one. Normally after so long the contents of a deleted file would have been overwritten, which does destroy it. Jordan Tanner was proficient with computers. He had an extra-large hard drive installed on his terminal, which he partitioned. His brother Tyrone who took over from him doesn't use a tenth of its capacity."

"How do you know all this?"

"I worked part-time at the *Sentinel* in college. I still have a few friends there. It's common knowledge baby brother prefers to dictate his editorials and let his secretary manipulate the keyboard."

Except Jeff hadn't known that. It was also apparent that Pager didn't think highly of Jordan's younger brother. "You think Tyrone deleted the file from the desktop?"

"Inconclusive." He placed his large hands on the back of the chair he'd vacated. "I imagine several people have access to the editor's computer. His secretary and of course the system administrator who changed permissions and passwords when Tyrone took over." He stepped away from the chair.

"Hang on," Jeff said to halt his retreat. "Are you serious about conducting your own investigation?"

"Yes, Mr. Rowan, I am."

"You're a damn fool."

Pager grinned. "I've been called that before, and by people who know me a lot better than you do. It hasn't stopped me in the past."

"I'm in charge. You take your orders from me."

"I'm a great admirer of age and wisdom."

Jeff tried not to smile, but it was impossible. "If we're going to work together, you can stop with the Mr. Rowan business. My name is Jeff."

The other man reached across the desk with an outstretched hand. "Call me Derek."

SATURDAY AFTERNOON Kelsey let herself in the back door of the house she'd grown up in.

"Hi, honey." Catherine was setting cups and saucers on a brass-trimmed wooden tray. An open tin of assorted biscotti sat beside it, while the gurgling coffeemaker on the side counter filled the room with an enticing aroma.

Kelsey kissed her mother on the cheek and caught a whiff of scent, something Catherine didn't normally use, because it would detract from her professional image.

"Cologne?"

"It's Saturday afternoon and I'm off duty," her mother said defensively.

Getting together with a hired detective struck Kelsey

as a business meeting, not a social one. Or maybe her mother simply wanted to feel like a woman for a change, instead of a police chief. Since she'd been widowed, she'd buried herself in her work.

"Four cups?" Kelsey snagged one of the cookies. "Who else is coming besides this private investigator you want me to talk to? I still don't understand why. I've told you everything I know."

"Derek will be joining us. He should be here in a minute."

A tiny shiver gripped Kelsey's stomach. "Derek? What has he got to do with this?"

"He's helping out," Catherine replied. "Get me that glass serving dish, will you, please?"

"But…" Flustered, Kelsey gaped for a moment before reaching into an overhead cabinet and removing the plate. She put it on the counter beside the tray. "You said you were hiring a private detective to investigate Dad's death, that you couldn't trust people on the force."

Her mother opened a drawer, removed a round paper doily which she placed on the dish and started arranging biscotti on it. "Derek is different. I know I can trust him."

Kelsey wanted to argue the point, but she wasn't sure how she could without giving too much away. Her mother thought the sun rose and set on Derek Pager; her dad had, too.

The doorbell rang.

"That's him now. Would you answer it, please?" Catherine asked. "I'll bring the refreshments."

Kelsey didn't move. "When is that other guy supposed to get here?"

"His name is Jeff Rowan. In a few minutes. He was very punctual when he was here Thursday." Her lips twitched. "And Derek is always a few minutes early."

The bell sounded again.

"Go ahead." Catherine began refilling the sugar bowl from the canister on the counter. "I'll be in as soon as the coffee is ready."

Kelsey wasn't fooled. Her mother wanted to give them private time together. As if it would make any difference. The clock said the P.I. was due in less than three minutes, hardly sufficient time to resolve the irresolvable. She was tempted to suggest that she take the tray while her mother greeted her guests.

The bell rang a third time.

"Please, don't keep him waiting, honey," her mother said, as she poured half-and-half into the creamer.

Unhappy at the prospect of having to deal with the man she'd rejected, Kelsey nonetheless obeyed. Her pulse, already up by the time she reached the door, accelerated another notch when she opened it. He stood before her, tall and very male, in buff-colored Dockers and an electric-blue knit Polo shirt. His toothy smile made her heartbeat race even more.

"Hi, Kelsey." He slipped into the foyer quickly, as if he was afraid she might slam the door in his face. "It's good to see you."

She was unsure of what to do next. Suppose he placed his hands on her shoulders and bent to give her a kiss? The thought brought heat to her face and a jolt of panic.

"How have you been?" he asked, jamming his hands in his pockets. "You look well."

"Mom is bringing coffee to the living room."

"Oh, let me give her a hand."

Resentment percolated as she realized she was following him through the dining room. He'd spent many hours here when they were in college together.

"Hi, Mrs. Tanner," he said as he entered the kitchen. "Can I help you with that?"

Catherine had just gripped the handles of the loaded tray. "Thank you." She stepped back and let him take it.

"I wish you'd told me he was going to be here," Kelsey muttered to her mother after Derek had passed through the swinging door to the dining room on his way to the living room.

"Would you have come if I had?"

"No," Kelsey said emphatically.

Catherine stared at her. "I don't understand what's going on between you two because you haven't deigned to enlighten me, so you'll have to forgive me if my decisions don't meet your expectations." She held her daughter with a sharp glare. "This meeting is about your father's death. If you don't want to be here, you're free to leave. If you stay, I expect you to be civil."

Her mother didn't often lecture this way, so Kelsey knew she was in the doghouse. Which added another layer of guilt to a pile that was already insurmountable. She'd tried a few times to explain what had happened, why she'd chosen the life she had, but she was never able to bring herself to say the words. The word.

"I'll hang around for a while."

They entered the living room as Derek was placing

the tray on the coffee table. His bent posture emphasized the narrowness of his hips, the sweeping V of his broad back. Kelsey looked away.

Relief swept over her when the doorbell rang this time. "I'll get it," she sang out.

The man at the door was not what she had expected. Her mother had said he was a former police detective. Kelsey had assumed she meant retired until she mentioned something in passing about his having left the force under less than ideal circumstances. Given all the problems the department was having, Kelsey had pictured a hard-nosed bully, or maybe a balding, red-nosed bumbler with a dirty collar and bad breath.

Not this guy. He was old enough to be her older brother, but too young to be her father. His clothes were stylish but conservative, and he carried an expensive leather attaché case. He might have passed for a yuppie. His hazel-green eyes were sharp and intelligent and so riveting they made her uncomfortable. He was good-looking, she realized. Brown hair that probably bleached out if he spent much time in the sun. Chiseled features, especially his mouth. A strong face, yet she sensed gentleness as well.

"You must be Chief Tanner's daughter," he said, in a mellow baritone.

"Sister Kelsey." She offered her hand which he took after a slight hesitation. Being perceived as untouchable was something she was only beginning to get used to—and like.

"I didn't realize you were going to be here," he said.

"Mother likes to surprise people. Shall we join her in the living room?"

CHAPTER SIX

JEFF HADN'T COUNTED ON a nun being part of the equation. Kelsey Tanner also didn't resemble any nun he could ever remember seeing. The white-trimmed gray veil failed to hide the fact that she was beautiful. Spotting a photograph of Jordan Tanner on the telephone table in the foyer, Jeff realized his daughter had taken the best features from both her parents. She had her mother's oval face, her father's milk-chocolate complexion, big, wide-spaced amber eyes and a remarkably sensuous mouth. Her less-than-chic attire didn't disguise a slender, yet voluptuous, figure. She also moved with the grace and dignity of someone brought up in luxury.

Catherine was pouring coffee when they entered the living room. Derek rose and came forward to shake his hand.

"Chief," Jeff said, before she had a chance to greet him, "may I speak to you for a minute, in private?"

She looked up, and with a worried glance at her other guests, put down the coffee carafe. "Of course."

She led him into a long, low-ceilinged dining room. A table that could accommodate twenty dominated the space.

With one hand clutching a black-lacquered sideboard, inlaid with mother-of-pearl dragons and griffins, she turned and faced him. "Is something wrong? Have you found—"

"I'm wondering what your daughter is doing here? This isn't a prayer meeting."

"She's the one who alerted me about the missing uranium. I thought—"

"Good for her," he said, "but you seem to be missing my point, Chief."

"Call me Catherine."

She was doing it again, distracting him…or trying to. Was it calculated?

"I asked her here today so she can tell you firsthand what she knows. Ask her whatever you want. She won't break just because she's a nun. Maybe if Jordan had lived, she—"

What was she about to say? That if her husband were alive Kelsey wouldn't be wearing a veil?

"She made the connection on her own between the missing yellowcake and Jordan's death," Catherine said. "She's smart. Maybe she won't have anything to contribute, but I don't want to take the chance that I've missed something. I'm too involved, Jeff. I need your objectivity."

She had him cornered. Either he gave in to this request or he marched. And he didn't want to do that.

"I probably should have told you beforehand that she would be here. This is important to her, Jeff. She and Jordan were very close, in some ways closer than she and I were."

He knew it wasn't unusual for girls to be attached to

their dads. Then, too, this father and daughter also shared a racial identity. Did that make Catherine sometimes feel like an outsider?

"There's more going on here, Catherine. What is it?" Her first name had come out without his thinking about it.

She bit her lips and squeezed out a watery smile. "I'm hoping that by getting Kelsey and Derek together they might start talking to each other, resolve whatever differences they have. Or I can at least get a clue about what went on between them."

He grinned. "The chief of police playing matchmaker?"

Shiny silver sparks sizzled in her blue eyes. He shouldn't enjoy watching her fight the impulse to lash out at him. Just respect her ability to do so. But she was bringing out a playful—she would probably call it a perverse—side he rarely displayed on the job.

"Okay—" he touched her elbow to guide her back "—let's go see what we can find out."

She eyed him warily as they returned to the living room where Kelsey and Derek were sitting on opposite ends of the two couches sipping coffee. The atmosphere between them was charged, as if they'd had a disagreement and were furious with each other.

Jeff glanced at Catherine, who had resumed pouring coffee. Her movements were not quite as fluid as they might have been.

She held out a steaming cup to him, and in her eyes he saw it, a plea for tolerance. He sat on the same couch as Derek.

"Where should we begin?" Catherine asked.

Jeff looked at the young woman across from him. "Since you were there when Summers approached your dad, Sister Kelsey, I'd like to hear from you exactly what happened and what was said."

She nodded and repeated what she'd already told her mother.

"Did he appear nervous, excited, angry?" Jeff asked.

"Not angry. More like proud he knew a secret." She paused. "He hesitated, though, when Dad asked him if he had any proof, sort of glanced around to see if anyone was listening."

"Were they?"

She shrugged. "Not that I noticed. He did lower his voice when he said yes, though."

"Did your father say specifically how he was going to check his claim, either to him or to you?"

She brushed back the right side of her veil. "He didn't talk about his work much, unless it was to get opinions on a subject for his editorials."

"He must have placed some credence in Summers's assertion," Jeff said, "because Derek was able to recover the editorial your father wrote the afternoon before he died."

Both women turned to the rookie. Catherine's eyes held admiration. Her daughter's were less certain.

Jeff picked up the attaché he'd left leaning against the side of the couch, removed printouts and gave one each to Catherine and Kelsey.

"Can you verify that he wrote this?" he asked. "It seems authentic to me, but you're more familiar with his writing than I am."

They took a couple of minutes to read it. Derek's attention was centered on Kelsey, a fact she seemed all too aware of because she squirmed and regarded him with a frown before returning to the paper in her hand.

"I don't remember ever seeing this," said Kelsey.

"It was never published. In fact, it had been deleted from his office terminal."

"Then how—"

"Derek told me he was a computer genius. I should have believed him."

Kelsey blinked but refused to look at the young man sitting no more than ten feet away.

"It's Dad's," she finally announced. "His voice, his style and syntax."

"Why do you doubt he wrote it?" Catherine asked. "What would be the point of planting this on his computer and then deleting it?"

"None," Jeff agreed, "but I had to make sure. This is the only link we have between Summers and your husband. It constitutes evidence of a possible motive for what happened to both of them, assuming Summers's fall was staged."

"You think it was?"

Jeff nodded. "I did some research on Mr. Summers. He was retired on disability eight years ago, following an on-the-job accident in a freight warehouse. Nothing suspicious in the incident itself, as far as I can tell. He wasn't watching where he was going and slammed his right knee into a parked forklift. Damaged his knee so badly it left him with a stiff leg. He had to take stairs one at a time."

"You're saying he wouldn't have been able to climb a ladder to his roof," Kelsey said.

"I imagine he could have, but it would have been slow and tedious. The question is why would he? He was having his house reroofed by a reputable company. The work was less than half finished, too early to perform an inspection. Besides, his son was overseeing the work. He would have been the one to check things out."

"Isn't that the point?" Kelsey asked. "He was foolish enough to climb on a roof when he shouldn't have and fell as a result."

"It's a reasonable premise, one nobody seemed to question at the time."

Kelsey placed her cup on the coffee table and rose to her feet. "I have to go or I'll be late for vespers. Nice meeting you, Mr. Rowan. I'll call you next week, Mom."

Derek sprang to his feet, his eyes following her as she crossed the room.

"I'll be right back." Catherine trailed after her daughter. A muted exchange ensued in the entryway. She returned a moment later, her mouth set, and motioned for Derek to be seated.

"What do you want me to do next?" he asked Jeff.

"Get me the complete file on the Summers's case. I don't imagine there will be much, but it might contain something that'll point us in a direction."

"I'll have it for you tomorrow."

The young policeman left a minute later, after thanking his hostess and again shaking Jeff's hand.

"A real gentleman. Is he always that polite?" Jeff asked.

Catherine chuckled and started gathering cups and

saucers onto the tray. No one had touched the biscotti. "He's come a long way from the ghetto."

Jeff remembered the ease with which the guy had worn gangsta duds the day before. Would the real Derek Pager please stand up.

"So what happened? Between them, I mean?"

"I wish I knew." Catherine led him through the dining room and held the swinging door for him to enter the kitchen.

He deposited the tray on the island. "You must have asked."

"Of course I did." Irritation heated her words. She circled the work center. "Several times. But the only answers I get are platitudes."

"She wants to serve God."

"Something like that." Catherine placed the dirty china and silverware in the dishwasher. "She was taught by the School Sisters of Our Lady in elementary school, and now she's joined them."

"Has she always wanted to be a teacher?"

"Not that I was ever aware of. She majored in biochemistry at Rice, graduated cum laude. That's not a subject you teach second-graders."

"You're not happy with her decision."

Catherine set the dishwasher on rinse-and-hold and hit the button. Over the machine's low rumble, she said, "I could accept it if I understood it, but I don't. She was an affiliate of the School Sisters in college. We thought of it as another club on campus, one dedicated to helping them out. Then, the day after she graduated, she announced she was becoming a postulate, the first step of professing, of making a lifelong commitment. Now she's advanced to novice."

Beneath the confusion, Jeff sensed another emotion. He leaned against the counter and folded his arms. "You're angry with her."

Catherine replaced the uneaten biscotti in the tin and put it in the overhead cabinet beside him. He found himself staring at the swell of her breast under the upraised arm.

"I know I shouldn't be, but I am," she said. "Not so much with the decision—though I'm not happy about it—but with her shutting me out."

"Maybe she thinks you should accept her choice."

"Well, I can't, and that's what really makes me angry. Angry and disappointed. I'm her mother."

She slammed the cabinet door and turned to him. "My husband is dead, and now my only child has chosen a life that renounces marriage and family." She picked up the tray, wiped its surface with a damp cloth and upended it in a lower cabinet. "I'll never have grandchildren."

He offered what he hoped was a reassuring nod, though he would much rather put his arms around her. Strange how this strong woman drew out his protective instincts.

"You're too young to be thinking of grandkids," he said.

She snorted. "I'm forty-five, Jeff. I have women friends younger than I am who already have a slew of them."

"Do you think you'll ever remarry?"

For a moment he thought she was going to tell him it was none of his business.

"I loved Jordan," she said. "I can't imagine living with any other man, much less feeling again what I felt with him."

He watched her quick, efficient movements as she wiped down the counter. There was a banked fury in them. Jordan Tanner must have been one hell of a guy, he thought enviously. "Would he want you to spend the next forty years alone?"

Her tidying up jerked to a halt. She tightened her grip on the washcloth as she hissed out a breath. "It's not about what he would want anymore, is it?"

"No," he said quietly, "it's about what you're willing to do to take control of your life."

She stopped again, raised her head and studied him, her eyes narrowed with the hostility that comes from being hurt. "Preaching doesn't become you," she said, and resumed scrubbing a spot that was already clean.

He held out his hands, palms down, fingers splayed. "Sorry. I didn't realize I was."

She examined the pristine room, apparently scouting for something to keep her occupied. He had the feeling she did that a lot.

"Who profited from your husband's death?"

She whirled around frowning, though she must have asked herself that same question. Cops who'd worked homicide always did. Inhaling deeply, she leaned against the counter across the room from him.

"Financially? I did." She took in her surroundings with the sweep of her hand. "As you can see, we're not poor. None of this would have been possible on a cop's salary, not even a police chief's. Tanner money bought this house and the other luxuries we enjoyed." Past tense, he noted. "There was, however, a two-million-dollar life insurance policy payable into his estate. One million for me, one million for Kelsey."

"So she's wealthy in her own right."

"At twenty-one my daughter began receiving a small private income from an annuity we set up for her when she was a baby."

"And the million bucks?"

"As the executor of Jordan's estate, I've placed it in a special trust which she can't draw from until she either takes her final vows or leaves the convent."

Jeff raised his eyebrows. Grieving hadn't dulled this mother's instinct to protect the family assets. "I don't imagine she was very pleased with that."

"She'll get over it."

Catherine's cold determination caught him by surprise. She was angry, yes. Was she also vindictive? Or was this manipulation her way of protecting her child from herself?

"When does she take these final vows?"

"Not for at least five years." She crossed her arms beneath her breasts. "Surely you're not suggesting the sisters killed Jordan for Kelsey's inheritance?"

He lifted a shoulder, eager to release the tension building between them. "It doesn't seem very likely, does it? But I don't have to remind you that filthy lucre is a leading motive for murder."

"It wasn't in this case."

"So what was?"

Her response was a frustrated shake of her head.

"Aside from money," he continued, "who benefited from Jordan's death?"

"Theoretically his brother Tyrone, but that doesn't wash, either. He's taken over the *Sentinel* only because his father isn't able to handle the pressure of the job anymore. And Ty hasn't exactly been a sterling success."

"Why?"

"He calls himself an investor. In fact, he's a dilettante who bounces from one project to another. Over the years he's made a profit on a few of them, but more often he loses money. His father has been bailing him out for years."

"An enabler," Jeff commented. "What kind of deals?"

"A couple of high-end restaurants that folded within a year."

"It's a tough business."

"Especially when you have your eye on the hostess's T&A instead of the kitchen's P&L."

So her brother-in-law liked to play around. Jeff tucked the information away for future reference.

"There were some real estate ventures that were also more speculation than research," she said. "I could go on."

He got the picture. "Based on the venomous tone of editorials he's published against you in the last few months, he doesn't like you much. Why is that?"

Brushing back a stray wisp of golden hair, she snorted. "Maybe because I see him for what he is. Handsome, charming, lazy, selfish, deceitful and unrepentant. He has a lovely wife he cheats on and three adorable children he ignores."

The intensity of her reply took him momentarily aback. "Why then would his father put him in charge of the newspaper?"

"I imagine Marcus is hoping he'll stick with this job."

"How old is Tyrone?"

"Forty-two."

"And his father is still waiting for him to settle down?"

"Hope springs eternal. If you're thinking Ty had his brother bumped off so he could take over the paper, you're barking up the wrong tree."

There were other reasons siblings killed each other. "How did the two of them get along?"

She cocked her head to one side. "Ty looked up to Jordan but he was also jealous of his success, his prestige in the community. For his part, Jordan did what he could to protect his kid brother. Don't get me wrong. My husband wasn't like his father. He didn't hesitate to tell Ty what he thought about his schemes. But if he could legally and morally help him, he did."

"All things considered, it sounds like a healthy relationship, at least on Jordan's part."

"My husband was a loving and caring man," she said with quiet persistence. "You and I have been cops long enough to know there's no such thing as an ordinary family. The Tanners are as unique as any. Jordan was the levelheaded one that kept it from being completely dysfunctional." The note of sadness and loneliness Jeff had come to recognize crept into her voice again.

Jeff hated having to add to her pain, but there was no alternative if they were going to get to the bottom of her husband's death. He'd come to accept that Jordan

Tanner had been murdered. And he wanted to learn more about the woman he'd left behind.

"What can you tell me about Jordan's last.day?" he asked.

CHAPTER SEVEN

"HE ARRIVED at his office that Wednesday morning round eight," she said, "chaired a meeting of the editorial board at nine, then went to see the mayor at ten."

"What for?"

"The paper was covering the upcoming school board elections, and the mayor was worried that a couple of the candidates were getting bad press."

"Were they?"

"No more than they deserved," she said. "Jordan's policy was to report everything that could have a bearing on a candidate's ability to serve, including character issues. For instance, Davy Cordova had been arrested for drunk driving twice in the previous year and had a long record of family violence and assault. Philippa Moore had been implicated in several money-laundering investigations at the credit union where she was a member of the board. The charges were always dropped, but on technicalities, not evidence."

"What was Jordan's response to the mayor's concerns?"

"We never got to talk again after he left the house that morning, but he would have refused to hold back pertinent information on public figures of either party just because it might make them uncomfortable."

"How long did this meeting last?"

"About three-quarters of an hour. He left city hall around ten-forty-five, according to the mayor. He signed the log at the front desk of the athletic club at three minutes after eleven, so he must have gone straight there."

"Was the athletic club part of his normal routine?"

She nodded. "Three times a week. On Mondays and Wednesdays he ran outside on the jogging path through Memorial Park. Fridays he played racquetball or squash." She bit her lip. "He kept in good shape, Jeff. He watched his diet, did all the things the doctors tell us to do, and then he dropped dead."

"The autopsy said it was a heart attack."

She breathed out. "Brought on by dehydration. The temperature that day had reached a hundred degrees by noon. Which was why Tyrone decided not to go with him. The medical examiner learned later that Jordan had drunk a couple of cups of coffee at the mayor's office. Coffee's a diuretic, so Jordan could have been low on electrolytes without realizing it when he started his run."

"He wouldn't have taken water with him?"

"He drank Gatorade on his runs, but apparently not that day."

"Though it was sweltering. Why?"

"It didn't make sense to me, either. Jordan was too smart not to take fluids."

"He could have stopped at fountains in the park."

"That's what everybody said. Then Stuckey reported seeing him drinking from a Gatorade bottle."

"Did you attend the autopsy?"

She shivered. Jeff understood why. As a homicide cop she would have attended more than one postmortem. It took a strong stomach and a determined mindset to see a corpse cut open. He was willing to credit her with the professional mettle in the case of a stranger, but emotional detachment when the body on the slab was the person you lived with and had made love to was another matter.

"I wasn't that brave," she said, her voice brittle rather than strong. "When I brought you into my office and fired you, why didn't you fight me?"

"What?" The jump in topics caught him off balance. Disturbing him was something this woman seemed to be exceptionally good at.

"I sent you packing, and all you did was glare at me and walk away. Why didn't you challenge me, if not then, later?"

He was struggling to keep up with her. What did his not ranting at her have to do with her husband's autopsy? Suddenly he understood. While she was dealing with him, her husband's body was being sliced open on a pathologist's table. She'd been expecting a fight, probably welcoming it as a distraction from the ugly images parading through her mind.

"I couldn't have won. Not then. Not there." He had the strangest feeling he'd let her down, instead of the other way around. "The deck was stacked. The atmosphere in the department had been polluted against me. I was better off getting on with my life."

"You caved in," she said with a hint of contempt.

"If you remember, Chief, you were the one who screwed up. Or was that admission in my office the other day just a ploy to rope me into this obsession of yours? Maybe you think I really am a racist."

She glared at him. He'd regretted his outburst even before the words had left his mouth. Her lips thinned to a straight line. "I expected you to fight me because it was the right thing to do," she said, "not because it might be profitable."

She was calling him a wimp. No one had ever accused him of cowardice before. Her uncanny ability to reverse tables had his blood drumming with sudden temper, but there was admiration behind it, too. She was good at what she did, and he was glad they were at least theoretically on the same side this time. She'd make a formidable enemy.

He wandered over to a wrought-iron chair in the breakfast nook and sat down. She was right. He had fled rather than fought. He hadn't considered it running away but exercising the wisdom to realize what couldn't be changed. Now he had to question that decision.

He was also becoming too aware of Catherine Tanner as a woman, and that wasn't good. She was a client, yet his reaction to her spooked him, made him feel vulnerable and unprofessional. He couldn't afford that, either. This was a job, nothing more.

"Maybe I'm putting too much into what this Stuckey character claims he saw," she acknowledged. "The guy probably can't remember what he drank yesterday, much less what took place a year ago. He could have imagined it, or gotten it confused with something else.

A man actually did have an epileptic fit in the park a week before, and the paramedics had to be called. Maybe Stuckey's mixing that up with Jordan's death."

Without thinking, Jeff reached across the table and took her hands in his, then probed her sad eyes. "But if he's telling the truth, it means Jordan was poisoned."

She tried without success to hold back tears.

He got up, circled the table, extended his hands. Tugged her gently to her feet, wrapped his arms around her. She didn't respond at first, then slowly she hugged his waist and rested her head on his shoulder. She felt so right there. He wanted to kiss her, but had to be content with pressing his lips into her hair. A minute passed and she was crying softly, her tears dampening his shirt.

"I'll find him, Catherine," he murmured, "I promise."

LATER THAT EVENING, trying very hard not to dwell on the memory of Catherine's body pressing against his, of the way they fit so comfortably together, Jeff danced his fingers over his computer keyboard. Since the environmental cleanup of the old waterfront district was a matter of public record, he had no difficulty finding out which of the Rialto facilities the Superfund was handling. The larger question was who was leasing the warehouse when it shut down in '77.

Uranica Corporation.

He checked a variety of resources but could find no record of the company anywhere in the U.S. or Canada. He extended his search to Central and South America. Nada. Europe. Zero. Asia. Zip. He considered calling Derek Pager. Maybe the computer genius could come up with a lead, but then he thought of someone else. First, though, he sent an e-mail to a friend of his in the FBI.

The following morning he received an answer back.

"No record of Uranica Corp on file."

Another dead end.

Sunday was a good day for visiting people, so just before noon he phoned Kermit Nagle. He had met Nagle several years ago when he was investigating a double murder in Sunnyside. Nagle was a neighbor of the dead couple, and his memory for quirky details had proven a godsend in identifying the killer, who was later apprehended. Jeff had also found the middle-aged former mining engineer to be far more intelligent than his offbeat, politically incorrect and sometimes irreverent humor suggested.

Ten minutes later he was on his way to the man's house.

The Nagle yard reflected Kermit's past profession. A small duckbill ore car sat on a short length of steel track in the flower bed near the front door. Leaning against it were a couple of well-worn shovels and a rusty pick. A weathered kerosene lantern completed the display. Jeff reached for the bell, but the door flew open before he had a chance to push the button.

Years of relative inactivity had added bulk to Kermit's wide frame, but didn't disguise the essential brawn beneath it. He had massive shoulders and big, scarred hands. His nose had been broken twice, once while working, once in a barroom.

Those hell-raising days were long gone. Kermit Nagle had retired from mining ten years ago at the age of forty-five. He now lived on his investments and the supplemental income he earned writing short stories, shoot 'em up westerns and offbeat murder mysteries.

Announcing that his wife was out spending his hard-earned money, he led Jeff into his book-filled office. The "safe" in the corner behind his desk was actually a small refrigerator.

"Stella wants me to shed thirty pounds," he grumbled, "so she has me off my brew and on diet cola." He shivered dramatically. "I keep telling her the stuff is bad for you, but she won't listen. No reason you can't have one, though." He opened the fridge, which was filled with canned beer and soft drinks.

"Misery deserves company," Jeff said. "Cola is fine."

Frowning—no doubt in disappointment that he wasn't being given an excuse to defy "the little woman"—Kermit extracted two cans, handed one to Jeff and parked himself in an old-fashioned wooden swivel chair. They popped the tops. "You said you had some questions I might be able to help you with."

Jeff hadn't wanted to give any particulars on the phone. "What can you tell me about uranium?"

Kermit raised an eyebrow and reached over to a side table, picked out one of the various rocks scattered there and tossed it to Jeff. "Here's a sample."

Jeff caught it, though his instinct was to shy away from the substance that conjured up images of people glowing in the dark. The gray, baseball-size rock was heavy, coarse and unimpressive.

"It's not dangerous," his host assured him.

"But it is radioactive, right?"

From the drawer in the same table Kermit removed

a piece of equipment that resembled a voltmeter. He pressed an on-off button, adjusted a dial and extended the instrument across the desk. The device clicked more rapidly as it neared the rock.

"This is fairly low grade," he said. "Not much more than you might get from a piece of granite."

Jeff gaped. "Granite's radioactive?"

"Most potassium-rich rocks are to some degree."

Kermit laughed and held the Geiger counter over Jeff's wrist watch. The clicking again accelerated. "You have a radium dial. There's no danger in the miniscule amounts we're dealing with here. I worked a couple of uranium claims back in the sixties. We mined it the way we did any other mineral, mostly because we didn't know any better. Nowadays you have to take all sorts of precautions. Except nobody's mining it anymore."

"Why not?"

"Not worth it. Back in the fifties and early sixties processed uranium—yellowcake—was going for anywhere from six to eight dollars a pound. By the mid-seventies it had skyrocketed to over forty, before beginning a slow decline. Then came Three Mile Island and Chernobyl. The bottom fell out of the market completely, and the price of yellowcake plunged to four or five bucks a pound. It's back to ten or twelve dollars now, I think, but that's still not enough to cover labor and heavy-equipment expenses, much less the cost of processing it under the new strict environmental regulations. Today there are only a handful of mining companies left that even deal in the product, mostly overseas."

Jeff regarded the soft drink in one hand, the chunk of radioactive mineral in the other.

"We have plenty of uranium stockpiled to meet current demands for nuclear power and weapons," Kermit went on. "The big concern today is what to do with the waste products. There have even been proposals to put it in rockets and send it deep into outer space. Now if you could come up with a peaceful, productive use for the spent fuel, you'll get the Nobel Prize for saving the world and become very, very rich."

Jeff put the rock on the desk in front of him, convinced he wasn't going to be able to solve that particular problem. His interest was closer to home. "Ever hear of a company called Uranica?"

Kermit stroked his chin, then shook his head. "Nope. Should I?"

"They leased a warehouse on the Houston waterfront but abandoned the place and the yellowcake stored there in the late seventies."

Kermit sucked down the rest of his cola and tossed the can into the wastebasket at the side of his desk.

"You're referring to the forty barrels the Superfund had to dispose of."

On the way over, Jeff had debated with himself about how much he could tell Kermit. Instinct and experience told him he could trust the guy, and leveling with him might reveal new information.

"There's reason to believe sixty barrels were left behind."

Kermit's bushy eyebrows rose, as he whistled through his teeth. "Twenty barrels are unaccounted for?"

Jeff nodded. "We can't be sure. That's why I want to find out what happened to Uranica Corp, so I can check their records."

"If they have any," Kermit supplied. "Back in the boom-and-bust years of the Cold War, uranium companies were formed overnight, a lot of them by con men. A few made huge profits, mostly in stock trading rather than operations. Many operations that actually found uranium folded because the people running them didn't know what they were doing. For the legitimate ones, buyouts and consolidations were the only roads to survival." Kermit scratched his head. "Uranica. Sounds like any one of dozens of fly-by-night outfits." He paused to stare at the ceiling, then shrugged. Reaching back into his safe, he extracted two cans of beer. "This requires serious cogitation."

Jeff laughed and accepted the proffered brew. "The sun is over the yardarm somewhere. Thanks." He sipped away the foam that bubbled out when he sprang the top. "What would twenty barrels of yellowcake be worth?"

"Officially? At the current price, you're looking at ten to twelve thousand dollars a barrel. Multiply that by twenty barrels…upwards of a quarter of a million. On the black market, I would guess it could fetch ten times that. Maybe more."

"Terrorists have deep pockets these days," Jeff noted. "How can I find out what happened to Uranica? I've done the usual search for registered corporations, domestic and foreign. Nothing. The FBI says the company doesn't exist. Claims they interviewed a bunch of senior miners out west, but none of them ever heard of it."

"Those old-timers wouldn't talk to the feds. Might as well put on a suit and ask a hillbilly where you can buy good moonshine." Kermit pursed his lips. "I wonder…"

Jeff waited.

"Let me make a few phone calls. I have some friends in Arizona and Nevada who've been around most of the mines in the southwest. One of them might be able to tell us what happened to this outfit."

"One other question," Jeff said. "Assume someone did steal the twenty barrels of yellowcake and sell it to terrorists. What would they do with it, and how would we find it?"

"That's two questions." Kermit upended his beer can, stretched back in his chair and stared again at the ceiling, as if the answers were written there.

"They would have to get it out of the country," he said, "to a place with a nuclear weapons program, like India or Pakistan. Creating an atomic bomb isn't something you do in your basement or backyard. You need a nuclear reactor to turn the raw product into useable material. As for getting it there—"

He stuck out his lower lip. "Hundreds of cargo ships go through here every year, each carrying thousands of containers. A barrel weighs around six hundred pounds. Assuming they left the powder in the barrels and didn't split it into smaller units for easier transport, you're still not looking for excessive weight or distinctive shapes."

"But it would be detectable with a Geiger counter."

Kermit frowned. "That's one of the ironies I don't understand myself. Yellowcake isn't particularly radioactive. If it was enclosed inside a shipping container, it probably wouldn't emit any more radiation than any other cargo."

Jeff blew out a breath in frustration. "Are you saying we can't trace this stuff?"

Kermit shrugged. "It'll be tough. Your best bet will be to work backwards. Isolate shipments going into target ports from Houston, then see if you can determine if they were suspicious."

"We're looking for a needle in a haystack."

"A hot needle that could set the whole barn ablaze."

CHAPTER EIGHT

"YOU'RE NOT ASKING MUCH," Derek told Jeff in his office the next day.

The task was daunting, but Jeff also got the impression the computer geek was eager for the challenge.

"I won't be able to do this overnight," Derek warned him.

"Take a couple of days if you need to," Jeff said with a facetious grin. The assignment could take months.

"Great. I'll do it between naps and chocolate bars."

Jeff could see the guy's mind was already sorting through ideas on how he could break into the computer systems that stored the port of Houston's data.

"I'll do my best," Derek said, "but I can't promise anything. The sheer volume of information—"

"This is important," Jeff reminded him. "Yellowcake in the wrong hands—"

"Could make the twin towers look tame."

"Provided, of course, Kelsey's recollection of what happened is accurate."

"She doesn't lie," Derek snapped.

"I'm not suggesting she does," Jeff said, "but one thing you'll learn in police work is that people's memories are often flawed. Eyewitness accounts can be very unreliable, especially after they've been filtered through a traumatic series of events."

"There's nothing wrong with her memory."

"I guess you would know."

Derek's expression hardened. "What's that supposed to mean?"

"I understand you two were pretty close in school. Her mother tells me she expected you to get married. Why didn't you?"

Years of interrogating bad actors or just trying to eke information out of unwilling subjects had taught Jeff that sympathetic silence often accomplished more than a direct question.

Derek slouched into the visitor's chair. "I was waiting until the night of our graduation to give her a ring. I thought it would be more romantic. I guess I waited too long."

"Do you think your proposal would have been unexpected?"

"No, we'd talked about getting married, having kids, even where we wanted to live. I couldn't afford to buy a house in the Memorial district like her folks, and I'll probably never make enough to own a mansion in River Oaks, like her grandparents, but we could have done all right."

"She's an heiress. She has money," Jeff pointed out.

He shifted his jaw. "We'd already decided to live on our earnings, mine and hers, at least until we had kids."

"Sounds like a good plan. So how come you didn't ask her on graduation night?"

"She changed. She pushed me away, wouldn't let me get close to her."

"Why?"

The intensity in Derek's dark eyes dimmed, as if he were searching inside, not out. "I don't know. Maybe because she was ashamed of doing so badly in her finals. She was about to graduate *magna cum laude,* then…she barely passed her exams."

"Did she often freeze up on tests?"

"Not Kelsey. She had one of the highest grade point averages on record. Then, in a matter of a week, she blew it."

Catherine had mentioned Kelsey graduating *cum laude.* Jeff had been impressed with that; he hadn't realized it represented a tumble from an even higher peak.

"So what happened?" Under other circumstances, Jeff might have conjectured that she'd met someone else, but her going into a convent seemed to nix that theory.

Derek shook his head. "I don't know. But she went into such a depression afterward that she hid away from everyone. Including me. Especially me."

"She didn't explain?"

"Claimed she panicked, kept apologizing for letting everybody down. I was disappointed for her, but I didn't care about her grades. She drove off after getting her diploma without telling anyone where she was going and didn't come home that night. Her parents were as frantic as I was. Mrs. Tanner… The chief even put out an unofficial bulletin for her. Kelsey showed up the next day and announced she was going to become a nun. I found out about it from her father. She didn't even have the guts to tell me herself."

"Had she ever talked about doing this before?"

"Not once."

"What was her father's reaction?"

"He said to give her space, that she was obviously upset and needed time to calm down, sort things out and forgive herself."

"Did you agree with him?"

He lifted his shoulders in a defeated shrug. "What choice did I have? I couldn't very well climb the convent walls and drag her to the altar."

Jeff chuckled, hoping to lighten the mood. "No. I suppose those days are gone."

Derek's face remained stern.

"Why do you think she bombed? Was she overconfident? Did she just not bother to study?"

"She studied all the time. The weekend before exams, she went to the compound to cram."

"Compound?"

"The Tanner family retreat up at Lake Conroe. Kelsey took me there once. A dozen acres with a cabin." Derek scoffed. "Hardship living by Tanner standards. Only three bedrooms, two baths, a kitchen and a living room. At least double the size of the place I grew up in."

A note of bitterness crept into his words, a slip Jeff suspected was rare. Straightening his shoulders, the young cop added, "Anyway, she went there to study."

"Did you go with her?"

"I told you, she went alone. I had exams coming up, too."

Jeff smiled. "Yeah, being cooped up with a beautiful woman in an isolated cabin for a weekend, I wouldn't get much studying done, either, except maybe anatomy."

Derek sprang from his seat. "She's not like that." His hands were curled into tight fists.

"Hey, calm down, guy," Jeff urged, baffled by the explosive reaction.

"I've never touched her, not that way. She's a virgin," Derek blurted out, then averted his eyes. "She said she was saving herself for our wedding night."

Jeff nearly gaped. It was a rare admission and raised a plethora of questions. Kelsey may be a virgin, but he doubted the tough kid from the ghetto was. Did he seek physical gratification with someone else? Had Kelsey found out? Was that why she dumped him? If she'd been saving herself for him, as he claimed, catching him fooling around with some tramp could explain her depression.

Maybe Catherine ought to delve a little deeper into Derek Pager's personal history. In the meantime, Jeff had a visit to make to city hall.

LATE THAT SUNDAY EVENING Catherine was finally able to get hold of Risa Taylor at home. She and Grady Wilson who was also a cop, had finally been able to coordinate their schedules so that they had several days off together. They'd spent them in New Orleans.

"It's as hot and sticky there as here," Risa said. "If we had any sense we would have gone north, far north."

"But they wouldn't have good Cajun food and mint juleps there," Catherine pointed out.

"Yeah. Or the jazz. What's up?"

"As a matter of fact, I want to ask for a favor."

"Anything, Chief, you know that."

"I'm trying to find a vagrant by the name of Harvey Stuckey." She gave a brief rundown of the story he'd told Abby and a rookie about seeing Jordan collapse.

"I assume you want this off the record."

"Until I can talk to him personally and determine how credible he is. Abby's convinced he's telling the truth, but—"

"If he's an alkie, his idea of truth may be different than yours," she observed. "But I understand. I'll ask Grady to put out a few quiet feelers, too, if that's okay. Have you got anyone else working on this?"

Catherine wasn't ready to out Jeff yet. That would come later. "I've already talked to Mei Lu, but working white-collar crime, she isn't likely to run into this guy."

"I'm supposed to meet with Lucy and Crista tomorrow after work for drinks." Lucy worked in missing persons and Crista was on the Chicano squad. "Wish you could join us, but I know you have other things on your plate right now. Do you mind if I tell them about this and ask them to keep their eyes and ears open? All hush-hush, of course."

"Thanks, Risa. That would really help. Unwinding with a cool one sounds wonderful. Maybe one of these days… I was getting ready to call them—"

"Consider it done."

"I feel so bad about not keeping better in touch with the group. I guess the last time we were all together was at Jordan's funeral."

"Just remember we're always here for you, Catherine."

It felt good to be called by her name instead of rank.

"That means a lot, Risa. Thank you."

Catherine hung up the phone with a sense of long-ing for the days before she was made chief. When she and her female students from the academy had been tight. When they shared girl talk and sat around a table in their favorite watering hole, bitching about the male chauvinist pigs they had to work with.

The bond had faltered when Risa was accused of killing her partner. They'd mended the breach since then, but the old sense of "us against them" hadn't been completely recaptured. Catherine's position as police chief had prevented her from providing the kind of close personal support she'd wanted to give. Maybe this joint effort would help them close ranks again.

"WHAT DO YOU KNOW about Jordan's last meeting with the mayor?" Jeff asked.

Fifteen minutes after coming home from the office Monday evening Jeff had called to ask if he could come over. Of course she said yes, then changed her clothes with a strange feeling of anticipation.

Her crying jag in Jeff's arms two days before had stirred needs she'd managed to sublimate till then. A year was a long time to go without physical contact, es-pecially when the previous twenty-five had been filled with touching and being touched.

"It was to discuss coverage of the upcoming school board election," she reminded Jeff. They were standing in the kitchen clutching cold soda cans.

"Jordan told you that beforehand?"

"He got a call from the mayor that morning while we were getting dressed. We were both running late." *Because we'd made love—for the last time.* "I confirmed it with the mayor afterward. I wanted to know everything that happened to him that morning." She moved over to the breakfast nook, sat down and peered up at him. "I explained all this to you the other day."

"Did you know Buster Rialto was also there?"

She gaped at him. "Rialto? No, I didn't. Why? And how did you find out?"

"Sally, the mayor's secretary, is an old friend of mine. It seems the school board issue was a subterfuge. The real purpose of the meeting was to mediate an agreement between Rialto and your husband for the *Sentinel* to hold off publishing the discrepancy in the amount of yellowcake stored in Rialto's warehouse until an independent investigation could be completed."

"Wait a minute. The editorial announcing that wasn't published. How did the mayor even know Jordan was aware of the discrepancy?"

"Exactly." He tipped his can. She watched his Adam's apple bob as he swallowed.

"Jordan would never have agreed," she insisted, disconcerted by her reaction to Jeff, by the temptation to stare, to soak up the energy he exuded.

"Sally didn't catch everything, but from what she did hear, Jordan flat-out refused, said it would take too long and get swept under the rug without media pressure."

Catherine forced herself to turn away, to gaze out the

bay window—at anything but the man standing a few feet away.

She wasn't surprised the mayor had deceived her. Stan Walbrun was first and foremost a politician. Telling her what she expected to hear would be second nature to him. The growing feeling of being surrounded by conspirators was depressing.

"Do you mind if we go outside?" she asked. "I haven't done any gardening in ages and I need the therapy."

The sun was setting. Perhaps half an hour of decent light remained. She led him through the back door, onto the gray flagstone patio and around the corner to the potting shed she and Jordan had built together.

"Your yard is beautiful," Jeff said.

"Thanks to Emilio. He's in his late seventies and doesn't move very fast, but somehow everything gets done."

"Slow and steady. There's a lot to be said for that."

The innocuous statement suddenly conjured up the kind of erotic images she had no right to be contemplating.

From the workbench she picked up a flower basket and a plastic bucket containing garden tools and made her way to the rose garden outside her bedroom.

"The big question—" she cut a long pink hybrid tea "—is how Rialto knew Jordan was going to blow the whistle on the missing barrels one day after he'd met Summers, who just happened to fall off his roof that evening."

"Could Jordan have discussed it with someone, someone who would relay the information to either the mayor or Buster Rialto?"

"I spoke to everybody who was at the editorial meeting that morning." She snipped off dead heads and dropped them in the bottom of the bucket. "All they mentioned was the upcoming school board election and which candidates they would endorse. No one said a thing about yellowcake, the Superfund or the harbor cleanup." She cut another rose and placed it beside the first.

"But you couldn't specifically ask about it, either, since you didn't know."

"No, but I gave each of the staff adequate opportunity to introduce the subject. I spoke to them individually, so someone would surely have commented on it, unless they were all in on the conspiracy."

Jeff picked up the basket and held it for her when she measured out another blossom, this one a cheerful yellow. "How about reporters? Jordan must have assigned this story to someone."

"He might have given the story to Curtis Rainey, but Rainey was in Iraq at the time, covering the war. He wasn't due back for several days."

"Yet Jordan wrote the editorial," Jeff observed.

"It wasn't unusual for him to put his first thoughts down on paper, file it away, then refine it later when he had more definitive information."

She added a rose to the growing bouquet, this time a velvety, bloodred Abraham Lincoln.

"Jeff, I'm convinced Jordan didn't talk to anyone on the paper about this. So how did the mayor and Rialto get wind of it?"

He shifted the basket to the other hand. "Someone either had access to his computer or hacked into it."

"The mayor isn't above pursuing his own interests, including doing favors for friends and supporters—"

"People like Rialto."

She nodded. "I can't picture him being into high-tech spying, though. That would be more in Buster's arsenal."

"Maybe Derek can figure out if there's still a tap on the editor's computer. If Rialto's the person responsible, chances are he didn't remove the bugs just because the incumbent changed."

Aware of how close he was to her, how easy it would be for them to touch, she proceeded to another bush.

"So, as you see it," he said, following her, "Rialto got wind of Jordan's editorial, contacted the mayor and asked him to intercede."

She selected a stem with three blossoms on it and clipped. "They could have then remotely deleted the editorial."

Jeff shook his head. "Possibly, but I'd expect someone smart enough to hack through a firewall to know how to remove all trace of a file."

"Unless Tyrone was the one who deleted it when he took over as editor."

"Could you ask him?"

CHAPTER NINE

JEFF WATCHED HER tense up at the suggestion. No wonder, considering the attitude the *Sentinel* had taken against her since Jordan's death. "I'd rather not tip my hand."

"I bet Derek can tell us when the file was deleted. If it was in the middle of the night, chances are it wasn't Tyrone."

Jeff decided she was right. Puttering in the garden was good therapy for her. She moved with purpose and efficiency among her plants and shrubs, yet she had an innate grace that mesmerized...and aroused.

He'd never before encountered her intoxicating blend of strength, poise and vulnerability. Maybe that was why his marriage had failed, why he'd never stayed with one woman for more than a few months. With Catherine...he couldn't imagine growing tired of being with her.

Shadows were lengthening darkness crowding in. The night air, while still warm and thick, felt less suffocating, almost comforting. Catherine surveyed the yard, took a breath that came close to a sigh and slapped at a mosquito.

"We better go inside before we're eaten alive," she said.

He followed, not sure if the aroma he was inhaling was from the blooms he was carrying or the woman walking ahead of him. He had the definite feeling, though, that after tonight he would always associate the scent of roses with her.

She returned her gardening tools to the potting shed and relieved him of the basket. Their hands touched only briefly, but it was enough to provoke his awareness of the softness of her skin. The heat he felt now had nothing to do with summer temperatures. Her almost imperceptible hesitation suggested she too was conscious of their fleeting contact.

They entered the kitchen and almost shivered in the dry coolness of the air-conditioning.

"There's another issue you'll need to decide soon," he said, as she placed the basket on the counter by the sink.

She removed a ceramic vase from a lower cabinet. "Going public."

He raised his eyebrows, pleased that they were so closely attuned. He shouldn't be surprised. They were both experienced cops, after all.

"I've been considering it," she said.

"The mayor's secretary will keep her mouth shut about talking to me, if only because she wants to keep her job. But I'll need to contact other people, some of them on the force. I don't think we can count on everyone being as cooperative as Sally. You'll take flack when word gets out that I'm working for you."

She arranged the multicolored roses in the vase. "I can handle it."

He smiled. "I'm sure you can, but—"

"Be discreet, but not to the detriment of getting the job done." She set the bouquet on the table. "When the time comes, I'll hold a news conference if I have to."

"I'll keep it under wraps as long as I can."

"Thirsty?" She swung around to face him. Their eyes met…and held. "I have tea, or something stronger, if you'd prefer."

"Tea is fine."

Her knees felt watery as she removed a pitcher from the refrigerator and poured them both tall glasses of tea filled with ice. He declined the offer of sugar but accepted a wedge of lime. They wandered into the living room, which was now shrouded in growing darkness. Catherine switched on the table lamp beside a club chair. It had a stained-glass shade and a bronze base. Tiffany? He didn't know. It wasn't the kind of thing he would have selected for his own place, but in the context of this room, he decided he liked it.

"This is an interesting house."

She chuckled and settled into an easy chair after turning on another light. "Interesting is a word people use when they don't like something but are too diplomatic to say so."

He cocked an eyebrow. "Not in this case. I do like it. Reminds me of Frank Lloyd Wright's architecture."

This time she was the one to raise a brow. "Not many people recognize the similarity."

"It wasn't built by him?"

"Jordan designed it. He considered going into architecture at one time."

"Why didn't he?"

She laughed, and Jeff realized it was the first time he'd heard her do so with genuine, relaxed amusement. He liked the sound and wanted to hear more of it.

"He hated math," she said.

He grinned in return. "I can see how that could be a problem." Reluctantly breaking eye contact, he surveyed the room, its straight lines, the modest, almost inconspicuous ornamentation that lent an air of grace and dignity without drawing attention. "I like his tastes."

Over the rim of her glass she studied him before taking a sip. "The two of you would have gotten along very well." She spread her elbows on the arms of the chair, the glass held with both hands in front of her. "I'm sorry you never met him—or he you."

Jeff sensed sincerity in her statement. In most of the successful marriages he'd observed, starry-eyed love gradually morphed into a kind of comfort zone. In the case of Catherine and Jordan, he had the feeling the romance had never faded, making them very lucky, and her plight all the more tragic. In spite of her loss, her sorrow, he envied her experiencing something he'd only dreamed about.

Restless, she climbed to her feet and stood in front of the picture window overlooking the shadowy garden, the melancholy on her face reflected in the glass.

"I have to admit I didn't particularly care for this house at first," she said, as much to herself as to him.

"Why is that?"

"Unfamiliarity more than anything else. The home I grew up in was very traditional. Soft lines. Rounded corners. Superfluous frills. This seemed austere by comparison."

"But you like it now?"

She nodded. "In my mother's house, a potted plant was just another item cluttering up a room. Here each item of furniture has individuality, its own personality, and a simple bouquet becomes a showpiece because it doesn't have to compete with imitations of nature."

Jeff realized that the décor which was essentially masculine in its straight lines and uncompromising angles actually favored a woman because it emphasized her femininity and grace.

He rose and went to her. Relieving her of the sweaty glass, he placed it on the white marble windowsill, then turned her to face him, his hands holding hers.

"He was a lucky man."

Her features crumbled, and she leaned into him. He had no choice but to put his arms around her. To comfort and offer solace. But that wasn't what he was feeling. He was too aware of her body touching his, of her muffled sobs against his chest.

He stroked her back. The warmth of her skin under the thin cotton blouse sent heat rushing through him. On a hiccough, she eased away.

"I'm sorry," she murmured. "That's the second time I've done that. You must think I'm a hysterical old woman."

He inhaled her scent, buried his nose in her hair. "Neither hysterical, nor old," he murmured, "But definitely a woman."

She tightened her grip on him.

"We all need a shoulder to lean on from time to time," he said. "Mine is available whenever you want it."

She tilted her head up, gazed at him with a bitter-sweet smile.

They stood together, belly to belly, breasts to chest. No tears this time, just an exchange of body heat.

He brought his mouth down to hers and softly kissed her. They remained still, their lips touching, each aware of the other's breathlessness. The moment lingered. He broke off but didn't separate himself from her. Their eyes locked. Hers were full of uncertainty and what he could only describe as longing. She raised her hands and draped them on his shoulders. He kissed her again. His tongue made contact with her lips. She parted them. He entered. She retreated, only to reestablish that tingle of intimacy again an instant later. As if by mutual understanding he withdrew. They separated.

The minute that followed was filled with silence. Jeff waited for her to ask him to leave. She didn't. He considered apologizing, but he wasn't sorry, and she didn't seem upset as much as confused. He was, too. He hadn't come to Catherine Tanner's house with the intention of kissing her. He wished the phone would ring or someone would come to the door. Anything to break the writhing tension between them.

"Will you call me tomorrow?" she finally asked in a voice that was soft, self-conscious. "And give me a progress report on your investigation?"

"I'll call you every day," he promised, "even if the only thing I have to say is that there's no news."

"Thank you."

"I'd better get going." He turned toward the front of the house. "I still have a lot to do."

They searched for something more to say, but nothing came. With mutual nods of farewell, she let him out the front door. The latch snicked closed behind him. A line had been crossed. The question was how far over it he dared go.

JEFF DROVE HOME in a trance. He hadn't planned this. He hadn't seriously entertained fantasies of their relationship rising above the professional. That he found her attractive was nothing more than the normal male reaction to a striking woman. Or so he tried to convince himself. Which brought up the question of what exactly there was about her that he found so alluring. She wasn't stunning in her beauty, not in the classic sense. She had charm and dignity, but those were hardly qualities that aroused a man's passions. Something did, because his libido was on high alert.

She was in her midforties, six years older than he. The age difference should be a turn-off, men were supposed to prefer their women younger. But of course there was nothing conventional about this situation. She was the chief of police in a city of nearly two million. He was the ex-cop she'd fired from the force. No, there was nothing conventional about any of it.

"I should have turned down this job," he muttered to himself. Instead, he'd kissed her. And she'd kissed him back.

He stopped for a red light and for the first time in years wished he had a cigarette. Seeing the smoke curl around him would suit his mood right now and match the state of his thinking. Cloudy. Hazy. Amorphous.

The signal turned green. He pressed on the accelerator and was content to conform to the speed limit. His thoughts wandered, straining to find stability.

He pulled into his driveway, hit the automatic garage-door opener. The house was dark but for the light he always left on over the sink in the kitchen. He could barely remember the days when he came home to a wife waiting for him, maybe because that episode had been so brief.

He got out a frozen dinner and popped it into the microwave while he went out to the mailbox and gathered the day's delivery. Mostly junk. Somehow he'd gotten on a Victoria's Secret mailing list and was receiving their catalogues. Not looking at it was impossible.

Flipping it open, his eye caught a black lace chemise, the spaghetti straps of the low-cut top exposing the model's tantalizing cleavage. His mind flashed to a fantasy of Catherine wearing it, her full breasts caged in the delicate web of filigree. He slammed the magazine shut. What he needed was a cold shower.

CHAPTER TEN

"HEY, GIRL, you missed our date last time. You going to be able to make it today?"

Catherine gripped the phone and stared at the calendar on her desk. She and her sister-in-law got together for lunch every third Thursday of the month. Today. Her docket was full, but Annette had left that hour and a half open. Last month Catherine had cancelled their date to call a special meeting of Internal Affairs to deal with the recent arrest of a cop in a drug-dealing sting. Reporters had somehow gotten wind of the news before the dirty cop had even arrived at the station house for booking. She'd gone through the motions of warning those connected with the case of the dire consequences for anyone caught leaking information to the public, but the threat was hollow. The culprit, a friend of Eddie Fontanero's, was covering his tracks and the press would never give up its source.

"So far, so good," Catherine answered. "I picked last time, even though I stood you up. So today you choose the place."

Melissa's rich voice held a note of humor. "How about the Cheesecake Factory."

Catherine groaned. "You're putting temptation in my way, girl, endangering my very soul, or at least my waistline."

The other woman laughed. "I've sometimes thought the purpose of hellfire was to try to get the grins off the faces of the damned."

"You're evil."

Melissa snickered. "Twelve-thirty or I'll start without you." She hung up.

Annette buzzed Catherine to remind her she had a meeting with the Family Violence Unit in five minutes to review procedures for removing children from abusive situations. That would be followed by one with representatives of the Junior Chamber of Commerce to discuss how to protect small businesses from vandalism.

"Is my lunch slot still open?"

"So far," her administrative assistant said.

"Keep it that way."

Of all the adult members of the Tanner family, Catherine was most comfortable with Tyrone's wife and the mother of his three children. Melissa was a Creole from nearby Louisiana. Tall, willowy, beautiful and sophisticated, she tended to revert to the patois of the bayou when she got excited—to the amusement of her husband and the raised eyebrows of her in-laws.

Catherine arrived at the Galleria five minutes ahead of schedule. By the time she had parked and crossed to the mall entrance where the Cheesecake Factory was located, she was running five minutes late. She mounted the stairs to the restaurant's second floor and found Melissa waiting near the maitre d's podium. A bright smile spread across her face when she saw Catherine.

"You made it, and right on time, too." She gave Catherine a sisterly hug.

As always, Melissa was dressed to the nines. She'd been a model when she met Tyrone and still worked hard at maintaining her figure. Her dark complexion was youthful and flawless. Her short-cropped hair was mahogany rather than black and, like Kelsey's, glowed with titian overtones. Today she wore a beltless burgundy and teal knee-length dress that accentuated her slender frame. The rings on her fingers sparkled with diamonds and precious gems. Following behind her, Catherine noted, not for the first time, that she was almost too slim, bordering on anorexic.

They sat in a booth across from each other.

"I know you've been busy," Melissa said after the hostess presented them with menus and departed, "but how are you, really?"

"I'm fine," Catherine assured her.

"You taking care of yourself? You look tired."

"Work." It accounted for some of her sleepless nights, though not last night. She'd tossed and turned, plagued with memories of Jeff kissing her. The first man, other than Jordan, to do so in twenty-five years. It was a strange sensation. Stirring and a little frightening.

Melissa tilted her head and studied her more astutely. "There's something different about you," she said, her eyes narrowed. "A hint of the old enthusiasm. I'm glad. This has been such a horrible year. In your place I doubt I could have survived."

Catherine didn't want to probe too deeply into the possible reason for her newfound joy, if that's what it was. "And you look fabulous."

Melissa appreciated compliments and accepted them with grace, but it seemed to Catherine there was a perpetual melancholy in her eyes, as if she recognized that stringent dieting and daily workouts weren't sufficient to keep her husband faithful. She laughed. "The big four-oh is quickly approaching and it scares the hell out of me."

Catherine snickered. "Having passed that point, I can tell you it's all in your head. I don't feel a day over thirty-nine. Besides, Jordan reminded me regularly that life begins at forty."

Melissa snorted. "He wasn't a woman. Men have all the advantages—"

A waitress came to take their orders. As usual, Melissa smacked her lips over all the succulent items on the menu, then ordered soup and a salad, claiming she was saving herself for dessert. Catherine selected a club sandwich but passed on the fries.

They talked about Melissa's children. Fourteen-year-old Tiana would be starting high school this fall, and her seventeen-year-old brother would be graduating in the spring. Ralston was several inches over six feet, thickly muscled and a star on his football team. He had already been scouted for an athletic scholarship, which his grandparents firmly opposed. Sports were an escape for many minority kids, but the senior Tanners disdained the notion of one of their offspring being stereotyped with a bunch of kids from the ghetto. Catherine knew Jordan would have told Ralston to go for it. He'd have brought his parents around to accepting it, too. She wondered what Jeff would think of the situation and the advice he'd offer.

She gave herself a mental shake. Why should she care what Jeff Rowan thought? Just because the man kissed her—and she kissed him back—didn't justify her practically obsessing over him like some adolescent.

Steering herself back to the conversation at hand, she said, "As long as what Ralston does isn't illegal or immoral, he should be true to himself." The food arrived. "He won't be happy living someone else's dream," she added, when the waitress had gone.

"You sound like Jordan," her sister-in-law blurted out, then bit her lip. "I'm sorry. I didn't mean to…"

Catherine smiled. "That was a compliment. Nothing to apologize for. Don't worry about mentioning him. He's never far from my thoughts anyway." *Except when I'm kissing Jeff.*

"I've always envied you," Melissa said. "What you and Jordan shared was so special." She dabbed vinaigrette on her spinach salad. "I'd hoped Tyrone and I would have that… I've tried to be the wife he wants, he—"

"He doesn't deserve you, Melly. He is what he wants to be, not what he should be. You're entitled to better."

Melissa concentrated on her food. "Oh, I couldn't leave him, if that's what you suggesting. He's not perfect, but…I have to think of the children." She forked up dark green leaves. "I've seen what divorce can do to kids. I won't let that happen to my children. Growing up is hard enough these days, being a teenager especially," she rambled on. "So many influences parents can't control. At least we owe it to them to give them a stable home, even if it's not perfect." She tried to smile. "Besides, I love the handsome bastard." Her eyes were glassy.

Catherine reached across the table and placed her hand on her sister-in-law's. "I didn't mean to upset you."

"You haven't said anything I haven't thought myself. A hundred times. Maybe someday I'll work up the courage to tell him to go to hell, but not until after the kids are grown."

Catherine picked up a three-tiered triangle of sandwich. "You're right about kids needing stability. I've seen too much of what happens when there isn't any. Over ninety percent of the felons we deal with come from broken homes, and not all of them poor ones, either. You're doing the right thing."

"I'm worried about Dante," Melissa said a minute later.

"Why?" At nineteen, their elder son was a freshman at Rice, majoring in architecture, his uncle's favorite art form.

"You know how he always looked up to Jordan as more than an uncle, more like a fa—" She didn't complete the word. "Ever since Jordan's death, Dante and Ty haven't been getting along."

"They've been fighting? Over what?"

"There doesn't have to be a reason. The two never seem to exchange a civil word anymore. Dante's schoolwork has suffered, too. He's going to summer school—"

"I thought that was to earn extra credits."

"That's what we've been telling people. The truth is, he failed two subjects and has to take them over in order to go on to junior year."

"I'm sorry to hear that," Catherine said. The boy had graduated with honors a year early from high school. Jordan had been as proud of him as if he were his own son.

"I wish there was someone he could talk to. Someone who could help him."

"Have you considered professional counseling?"

"He won't go," Melissa said. "He insists he has everything under control. If only—"

"Jordan were here," Catherine concluded. But then, there wouldn't be a problem. For her, either. She wouldn't find herself thinking about Jeff Rowan in ways that were inappropriate.

"How is Ty handling the situation?" Catherine asked.

"Not well. He's threatening to kick Dante out of the house. At one point I was afraid the two were going to start swinging at each other."

"That's not like your son." He'd always been a quiet boy, rather introspective, neither combative nor competitive.

"Which is why I'm so worried about him," Melissa said, concern in her soft voice. "I wish I knew what was bothering him."

"Girl problems?"

Catherine watched the shadow cross her friend's face. Dante had had the same girlfriend through high school and college. Kiesha was plain, bookish and shy, and their relationship seemed more platonic than romantic.

"He broke up with Kiesha right after Jordan died."

Not a good sign. Dante wasn't effeminate, but Catherine had heard occasional snide comments that questioned his sexual orientation. If he was gay and struggling with a decision to come out of the closet, it might explain the tension between him and his very heterosexual father.

"He doesn't seem to have many friends anymore, spends too much time by himself."

Catherine sympathized. "As you said, he and Jordan were close. We all handle grief differently. Maybe you just have to give him time to work things out and be supportive of him when he does."

Melissa was savvy enough to understand what her sister-in-law was alluding to. She nodded despondently. "Kids don't always turn out the way we expect them to, do they?"

"No, they don't." Catherine knew she was referring to Kelsey. "Sometimes we have no choice but to trust them to make the right decisions."

ON HER DRIVE BACK to headquarters after lunch, Catherine thought about her comment to Jeff that there was no such thing as an ordinary family. She hadn't always felt that way. Her own family had seemed pretty mainstream when she was growing up. A mid-level manager in a large retail company, her father was the bread-winner; her mother a housewife who cooked and cleaned, ran errands and enjoyed bingo on Thursday evenings.

The crack in their perfect world came when Catherine brought Jordan Tanner home for dinner one Sunday afternoon. The uneasiness on her mother's face and the near outrage on her father's had shocked her. She'd anticipated surprise, but not hostility. They were civil to their guest, but the tension had been palpable.

After Jordan left, her father showed a side she hadn't seen before. Supporting equal rights was one thing, he reminded her, but dating a black guy was another. Her dad made his position even clearer by using racial epithets she'd never expected to hear from him. He didn't forbid her to see Jordan again—he was smart enough to know he couldn't prevent her from associating with him—but he did tell her never to bring him to their home again. Catherine had been crushed.

"I don't think we ought to see each other anymore," Jordan said the next day.

"What have I done?" she asked, hurt by his seemingly cavalier attitude.

"You haven't done anything. I just don't want to come between you and your folks."

"They'll come around." She'd actually believed it at the time.

"You might think so, but they won't."

"So you're just dropping me. I thought we were friends."

"We can still be friends," he said, "but that's all. Maybe someday a black guy can date a white girl without starting a riot, but not yet."

"And the journey will never be completed without the first step," she snapped back.

He'd smiled, his dark eyes softening. "I care too much for you to let you be hurt."

"You can't keep me from being hurt," she'd said. "I'm just asking you to be there when I am."

His eyes widened in surprise. He started to take her hand, then pulled back. "Pioneering is dangerous work."

Feeling bolder, she touched his arm, accentuating the contrast in the colors of their skin. She wasn't going into this blind. "Then I guess we had better be strong."

The kiss that followed was the most intimate, the most passionate they'd ever shared. More than a kiss, it had been an acknowledgment of where they were headed as well as a commitment to an odyssey that would be larger than both of them. If their affair faltered, it would not be because of skin color.

A month later she got a part-time job as a waitress to supplement the scholarship she was receiving and moved into a one-room apartment with a girlfriend. The relationship with her parents deteriorated further when she refused to come to Sunday dinners unless Jordan was welcome.

In the last semester of senior year, she told them she was going to marry him. The news was received with tight lips and dark scowls. Her parents came to her graduation but didn't stay for the reception afterward, and they refused to attend her wedding. She walked down the aisle alone.

Even the birth of their granddaughter didn't melt their hearts, but then, their granddaughter was black, so why should it? The one breach in the wall of silence was when her mother sent a sympathy card after Jordan's death. That her father's name was not on it spoke volumes. Maybe one day they'd reconcile, but it didn't seem likely. Catherine was willing to overlook a great many slights by her parents, but she couldn't forgive them for acting as if their granddaughter didn't exist.

In the meantime Catherine had work to do, a killer to find.

CHAPTER ELEVEN

THE EDITORIAL IN the Monday morning newspaper was the most vicious attack on the Houston Chief of Police the *Sentinel* had ever printed. Tyrone catalogued the recent mishandling of evidence by the forensics division that had put dozens, perhaps hundreds of felony cases in jeopardy, and that might have sent a host of innocent people to prison, while letting the real criminals roam the streets. Not only did it call Catherine Tanner incompetent, it insinuated she was a key element in the continuing corruption within the force. Adding insult to injury, he then accused her of setting the course of women in law enforcement back thirty years.

Catherine sipped her coffee and tried not to let the vitriol turn it to acid in her stomach.

Her mind replayed the lecture she used to give to the women who came through the police academy.

"There will be days when you'll bump your heads against a glass ceiling that will feel more like a stone wall.

"You'll encounter verbal abuse, not just from the criminals you apprehend, but from victims who feel you aren't doing enough. From witnesses who don't understand legal requirements or think they're stupid.

From your fellow officers who resent your role, initially as their equals, and for some of you later as their superiors.

"Every day you will have to earn afresh the respect of your male peers and superiors. You'll have to learn to fight like men, while never forgetting you're women. Not all of you will succeed, but I can promise that those of you who persist will grow stronger."

It had been a good pep talk, one she'd been obliged to learn the hard way at a time when the only women in the force had been meter maids.

With the help of a man who believed in her, encouraged her and held her in his arms, she'd withstood the slings and arrows aimed at her.

She would survive this assault, too. But coming from within the family made its knife edge all the more sharp, all the more hurtful. Especially when it was written by the man she'd protected.

The mayor called her office twice. Catherine instructed Annette to tell him she was in meetings. Reporters from the city's three TV stations as well as two national cable news networks came by, eager for her rebuttal to the charges leveled against her. Annette sent them packing. Three members of the city council phoned with demands that she contact them immediately, and a host of private individuals left messages, both supporting and condemning her as a public servant.

Catherine kept her luncheon appointment to address the Rotary Club at the Windsor Hotel. Instead of just one or two reporters showing up for a quick photo op, she was met with a phalanx of media hounds. She considered stonewalling with "No comment," but decided it would be better to answer their questions.

Greeting them with smiles and easygoing rapport, she pointed out that she'd inherited the corruption mentioned in the editorial from past administrations. She took pride in the force's honesty in addressing problems and aggressively rooting them out. She sidestepped the issue of who or what was currently under investigation.

"Your brother-in-law has attacked you personally. Why is that?" asked a reporter from the local CBS affiliate.

"I don't think the attack was personal at all," she replied. "He's doing a job, looking out for the public good, and I think it's to his credit that he doesn't let our family relationship influence his objectivity. He's concerned about police integrity. So am I. Keeping the force clean is my job. My name is used in the article because I'm the person in charge."

"So there is no personal animosity between you?"

"We've always gotten along very well."

She left the luncheon satisfied that for the moment she'd defused the situation. Her responses had all been accurate, though she recognized that some of them sounded like excuses. After two years as the top cop the problems were solidly hers, regardless of when they started. She'd bought some time today, but probably not much.

THREE TIMES Monday morning Jeff tried to call Catherine—once from home, twice from the airport—to let her know where he was going and why. A courtesy he didn't extend to other clients. But she was a professional investigator and might be able to give him some insights. Besides, he enjoyed talking to her, hearing her voice, and he took pleasure in sharing things with her.

He also wanted to get her reaction to her brother-in-law's diatribe in the morning paper. He didn't doubt she could handle the situation, but a sympathetic ear wouldn't hurt, and he'd promised her a shoulder to lean on.

Twice he got a busy signal, the third time an out-of-area message. He was disappointed but not surprised. She'd probably been bombarded with so many calls she'd had to turn off her cell phone. He could have dialed her office number but doubted he'd have better luck getting through. Besides, this wasn't exactly an emergency.

He was flying to Las Vegas because Kermit Nagle had called him early that morning to say he'd found the president of the defunct Uranica Corporation. Jeff asked for his number.

"Be a waste of time and long-distance charges," Kermit said. "You'll have to go there and see the guy in person. Chase Hutton's been in the mining business since the fifties. He doesn't trust anyone he can't look in the eye."

The three-hour flight from Bush International arrived at McCarran airport at noon. Learning that Hutton lived outside the city, Jeff had reserved a mid-sized rental car. Since he'd brought only carry-on baggage, he was out of the busy terminal within fifteen minutes.

The directions he'd received sent him into the hills west of the glittering desert metropolis to the end of a very long, narrow, dusty road. The house was a small, concrete-block, flat-roofed affair that even a fresh coat of white paint couldn't have made homey. Jeff pulled up behind a dented fifteen-year-old Ford pickup under a sagging single-car overhang. He rolled down his window, turned off the ignition and stepped out into the stifling dry desert heat. Compared with the humid swelter of Houston, it felt almost bearable.

Yellow weeds poked through the green gravel desert landscaping surrounding the house. Even the prickly pear cactus near the building was wilted. Jeff pressed the bell button beside the peeling hollow-core door. Hearing nothing and getting no response, he knocked.

The door swung open a minute later. Jeff wondered if he might have tripped into the twilight zone, since there was no one there—until a wheelchair rolled into view from behind it.

"Rowan?" the occupant asked in a scratchy voice. He was a scrawny cadaver of a man with oxygen prongs stuck in his crooked, vein-riddled nose.

"Yes, sir. Jeff Rowan. I'm here from—"

"I know where you're from. Come in, damn it. You're letting out all my air-conditioning."

Jeff stepped inside. As the wheelchair retreated, he closed the wooden door behind him.

"Thank you for seeing me," he said to the man's narrow back.

"Don't get many visitors these days." Hutton spun the wheelchair around, whipping the long clear tube that was connected to a wheezing oxygen machine against a side wall. "Got beer and whiskey. What's your pleasure?"

"I'm not used to this dry heat. What I really need is a glass of water."

"That stuff'll rust your pipes." The old man clucked his tongue, his expression one of distaste. "Don't recommend the swill from the tap. Check the icebox in the kitchen. Seems to me there's some of that fancy spring water there." He snatched an empty beer can off a lamp table and held it out. "Bring me a cold one while you're at it, will you?"

The place was small enough that Jeff didn't have to ask directions. At the far side of the cluttered living room was a dining area and just beyond it what passed for a kitchen. It smelled of old grease and stale cigarette smoke. According to Kermit, Hutton was dying of lung cancer, a common enough malady among old uranium miners. The man looked ninety but was only in his midsixties, and had, apparently, outlived just about all of his contemporaries in the business.

Jeff found an unopened bottle of water in the back of the refrigerator, which was so ancient there were no shelves in the door. He also snagged a can of beer from nearer the front.

Returning to the living room, he thanked his host for the H_2O and handed him his brew. The old man waved the gratitude away and popped the top.

"You live here alone?" Jeff asked, noting the dinner-plate-size ashtrays filled with cigarette butts on the end tables.

"Gerta on the other side of the hill drops by every day to see if I'm still alive. One of these days I won't be." There was no hint of bitterness or sentimentality in the statement, simply an acceptance of reality.

"I understand you used to be the president of Uranica Corporation," Jeff said, taking the chair closest to the window air conditioner that only just competed with the blast-furnace heat outside.

"President and CEO. Had a good run for a while, too. Lived high on the hog for a couple of years, till the bottom fell out. My partner insisted the price would go back up, that there would always be a demand for the yellow powder. He was wrong, of course. Don't know why I ever listened to him."

"Where is he now?"

"Buried him in Chloride twenty years ago. Told him he should never have given up whiskey. It's the only thing that's kept me going this long." He picked up the glass from the table and took a generous mouthful, chased it with a swig of beer, then poured himself more liquor from the half-empty bottle of Jack Daniel's at his elbow. "Sure you won't join me?"

"I'm driving," Jeff said.

Hutton shrugged, then began rambling about his late partner with a sort of passive nostalgia. He would undoubtedly have woven a series of tales about the old days if Jeff hadn't managed to get him back on track.

"Sure, I still have the records. They're in the little bedroom. Should have thrown them out years ago." His chuckle had a grating sound. "Guess I always hoped there'd be a miracle, and I'd find myself rich again."

"Do you know how many barrels of yellowcake were left in the warehouse in Houston when you shut the operation down?"

Hutton scratched his gaunt cheek. "Sixty, as in seconds per minute, minutes per hour. I always liked to use those little gimmicks for remembering things."

"You wouldn't have anything to verify that, would you?"

"You calling me a liar, sonny?"

"Hell, no," Jeff said, as if he'd been the one insulted. "But if I go back to Houston and tell them there were sixty barrels instead of forty, they'll call me crazy. The only thing those bureaucrats believe is what's written on paper, and then they go to court and fight over what the words mean."

The old man cackled. "Reckon you're right about that. Them records is all there."

"Mind if I take a look?"

He waved a bony, blue-veined hand toward the other end of the house. "Help yourself."

The little bedroom was down a short hallway, across from the slightly larger one Hutton used. The files were in dozens of neatly stacked boxes, but the orderliness turned out to be pure deception. There were plenty of file folders, but most of them were empty, their contents dumped loosely in the bottom of the cardboard cartons.

Jeff sat cross-legged on the dusty carpet in the airless room and started sorting. After fifteen minutes he was soaked with sweat, but he'd begun to discern a semblance of order and was able to hone in on the latter years of the corporation's existence.

An hour went by. He returned to the living room to see if Hutton was annoyed at his being there so long, but the dying miner was asleep in his wheelchair, his raspy breathing slow and steady. Jeff resumed his search.

Another hour and a quarter elapsed before he found what he was searching for, a single sheet of faded pink paper, headed "Final Inventory," dated the day the warehouse was shut down in 1977. At the bottom were two signatures, one belonging to an Oliver Hendricks, Site Manager, the other to William Summers, Warehouse Custodian. Among the items on the list of things left in storage were sixty barrels of yellowcake—the smoking gun.

He folded the thin paper and put it in his pocket just as he heard someone come in the front door. He returned to the living room to find a big, brawny woman with mousey gray-streaked hair and a ruddy complexion facing him. she wore a loose-fitting print dress, and her hands were fisted at her broad hips.

"Who the hell are you?" she demanded. Jeff judged her to be in her midsixties.

"My name is—"

"Gerta, he's all right," Hutton mumbled, having been jolted awake by her raised voice.

"Jeff Rowan," Jeff said and offered his hand. She ignored it.

"What are you doing here?"

"Damn it, Gert," Hutton snarled, "I told you this morning he was coming about them old files in the back."

She looked bewildered for a moment and ready to fight. There had been a time, Jeff suspected, when she could have taken him on in a brawl and probably come out ahead. He sure didn't want to mess with her now.

"Did you find what you were looking for?" Hutton asked.

"Sure did, thanks. You've been very helpful."

"See, Gert, I told you someday I'd do something useful."

"Well, it took you long enough, you old reprobate."

"She loves me," Hutton said with wink.

She scowled, but Jeff noticed she didn't dispute the point.

"Thank you, Mr. Hutton," Jeff said and offered his hand.

The man in the wheelchair took it, his shake demonstrating more strength than Jeff had expected.

"Glad to help, son. Have a good trip back."

"Ma'am," Jeff said politely to the sick man's hatchet-faced guardian. He let himself out and was surprised at how clean the broiling outside air felt and tasted.

He drove back to the airport, turned in the rental car and checked with the ticket counter. There was space available on a flight to Houston leaving in half an hour. He called the hotel, canceled his reservation and boarded the plane seconds before the door was sealed. He would have liked to call Catherine and let her know what he'd found but decided it would be much more satisfying to tell her in person.

CHAPTER TWELVE

KELSEY WAS FURIOUS when she read the editorial her uncle had written about her mother.

"Hasn't he done enough?" she muttered, her eyes squeezed closed.

She had to stop him, but confronting him wouldn't do any good, even if she had the audacity to face him. How could she? She was too ashamed. What was done was done. She'd made her decision—in a way it had been made for her. But she could still do something to help her mother.

As a novice, she lived in the community with the other sisters, but she hadn't yet taken a vow of poverty. She still owned her own car, the same one she'd had in college. Nothing fancy. She had no desire to show off. She also hadn't wanted to upstage Derek, whose little Chevy truck was several years old. So she'd bought a Honda Civic. The silver sedan was unpretentious and inconspicuous. Her cousin Ralston, who was several years younger and full of himself, accused her of slumming. He loved impressing his girlfriends with the Mercedes sports coupe his father had given him on his sixteenth birthday. Ralston had also gotten a slew of speeding tickets, which he bragged he never paid. Kelsey was sure her mother hadn't fixed them, but someone had. Did her mother even know? Maybe not. Police chiefs didn't get involved in mundane things like traffic violations.

The senior Tanners lived in the River Oaks section of Houston, close to downtown, yet virtually hidden from the city by the huge oaks, pecans, elms and sycamores foresting the slopes of the narrow valley of Buffalo Bayou that became the Houston Channel a mile or two farther east. The district was one of the oldest and most prestigious of Houston's residential areas. Kelsey's great-grandfather had purchased the property back in the twenties, but it had been his son, Marcus, who built on it in the late 1950s. By then, the *Houston Sentinel* had risen from an obscure Negro weekly to a nationally recognized city daily, and the family fortune, which went back to the days of Reconstruction, could be publicly displayed.

Kelsey remembered her mother once talking about her first visit to the Tanner residence.

"I'd never been in a mansion before." She'd laughed as she said it, as if it had been a fun experience. Kelsey doubted it. She wasn't sure if her grandparents disapproved of her mother because she was white or because she was lower middle-class. Probably a little bit of both. Being a cop certainly hadn't helped.

"I'm sure I gawked," her mother had said, "and made a terrible first impression."

As if that justified the disdain with which they'd always treated her. And now Uncle Tyrone was making it worse, making it public. Kelsey felt her face grow warm with outrage, something she would have to both hide and control.

The Tanner mansion, like many of its neighbors, was a cross between Greek revival and American Gothic. Only one corner of the two-and-a-half-story yellow-brick house could be glimpsed from the road. A high wrought-iron fence surrounded the five-acre estate.

Kelsey pressed the button in the brick pillar at the foot of the driveway, announced herself to the crackly voice that questioned who it was, waited for the ornate lacework gate to slide open, then proceeded along the winding driveway.

The grounds were fastidiously maintained by a full-time gardener who took his orders directly and exclusively from Grandma Amanda. Kelsey parked under the portico and went to the front door. A dark-faced housemaid in a black-and-white uniform answered the bell almost immediately.

"How's Grandpa?" Kelsey asked.

"He's right fine, Miss Kelsey," Ophelia replied. "Oh, I mean Sister Kelsey."

Kelsey smiled. "Miss, Sister or just plain Kelsey is fine."

Though close to seventy, Ophelia looked twenty years younger. She talked about retiring but never seemed to get around to it. She'd been with the family over forty years and had earned the right to address Kelsey by only her first name, but she never did.

"He's in his study," the short, round woman said, closing the door. "Go right in."

Marcus Tanner's study was a square room at the back of the house with a view of a formal garden that screened the tennis court beyond it. He lowered the book he was reading when Kelsey entered.

Tall and raw-boned even in his seventy-third year he was a commanding presence. If his stride was less confident than it had been ten years earlier when he was heading up the newspaper, no one doubted there was still steel behind the weakened façade.

"A pleasant surprise," he said, showing straight white teeth. All his own.

She came over to his chair and kissed his cheek. "How are you, Gramps?"

"Passable," he said. "Passable. What brings you to see me?"

The question was asked pleasantly enough, but Kelsey didn't miss the rebuke in it. She wasn't a frequent visitor and always wondered if the reception she received was one of censure that she came so infrequently or that she came at all.

On the other hand, she hadn't been given the access code to the front gate so she could wander in and out at will, the way her cousins could.

She'd never met her white grandparents, though she knew where they lived and had even walked by their house a couple of times with friends one summer when she was in high school, hoping she might see them, that they might recognize her and invite her in, but no one had been around. Being rejected by her mother's parents should have made her paternal grandparents all the more special. After all, she was black like them. But they always made her feel like an outsider.

It had upset her when she was younger, but her father had helped her learn to accept it.

"Your mother and I love you, Kel," he'd said. "You are the most precious thing in the world to us. Don't ever forget that. We have each other. That's all that matters."

Except now he was dead.

"Have you read today's paper?" she asked her grandfather, knowing full well he'd examined every line of it.

"I suppose you're upset about it." He made it sound as if she shouldn't be.

"She's my mother, Gramps. How do you expect me to feel?"

"I understand."

"Do you?" She sat in the leather chair across from him and folded her hands in her lap. "I don't. Why do you hate her so? She's never done anything to hurt you. She's always been polite and considerate, and in return you treat her with scorn. Why?"

"Perhaps I know a side of her you don't."

What secret could he possibly be referring to? "Then how about enlightening me."

"It's none of your concern."

Kelsey felt her composure slipping. "You show contempt for my mother, then say it's not my business?"

She'd come here determined to persuade her grandfather in a quiet and courteous manner to make Uncle Tyrone stop. She used to meekly accept her grandfather's dismissive attitude, but not anymore. She was angry. Perhaps she would always be angry now, but she wasn't going to be ignored.

"I don't think you have a reason," she said. "You just hate her because she's white."

He flexed his jaw. She could see his temper rising, but he didn't raise his voice. "You're young and innocent. I prefer to leave it that way."

Did he have any idea how much those words hurt? No, of course not, and there was no way she could tell him.

"Tell Uncle Ty to back off," she demanded.

"He has a job to do, a public trust to serve."

"That's bullshit and you know it."

The shock on her grandfather's face told her she'd stepped over the line, gone too far. He said nothing, merely glared at her as if she were a rodent or insect. She jumped up from her chair, her hands balled into fists.

"Tell him to leave her alone, or—" She bolted from the room.

She was through the doorway when she saw her grandmother standing in the hall, scowling at her. Kelsey halted.

"Come with me," Amanda ordered.

Turning, she entered the sitting room at the front of the house without so much as a backward glance, totally confident her granddaughter would follow. Heat pounding, Kelsey obeyed.

Small and delicate, Amanda Tanner matched her husband in strength of character. As far as Kelsey knew, they never fought, never contradicted or disagreed with each other—a model of marital harmony, a compelling example of two people who had endured trials and hardships and gained strength from the joint experience. They also shared a coldness, not toward each other—their mutual devotion was unmistakable—but toward everyone else. Jordan had paid them the polite deference they deserved as his parents—except in the matter of marrying Catherine against their wishes—but he'd also found them emotionally remote.

"Don't you ever come into this house and speak to your grandfather in that manner again," Amanda commanded, standing ramrod-straight, her gnarled hands folded at her narrow waist. She waited, no doubt expecting her granddaughter to apologize for her inexcusable conduct, but this time Kelsey refused to bend. She'd always been afraid of this woman, even on those rare occasions when Amanda showed affection. In spite of her resolve not to betray her fear, Kelsey felt herself trembling in the old woman's presence.

"You want to know why we have no respect for your mother?" Amanda finally asked, her words clipped, disapproving. "I'll tell you. She's a slut. She set her claws on Jordan, but that didn't keep her from trying to seduce Tyrone at the same time. He rejected her advances, but that didn't stop her. I wonder how many other men she's entertained over the years. She's nothing but a tramp."

Kelsey's heart stopped. She went numb. The room started to spin. Her legs began to weaken.

"No." The word came out as a moan. "It's not true."

She stared at her grandmother through a white haze, saw the gloating malevolence in the old woman's beady eyes. She'd just called her dead son a cuckold and seemed to take satisfaction in it. What kind of woman was this?

Kelsey covered her face with her hands and realized she was in danger of sinking onto the thick carpet. Summoning up a reserve of energy from somewhere, she fled the room and the house. Her fingers shook as she fumbled to start the car. She would have crashed through the gate if the electric eye hadn't opened it in time for her to pass through.

Her mother and Uncle Ty? It couldn't be. She didn't believe it. Never. Except…

AFTER LUNCH, Catherine could no longer put off returning the mayor's repeated calls. She hoped he had seen her impromptu news conference and that it had placated him, at least temporarily.

"Kean, Rocha and Castillo are calling for your resignation," Walbrun told her. They were the three councilmen who had left messages, insisting she contact them at once.

"I have no intention of resigning now or anytime soon," she declared.

"I'm glad to hear it," he responded, but his lack of zeal conveyed diplomacy rather than sincerity. "I saw you on TV. You handled the press well."

"Why didn't you tell me Buster Rialto was at the last meeting you had with Jordan?" She kept her tone neutral, but the silence on the other end told her she'd drawn blood.

"I…didn't think it was important."

"In the future, Stan, I'd appreciate it if you'd let me

decide what's important. I don't think you'd like your staff keeping information from you."

"I'm not a member of your staff," he snapped.

"No, you're not," she said with a sigh. "But I thought you were my friend."

"I…I'm sorry, Catherine. I didn't mean any harm."

"Thanks for calling, and for your vote of support."

She replaced the receiver and was surprised to see her hand shaking. She didn't have time to dwell on it, however. Annette stood in the doorway carrying a sheaf of papers.

"You're going to have a cauliflower ear by the time you finish with these," she said and presented the stack of telephone messages.

Over the next few hours Catherine felt like an answering machine, repeating the same message over and over again. No, she was not going to resign. No, the level of corruption hadn't increased since she'd been at the helm. Yes, Internal Affairs was aggressively pursuing all allegations of police misconduct. No, she wouldn't discuss ongoing investigations.

It was after five when she finally turned her cell phone on again. A second later it chirped.

"I just got back from Vegas. I have something for you," Jeff said without identifying himself.

Las Vegas? What was he doing there? But her door was open, and she didn't want to take a chance on being overheard, so she didn't ask the question. She looked at the institutional wall clock over the door. "I'll be tied up here for a while yet. See you at eight."

"Your house?"

"Yes."

He hung up. She stared at the phone for several seconds and finally closed it. What could he have found in Las Vegas, Nevada? As soon as she thought of the state, she had a good idea. She smiled just as the phone on her desk rang. She picked it up and resumed her litany of answers.

CHAPTER THIRTEEN

JEFF HAD CAUGHT a rebroadcast of her interview with the press on the evening news. She was good. Even when she said Tyrone Tanner was just doing his job, that his attack hadn't been personal, she'd stayed cool and at ease. He admired that. Under the same circumstances he would have lashed out.

Taking a chance that she would not have had time for dinner, he stopped off at a supermarket and picked up a few things.

She looked a bit frazzled when she opened the door. Frazzled, but incredibly alluring. What was it about this woman that made him so aware that she was a female and he was a male? Whatever it was, it was powerful. And troubling. They weren't compatible, yet there was something flowing between them.

"What's this?" she asked, eyeing the bag of groceries in the crook of his arm.

"I thought you might be hungry."

Her face lit up. "You mean I won't have to pop another frozen dinner in the microwave? Watch out, Jeff Rowan, I just may have to marry you."

The shock on her face when she realized what she'd

said made him laugh, while the statement itself sent a disturbing, yet not unpleasant punch to his belly. He stepped over the threshold. "Don't worry. I won't hold you to that."

"I…I'm sorry," she said, still flustered, and closed the door. "I don't know where that came from."

He smiled, enjoying her discomfort. "The stomach?" he asked. "I guess that means you're hungry." He marched toward the kitchen, aware of her trailing behind him and the electricity crackling between them.

"Kelsey will tell you I'm not much of a cook," she said, by way of explanation and apology. "Jordan did most of the cooking. By myself…it just doesn't seem worth the effort."

"Well, there are two of us this evening, so you're spared eating out of plastic. You may have dishes to do, though."

"That's why I have a dishwasher." Her little chuckle was more carefree this time. "What did you bring?"

"I didn't know what you might have on hand, so I got the makings of an omelet. Is cheese and mushroom okay?"

"Perfect." Her face beamed.

"And salad, of course."

"Of course."

He'd bought a baguette, which she popped in the oven for a few minutes to crisp up, then they set about preparing the rest of the simple meal. At first, he had to ask where things were, but as he became more familiar with the layout of the kitchen, he began rummaging for himself.

He cleaned and sliced fresh mushrooms and complimented her on how she'd handled the media.

She washed and tore up lettuce and told him she'd had practice over the years.

He diced red onion and asked if she thought the pressure was off for a while.

She quartered small red tomatoes and assured him the campaign against her was only heating up.

He whisked half a dozen eggs with a few swift strokes and wanted to know if she thought it would get worse.

She shredded cheddar cheese and assured him it would.

While she set the table, he pulled the cork on the full-bodied pinot noir he'd picked up on the way over.

She presented him with two large bowled glasses.

He poured.

They touched glasses, and just before sampling the wine, their eyes met across the rims.

The room stood still, as if there were no world beyond it. The way she regarded him produced a kind of telepathy. She told him she enjoyed his company and that she was grateful not to be alone. But there was something more. Something that set off a tremor in him of a kind he'd never felt with other women.

"Bon appétit," he managed to say.

Instead of drinking, she lowered her gaze, then raised it in a doubt-filled smile that seemed to harbor tears.

"Thanks for coming over this evening," she murmured. "For doing this."

"My pleasure. Any time."

They sipped. Their eyes locked. He was about to take her glass and put it down on the marble counter-top beside his, so he could fold her into his arms and kiss her, but then the oven timer dinged. The moment passed, but not the desire.

She removed the bread from the wall oven while he heated a copper-clad skillet on the gas range and melted butter in it. After sautéing the mushrooms and onions, he tipped them into a dish, added another pat of butter to the pan and poured in the frothy eggs.

She placed their wineglasses on the table and leaned against the side counter to watch him. He added the other ingredients, then folded the puffy mixture over on itself.

"You're good at that," she said. "My omelets always end up as scrambled eggs."

He felt pleasantly self-conscious. "I've had my failures."

She brought their dishes. He divided the omelet and slipped the portions onto their plates, then topped each with sprigs of the parsley he'd found in the crisper of the fridge.

"Voilà," he said, and followed her to the table by the window.

CATHERINE COULDN'T EXPLAIN why she dimmed the kitchen lights before she sat down, leaving the two of them isolated in their own little world. She never had when she, Jordan and Kelsey had eaten their family meals here. For some reason, it seemed appropriate tonight.

No, not appropriate, she admonished herself. Dangerous. She was giving Jeff the wrong signals. He'd kissed her and she'd kissed him back. Pleasant, but she didn't want it to go any further.

Liar. That kiss had been more than pleasant. The

problem was that she wanted it to go further. He had stoked a fire that had been nothing but smoldering embers for a year. She wanted to be touched. She wanted to feel like a woman, and that awareness filled her with guilt. She missed Jordan so much that sometimes she wished she had been the one who had died.

Displacement. That's how a shrink would explain the attraction she felt for the man sitting across from her now. She was using him as a substitute for Jordan, who was gone and wouldn't be back. Not in this lifetime.

Jeff's question resurfaced. "Would he want you to spend the next forty years alone?"

She knew the answer.

Using the side of her fork, she cut into the omelet. Jeff had done a perfect job. The eggs were light, the seasoning perfect.

"So what were you doing in Las Vegas?" She hoped the change of subject would corral her errant thoughts. "You must have found someone or something."

The way the corners of his mouth tilted up told her she wasn't fooling him, but he was willing to play the game.

"Both." He took a sip of wine. "I went to see the president of Uranica Corporation, the company that stored the yellowcake in the Rialto warehouse."

Catherine stilled the fork on its way to her mouth, then lowered it. "And?"

"He's dying of lung cancer. Probably won't be around much longer. I also brought back the original, signed, final inventory of what was left behind."

"And," she repeated, trying to decide if his news was good or bad. "What did it say?"

"Sixty barrels."

She gave herself a minute to absorb the information, then she closed her eyes and slouched against the back of the chair. "So Summers was telling the truth."

She wasn't sure what she felt, what she was supposed to feel. Forty barrels would have meant Jordan died of a coronary. A tragic death but the will of God. Sixty meant there was a good chance he'd been murdered, and she had been cheated, robbed of the man she loved. Either way he was dead, and she was alone.

No, not completely alone, she thought, as she glanced at the man sitting across from her.

"We need to turn it over to the feds," Jeff said a minute later.

"Not so quick." She buttered a piece of the crispy French bread.

"You're not thinking of withholding this from them, are you? That wouldn't be a good idea, Catherine."

"No, but let's consider the sequence of events." She finished her omelet. "It's been my experience that federal agencies are slow in dealing with evidence they haven't uncovered themselves." She toyed with the stem of her wineglass. "And they like to play very close to the vest."

"No argument there." He set his fork on the empty plate. "But we're dealing with national security here."

"I want to go public with this, Jeff."

He ran his tongue across his teeth as he gazed at her. "I don't think they're going to like that."

"I know they won't," she agreed. "But once we turn that piece of paper over to them, they'll impose a gag order on us. That's why we have to go public first. With the cat out of the bag, there isn't much they can do. We won't have broken any law or interfered with any investigations in progress. That we know of," she added.

"Why antagonize people who can hurt you?"

She'd considered that but had come to a different conclusion. "They'll rant and rave, even make threats," she acknowledged, "but they won't hurt me because ultimately I'll be helping them."

She could see Jeff's mind working as he broke off a piece of bread and spread it with a thin layer of butter. "I'm listening."

"Your contact at the FBI said they tried to find someone associated with Uranica Corporation and were unsuccessful. That makes this scrap of paper an embarrassment to them. The first thing they'll do is try to discredit it. Even if they do validate it, unless and until they are successful in recovering the missing yellowcake, they'll keep their mouths shut about it."

He swirled his wine. "I have to agree with you."

"They'll do file searches of cargoes going to various countries and organizations. They may even locate the missing barrels, but it could take months, even years. By then the harm could already have been done. On the other hand, if we go public, we can produce leads—"

"Or start a panic." He crunched bread.

She'd considered that, too. "Not if we handle it right, explain that yellowcake is not dangerous in itself."

"Okay. But you'll have every kook for six counties around reporting little green men."

She laughed. "Probably. But so what? They show up for every manhunt anyway."

"True enough. We can hold back certain bits of information to help separate the valid claims from the bogus, like we do with most requests for information from the public."

"Exactly." She got up and began clearing the table.

"Those aren't your only reasons, though, are they?" Jeff pushed back his chair and joined her in removing the dishes to the counter.

"Want some fruit?" Catherine asked, her hand on the refrigerator door handle.

"Sounds great."

She removed two large apples from the crisper, put them on plates and grabbed a couple of paring knives from a drawer.

"I want to put Buster Rialto on the defensive." She sat down and halved, then quartered the fruit. "He's more likely to trip and fall if he's looking over his shoulder."

"He'll also be more dangerous."

"I can't shy away from a job because of that."

He grinned. "So you'll call a press conference and go public with this while I'm delivering the goods to the feds?"

"*We're* going public," she corrected him, and had to suppress a smile at seeing the amazement on his face. "Together. While a courier is delivering a photocopy of the inventory to the feds. We'll keep the original as insurance."

He shook his head. "I won't help your credibility, Catherine. I'm a disgraced cop, remember?"

"Let me deal with that. Now here's what I want to do."

CATHERINE HELD the news conference at one o'clock Tuesday in the lobby of police headquarters. Jeff was standing beside her. She read the statement they had composed together and was immediately bombarded with questions from the floor.

"Chief Tanner," a local TV news reporter called out, "you claim twenty barrels of uranium are missing from the warehouse owned by the Rialto Corporation—"

"I said twenty barrels *may* have gone missing—"

"How long have you known about this, and why didn't you report it when the Superfund began cleaning up the site?"

"Mr. Rowan brought me the information last evening. I have contacted federal authorities and turned the evidence over to them."

"What evidence?"

"I'm not at liberty to discuss specific details of their ongoing investigation."

"Have you discussed this with people at the Rialto Corporation?"

"I'm sure federal officials will be interviewing them very soon."

"Yellowcake is one of the items on the terrorist alert list of banned substances," another reporter called out. "Are you accusing Rialto Corp of supporting terrorists?"

Catherine held up her hands. "No one is accusing anyone of anything. All we know at this point is that there appear to have been sixty barrels of yellowcake on hand when the warehouse was closed in 1977, but only forty were found when the Superfund went in to clean the place out last year. There are all sorts of possible ex-

planations for the discrepancy. The original inventory
may have been in error, twenty barrels may have been removed legitimately and not correctly accounted for,
or—"

"Or they could have been sold or stolen," said a reporter in front.

"Speculation at this point is fruitless and counterpro-
ductive. The Department of Homeland Security will be
investigating this matter very carefully."

"How dangerous is yellowcake?"

"I'm no expert," Catherine said, "but it's my understanding that in its raw form it's not a public threat,
which is why it was allowed to languish in a warehouse
all these years. Yellowcake becomes a dangerous substance only when it undergoes enrichment." She held
up her hands and smiled. "Sorry, folks, chemistry and
physics are not my areas of expertise." Then she added
with a smile, "You'll have to find a nuclear physicist to
explain it to you. And hope you can understand what
they tell you."

A few reporters chuckled.

"Mr. Rowan, how did you come into possession of
this information?"

"I can't give you any details, but I can tell you the
source is reliable and the evidence credible."

"Chief Tanner, if Rialto has owned the warehouse all
these years," a woman in the back asked, "they have
been legally responsible for its security, haven't they?"

"Federal and state officials will have to determine
culpability and liability. If—and I emphasize if—it

turns out the yellowcake was not handled properly, they will decide on appropriate follow-up action."

"Mr. Rowan. Weren't you the detective in the Houston Police Department who was fired last year for racial profiling?"

"I left the HPD last year. The reason—"

"Don't believe everything you read in the papers," Catherine interjected.

"Are you saying he wasn't fired for racial profiling?" a strident voice called out.

"No, I'm not saying that."

"So he was fired for racial profiling."

"I'm not saying that, either."

"But he was fired."

Catherine raised her hands. "I'm neither confirming nor denying that Mr. Rowan is a member of the Houston Police Department. Now, let's move on."

A loud and hostile male voice boomed from the side of the room. "Isn't this all a smokes creen to divert attention away from charges of corruption in your police department?"

The reporter, whom Catherine recognized as the muckraker Tyrone had hired away from one of the weekly tabloids, had a clear agenda but she had anticipated the question. She paused to maintain her composure.

"Since I took over as police chief two years ago, we have made major strides in identifying and correcting problems within the department. I'm not claiming we're perfect. There is still a great deal of work to be done. I have dedicated myself to ensuring the people of Houston are safe and secure in their homes, workplaces, recreational facilities and on the streets of this great city."

The reporter tried to interrupt, but she waved her hand and spoke over him.

"Our police force of almost five thousand officers is one of the largest in the nation. In spite of allegations to the contrary, it is also one of the most effective law-enforcement agencies in the country. Our people are dedicated professionals who take their jobs very seriously. Integrity is the linchpin of our core values of honesty and devotion to duty. We cannot do the job alone, however. That's why we've established hotlines and procedures for people to contact us confidentially or even anonymously if they have information that may lead to the apprehension of criminals or correction of police irregularities."

She looked into the main camera. "I urge anyone having information about the missing barrels of uranium to contact our office or federal officials immediately. This is not simply a matter of criminal activity but of national security."

"Does that mean you don't have a clue what happened to the uranium?" a woman asked.

Before she could answer, the *Sentinel* reporter called out, "Do you have any cases of police corruption under investigation right now?"

She let a moment pass before responding. "I'm not going to discuss current investigations. Our internal affairs division is always watching for possible legal and ethical violations of our code of conduct. But let me add something else. Spurious, exaggerated and unsubstantiated charges of corruption serve no purpose except to undermine public confidence in law enforcement."

She hardened her gaze. "If the *Houston Sentinel* has specific information about current problems within this law enforcement institution, it not only has the right, it has the duty to present those facts to the people who can do something about them. Otherwise one would have to question their motivation in making what amount to hollow accusations."

As expected, this produced a storm of additional questions. "The recent editorial in the *Sentinel,* accusing you of being part of the problem was written by your brother-in-law," a news anchor shouted out. "Does he have a personal vendetta against you? And if so why?"

She held up her hands, saying, "I have no further comment. Thank you for coming."

Questions were still being lobbed after her as she stepped away from the podium and left the room.

Jeff also ignored requests for information directed at him and followed the chief out. Neither spoke until they reached the security checkpoint by the entrance to the parking garage. She turned to him and extended her hand.

"Thank you for coming, Mr. Rowan," she said loud enough for the guard on duty to hear.

"Good luck, Chief," he replied, then murmured, "You've pulled the tiger's tail. Now let's see if he bites or runs."

CHAPTER FOURTEEN

LUCY MONTALVO, who worked in missing persons called a few minutes after five.

"Just wanted to give you a progress report, Chief. No luck yet on finding Stuckey. The guy's elusive. As soon as we locate one of his cribs, he's moved on."

"Keep looking," Catherine said.

"Oh, we're not giving up. Caught you on TV today. Have to admit I was surprised to see Rowan with you. I'd forgotten how yummy that man is. If I weren't happily married…" She sighed. "Anyway, the two of you raised a few eyebrows. That's for sure."

"What's the overall response?" Catherine couldn't help asking.

Lucy laughed. "About what you might expect. One third think you're out of your ever-loving mind. One third think it's a brilliant move, and the last third couldn't care less."

It could be worse, Catherine thought. "Thanks for the update."

She left the office at seven and drove home. Tonight was the concert for the Houston Children's Fund. Her mind and her body craved a night in but not showing up was not an option. Pavarotti would be performing, having been coaxed out of retirement for this special event, and her in-laws would be there.

With very little time to change and get to the hall downtown, she munched on a Power Bar while checking her e-mail. A quick shower refreshed her a little. She slipped into her black silk evening gown, put the finishing touches to her makeup, had another glance at her e-mail and left the house.

This was not the first social event she had attended by herself since Jordan's death, but the pang of loneliness, of feeling abandoned, was still raw.

Jones Hall was already crowded by the time she arrived. Nearly six feet tall in her two-inch heels, she scanned the lobby for familiar faces, hoping to find someone with whom she would be comfortable. On the other side of the vast space Tyrone towered above the crowd. She was relieved he had his back to her, so she didn't have to acknowledge him or the other members of his family just yet.

Suddenly the sound and polite jostling of the crowd disappeared. Jeff was standing by one of the pillars.

Their eyes met. He smiled. Her pulse quickened.

They started toward each other.

"You're beautiful," he said, when at last they reached the middle of the room.

It had been a long time since anyone had told her that. She ate it up.

"I didn't expect to see you here."

"Not a gumshoe event, huh? Think I can get a refund if I turn my ticket in before the music starts?"

He was teasing, calling her a snob, but how many people were willing to spend five hundred dollars to attend a single concert, even if it was for a good cause?

"I'm glad you're here." She hadn't meant it to sound as if he was there exclusively for her. Then came the panic. Maybe he wasn't the one who'd shelled out the money.

"Are you with someone?" People rarely bought single tickets to these events, but then most of the people here were more affluent than he was.

The lights flashed, indicating the concert was about to begin.

"Where are you sitting?" he asked.

She gave him her seat number.

"I'm nowhere close, but I'll see you at the intermission."

Then he was gone, swallowed by the crowd.

She shuffled into the packed auditorium, resisted the urge to search for him, and took her assigned place left of center, six rows up from the stage. On the way she nodded a greeting to her father-in-law at the other end of the row. He chose to ignore her. So did Jordan's mother. Tyrone continued an animated conversation with the man next to him. Only Melissa waved an enthusiastic greeting.

During the first half of the concert Catherine couldn't help being swept up by the enchanting arias of Verdi, Puccini and Wagner. She remembered what it felt like to have Jordan sitting beside her, her hand encased in his, but then her mind wandered to the image of Jeff, handsome in his tux, his eyes catching hers and the longing they ignited.

As soon as the applause subsided she was out of her

seat and hurrying to the lobby. The fatigue of the day dissipated at the thought of being with Jeff.

The moment she stepped into the lobby he was at her side. Warmth swept through her when he placed his hand on the small of her back to guide her through the slow-moving crowd. She had to fight the temptation to lean into him.

Friends and acquaintances greeted her, forcing her to engage in casual conversation, when what she wanted was for everyone around her to vanish, everyone except the man who was touching her.

Well past the doorway now, Jeff steered her to one side, away from the streaming flow that fanned out into the high-ceilinged lobby.

"I had no idea you were interested in opera," she said. She'd already established she was a snob. Now she was babbling.

He took in the assembly around them with a glance. "I haven't always been. A friend introduced me to it a few years ago."

Images of a socialite in a white sheath, dripping with diamonds, flashed across Catherine's mind. "She must have seen your potential."

A smile crept across his face and made his hazel-green eyes twinkle. "He." His lips curled. "Sal Vecchio and I were detectives together in fraud. As far as he was concerned music and opera were synonymous. He played it all the time in our car. I learned to appreciate it by default." He grinned. "Or maybe it was self-defense."

They were surrounded by glitz and glitter, but she was far more aware of the man standing beside her and the warmth he generated. She used her program to fan herself. "I'm thirsty," she said.

"What would you like?" he asked. "I'll get it."

"Something soft, without caffeine."

"Be right back." He faded into the milling crowd.

Her in-laws weren't too far away, but she elected to people watch, rather than join them. She had no idea what kind of reception she would receive from the other Tanners and decided it would be best to let them approach her. Melissa was stunning in a full-length silver gown that hugged her slender hips and thighs and showed off enough cleavage that every man in the room was giving her the once-over.

Catherine shifted to her right to watch another part of the crowd, only to find Carlotta Rialto gazing up at her.

The seventy-something woman resembled everyone's favorite grandmother. Her ankle-length gown of black lace over satin epitomized elegance.

"I saw you on television today," she said in a sweet voice. Catherine knew she could be anything but. In spite of her public persona, Carlotta Rialto was reputed to be not just the head of her family, but a kind of "godmother" to the people she dealt with.

"I was very disappointed," she said. "It upsets me to think you suspect our family of being unpatriotic."

"Mrs. Rialto, I never said that or implied it. In fact, I was very careful to make sure everyone realized I wasn't making any accusations. At this point we have no idea what happened—"

"Oh, I'm so glad to hear that," Carlotta said with a saccharine smile. "We have a standing in this community, you know. Our name and reputation are so important to us we would do anything to protect it. I hope you'll continue to make certain everyone understands that."

As benign as the words sounded, Catherine had no doubt she'd just been threatened with dire consequences if she caused trouble.

"Pavarotti is wonderful, don't you think?" Carlotta said. "We're very privileged to get to hear him. Enjoy your evening, Mrs. Tanner."

She disappeared into the milling crowd. Catherine searched for Jeff and spied him fourth or fifth in the line that was snaking its way toward a portable bar. She was about to join him when she heard someone behind her call her name.

"Hello, Ty," Catherine said, trying to sound relaxed as she looked up at his dark face. The glint in his ebony eyes proclaimed both intelligence and humor. With the curl of his full lips he also projected a hint of mischief and danger that many women found fascinating, even erotic.

Catherine had been unperturbed by Carlotta Rialto, but this man put her nerves on edge.

"Where's Melly?" she asked.

Tyrone sipped from a flute of champagne that seemed ridiculously delicate in his large, long-fingered hand. "Went to the powder room. Are you and Rowan enjoying yourselves?"

She had the impression he wasn't referring to the music. She wished Jeff would return. Aware of how much she wanted him as a buffer, a protector, she felt like a coward. But she was stronger than that.

"It's a wonderful concert," she said.

"I must say, your choice of white knight surprises me."

"What?"

A woman nearby turned at her sharp tone, eyed the big black man and blond woman, then averted her gaze and rejoined her party's conversation.

"Jeff Rowan," Tyrone said. "The two of you have been mooning over each other all evening."

Catherine was stunned. She had no idea anyone had noticed.

Tyrone's grin was villainous. "I suppose a disgraced cop is about the best you'll be able to get these days. You know the old saying, sleep with a black, you can't go back. You realize, of course, that no decent white man will want you now. I mean, how could he compete with the memory of a good black lover?" He glanced again at Jeff. "He'll never be able to satisfy you."

She felt the heat rise to her face and knew it must be crimson, not from embarrassment but from staggering rage. The impulse to slap him across the face was overwhelming, until, as she was about to bring her hand up, the last shred of reason told her that was precisely what he wanted her to do. Create a public spectacle. Her muscles quivered with suppressed fury, but she managed to keep her arm by her side.

"Catherine, are you all right?"

Tearing her gaze away from her brother-in-law, Catherine focused on Melissa.

JEFF STOOD in line, chatting with the people around him, every few seconds glancing over at Catherine. It wasn't until a huge black man approached her, however, that he became concerned. During the course of their conversation her color rose then fell, leaving her pasty-faced. She wasn't just upset, she was irate, maybe even frightened.

Though he'd finally ordered their drinks, he considered bolting to her side until he saw a stunning black woman in a shimmering silver gown join them and the atmosphere relaxed. Jeff gave the bartender a generous tip and wended his way back.

"You must be Jeff Rowan," the big man said, as Jeff approached. "I saw you on TV today. That was quite a press conference."

Jeff handed Catherine her lemon-lime soda.

"Jeff, this is Tyrone Tanner," she told him. Her social poise was back, but he could feel the controlled storm just below the surface.

All of six-feet-six, broad-shouldered and flat-bellied, the editor of the *Houston Sentinel* was both impressive and imposing. He thrust out his hand and smiled a smile that lit up his whole face, beaming pure charm and goodwill. In that instant Jeff understood how the guy got away with so much. He possessed the kind of charisma that made men want to like him and women gape. That brand of personal magnetism could be intoxicating.

Jeff wasn't surprised at the strength of the man's handshake.

"And this is his wife, Melissa," Catherine said.

"Ms. Tanner." He took her small, more delicate hand. For a moment, as she offered the usual social niceties, he glimpsed anxiety in the woman's deep-brown eyes.

The lights flickered, signaling the end of the intermission.

"We better get back," Tyrone said. "Enjoy the rest of the concert." He shepherded his wife toward the door to the auditorium.

"What did he say to you?" Jeff asked, as they proceeded toward another line.

"Nothing I haven't heard before."

Jeff clasped her elbow and turned her to face him. "Whatever it was, it got you pretty riled. I thought you were going to punch his lights out."

She rolled her eyes. "That obvious, huh?"

The crush of people forced them to move forward again.

"To me it was. So what did he say?"

Out of the corner of her mouth, she said, "He seems to think there's something going on between us."

Catherine watched him struggle with the concept. Did he want to deny it? Remind her they were business associates, nothing more, that a kiss didn't make them "us."

She'd loved only one man her entire life, and he was dead. Maybe what she was feeling for Jeff Rowan was nothing more than need growing out of loneliness and frustration. Maybe any man touching her the way he had would have provoked the same response.

What about the vile things Tyrone had said, that no white man would ever want her now? She'd never thought of Jordan as black. He was simply a man. More important, he was *the* man who loved her.

Now she found herself attracted to someone else.

Jeff held her arm as they inched along. She'd been

unwilling to answer his earlier question. Would Jordan have wanted her to live the rest of her life alone? She would never have been unfaithful to him while he was alive. Was she being unfaithful to him now because she wanted Jeff to touch her, to put his lips to hers, to make her feel again just a little of what she had felt before?

"What exactly did Tyrone say that spooked you?" he repeated.

Should she tell him? What would his response be?

No, she decided. It wasn't worth repeating. "That I must be desperate to be interested in a disgraced cop."

Jeff's grip tightened, not enough to hurt, merely an unconscious response to the slight.

They reached the point where they had to separate. He stepped aside to let other people pass.

"We need to talk," he said.

"Don't wait for me after this is over, just come to the house."

His smile had her itching to run her finger along the cleft of his chin. "I'll be there."

She wanted so much to kiss him. Instead she forced herself to turn away and saunter to her seat.

She couldn't have described what was played or sung in the second half of the concert. Love arias, probably. At least that's what the memory of them felt like when she later made her way out of the hall and hurried to her Lexus. Her reserved parking space was near the exit so she could get out quickly if duty called.

The fatigue of the long day was beginning to catch up with her by the time she arrived home. It was after eleven. Had she not invited Jeff over, she would have taken off her clothes and crawled into bed. The idea had a lot to recommend it. Instead she exchanged her evening dress for a satin robe that was both modest and stylish.

In the kitchen she checked the wine supply, trying to decide if Jeff would prefer red or white. Perhaps he'd rather have brandy or port. She poured herself a glass of cream sherry and felt her tired body begin to mellow out at the first sweet taste.

The doorbell rang just as she was about to ensconce herself in the living room and turn on the TV to one of the news channels.

Jeff's hair was unruly when she let him in, as if he'd been raking his fingers through it. Fatigue crinkled the corners of his eyes.

"I won't keep you up," he said, as he stepped into the entryway.

"Take off your coat and let's sit down."

He unbuttoned the tuxedo jacket but didn't remove it until they were in the living room, where he draped it over the back of a chair.

"I'm having sherry," she said. "I also have beer and wine, brandy, whiskey—"

"Maybe some Scotch."

She led him to the wet bar and started to fix him a drink, but he motioned her to the couch and poured the twelve-year-old single-malt himself.

"Actually, what I wanted to talk to you about could have waited until tomorrow." He settled beside her, facing the grand piano and picture window that looked out on to the night. "I just thought… I talked to Derek this afternoon. He did a further check on Jordan's last editorial. It was deleted from his office terminal about three days after he died, by a person who had logged on using Tyrone's new password."

"So Tyrone deleted it." She sipped her drink.

"It appears so." He extended his arm across the back of the couch. His hand wasn't touching her neck, but its heat cascaded down her shoulders, her chest and collected lower.

"So where do we go from here?" he asked.

How about the bedroom?

CHAPTER FIFTEEN

WHEN JEFF DIDN'T receive an answer, he said, "It's pretty obvious Tyrone considers you the enemy. I have to ask why."

She couldn't tell him. She wouldn't. She hadn't even told Jordan.

"I think he's infatuated with you," Jeff said. "Probably always has been."

"What?" She'd started to lift her wineglass to her lips, but a shiver forced her to put it back down.

No decent white man will ever touch you. No white guy will ever be able to satisfy you.

"Don't let yourself be alone with him." Jeff's voice was soft, caring...seductive. "If he comes to the house when you're alone, don't let him in."

It was good advice, and she planned to heed it. She couldn't allow herself to be intimidated by Tyrone.

"I can take care of myself."

"I mean it," Jeff murmured as his fingers coursed over her shoulders, cupped the back of her neck. He inched closer, his thigh pressed against hers, solid, warm, welcoming. He leaned into her. Their eyes met. Slowly he brought his mouth to hers. Her hands expanded against his chest, not in rejection, but finding comfort in the tantalizing contours of his hard muscles.

He threaded his fingers into her hair, held her captive as his tongue plunged between her teeth. A warning bell rang in her head. No, not a warning, she amended, more a carillon.

An erotic jolt swept through her. She felt herself begin to melt. She could still say no, but she didn't want to. His other hand caressed her left breast, a tender massage that had her begging for more. Her nipples hardened. Lust bunched and pinched in her belly. Breathless, she broke off the kiss.

"I want you, Cate."

No one had ever called her that. She'd been Cathy as a kid. Jordan had sometimes called her Cath. But no one had ever called her Cate. This was Jeff's name for her. She liked it.

His hazel eyes searched hers for a response.

"I want you, too," she murmured, then lowered her gaze, unwilling to let him see how much, or glimpse the full impact of the desire reflected there.

He rose to his feet, extended his hands and pulled her up. Their knees touched. He swept her into his arms and kissed her again, pressing his body to hers, letting her feel his arousal.

She led him halfway down the hall to a room on the right. It was shrouded in darkness but for the moonbeams streaming through a double window on his left.

Turning to him, she wound her arms around his neck. His mouth was hot and eager. As they deepened the kiss, he untied the belt of her gown. With shaky fingers she loosened his bow tie, felt the racing throb of his pulse as she unfastened his collar button. Undoing the ones below it, she slid her hands beneath the starched fabric and rubbed his warm flesh.

Suddenly they were struggling to get out of their clothes. He tugged the silky robe off her shoulders. She pulled his shirt out of his pants. He unsnapped her bra and drew it away. A whimper escaped her when he touched her nipples. She unbuttoned his waistband, felt the heat of the bulge beneath it. His trousers tumbled to his ankles. He tried to step out of them, but his shoes tangled in the cuffs.

With a nervous laugh, she knelt and untied his laces, slipped the shiny shoes off his feet and looked up as he stepped out of them. His hands extended to her, he raised her into his arms and almost lost it when her naked breasts made contact with his bare skin. Her nipples were hard against his rib cage. Their kisses became frantic. Lips still locked, they stumbled toward the double bed. In seconds they were shucked of the last remnants of clothing.

They sat on the edge of the bed. With one hand he fondled her breast. The other he knotted in her hair. Her pulse chugged and hammered as she spread her hand along his chest, grazed the fine sheen of hair over taut muscle. Liquid heat welled inside her, leaving her wet and needy.

His teeth and lips nibbled their way down her neck to the hollow at its base, slithered down her chest and captured a sensitive nipple. He tasted, then moved to the other. Eyes closed, she lay back on the downy pillows and let out an ecstatic moan when he continued his journey across her belly. Her breathing became fitful, ragged. Her heart pounded wildly. She exploded with a gasp when his ravaging tongue explored lower.

Jeff's needs were insatiable now. His hands and mouth couldn't get enough of her. His body ached with the desire to possess her. Then, in a move he hadn't anticipated, she was on top of him, doing things that were agonizingly pleasurable. He wouldn't last at this rate. Couldn't.

When she lowered herself onto him, he knew he was lost. He gazed up at her, her face ethereal, glowing in the pale moonlight. She smiled down at him, taunted him with her body, tantalized him as she alternated motion and restraint. The sweet torture she imposed was a whiplash of unbearable pleasure. He breathed out and in, his heartbeat a jackhammer in his chest. His body was more alive than it had ever been before. His existence, his fulfillment were all centered on this incredible woman.

He reached up and gathered her breasts in his hands. Head thrown back, mouth open, she closed her eyes. Her movements slowed, then sped up. He was helpless, a captive, the most unbelievably happy prisoner. She let out a cry and suddenly they were toppling, freefalling, plunging, crashing.

CATHERINE WOKE with a shiver. With nothing covering her, she instinctively curled up against the warm male body beside her. She was jolted awake when she realized it wasn't, couldn't be Jordan. A wave of loneliness washed over her, followed by the sharp stab of guilt.

Fully awake now, she studied the man sleeping beside her. Remorse poked around inside her, but not disappointment. Their lovemaking had been fabulous. He wasn't her husband, yet she couldn't accept shame for what they had shared. A playful grin twitched her lips.

You're wrong, Tyrone. So very wrong.

Still smiling, she slipped off the bed and tiptoed to the closet where she retrieved a light blanket from the top shelf. Lying down beside Jeff, she covered them both, then snuggled once more against his warm body. Content, she dozed off.

A shake of the mattress brought her back to consciousness. She opened her eyes to see Jeff sitting up beside her. Pale sunrise glowed through the windows.

"Where are we?" he asked in a voice still muffled by sleep.

"In one of the spare bedrooms," she replied.

"Spare bedroom," he muttered, as if his brain was having trouble processing the information. Pensively he nodded. "Not *your* bedroom."

She was tempted to say this one had been closer, which was true, but that wasn't the reason she'd selected it. As much as she'd wanted Jeff Rowan last night, she couldn't bring herself to make love to him in the bed she had shared with Jordan. Could Jeff understand that, or would he consider it a slap in the face, an indictment that he was a sex partner, not a lover? She bit her lip in anticipation of the verdict.

"I'd better get out of here." His tone was brusque. "It wouldn't do to have people see me leaving your house after spending the night."

"Jeff," she called out in a plea for understanding.

He abandoned the bed and strode naked to a door on the left, opened it, discovered it was a closet, closed it and stepped to the one next to it. Without casting her a glance or saying a word, he disappeared into the bathroom.

Minutes passed before she heard the shower. Leaving the snug refuge of the bed, she entered the steam-filled room. His tall, manly form was silhouetted on the shower stall's frosted glass door.

He spun around when she opened it and slipped in beside him. The hesitation, the wariness in his eyes softened into hunger when she draped her hands on his broad shoulders, raised herself on tiptoe and planted a tender kiss on his lips.

"You look mighty appealing this morning," she murmured in his ear, his unshaven cheek scratchy against hers.

His hands clasped her hips. He searched her eyes.

"Please don't be upset with me," she begged. "I—"

His smile was rueful. "I'm not upset," he assured her, then added, "though I do find you disturbing."

She scrutinized his growing erection. "Oh, dear. That's all my fault, isn't it?"

He grinned at her. "Every bit of it."

"And I suppose it's up to me to do something about it."

His greenish eyes twinkled. "Up to you, definitely." He sucked in a sharp breath when she cupped him. "I'm in your hands," he slurred. "I'm all yours. Do with me what you will."

The water was beginning to cool by the time they emerged from the foggy stall and toweled themselves dry. The sun was full up by then. So much for a discreet departure.

"Come on," she said, when he was buttoning his tuxedo pants over his wrinkled white shirt. "I'll fix you breakfast."

"You don't cook, remember?"

She chuckled. "English muffins or bagels, orange juice, and I can make coffee. But you already know that."

"Good coffee." He planted an affectionate kiss on her damp forehead.

"About the bedroom—" she started, then bit her lip.

"You don't have to explain," he told her. "I'm not offended, if that's what's worrying you. He was your husband, Cate. I'm not." He took her hands, lifted them and touched his lips to her knuckles. Over their joined fingers, he said, "And for the record, he was a lucky man."

She hadn't expected a tear to spill down her cheek, but it did. He wiped it away with the coarse pad of his thumb, the contact gentle, caring. He held her eyes with his. "One very lucky man."

"DETECTIVE TAYLOR IS HERE to see you," Annette announced over the intercom.

"Send her in," Catherine told her.

"I have the info you wanted, Chief," she said on entering the office.

Following Derek's determination that it was Tyrone who deleted Jordan's last, unpublished editorial, Catherine speculated there might be a tie between him and Buster Rialto. After all, Rialto stood to gain by the yellowcake discrepancy not being disclosed. Since Risa was currently involved in an ongoing investigation of gambling and prostitution, and Rialto was believed to be up to his armpits in both, Catherine had asked for her help.

"We checked telephone records, as you suggested, and found a reasonable number of calls placed by Rialto's staff to the *Sentinel's* advertising department and a few calls from Rialto's home to Tyrone's, presumably to coordinate social appointments. We also discovered a remarkable number of cell phone calls going both ways at hours that seem out of whack with either business or evening events."

"Telephone logs," Catherine muttered. "How close are we to getting taps authorized?"

Risa shrugged. "We've asked the D.A. a couple of times but always get shot down. He claims there's nothing suspicious about friends talking to each other at odd hours. We don't have a smoking gun to justify invading the privacy of a prominent citizen."

The D.A. was running scared.

"I want a copy of the telephone records you have so far," Catherine told her.

Risa smiled. "I figured you would." She reached into her tote-sized handbag, removed a brown business envelope and handed it across the desk. "It's all there. Dates, times, numbers."

After Risa left, Catherine placed it in her attaché case. Using her cell phone she dialed Jeff's number.

"We need to meet. The three of us. But I won't be able to get away until late, after nine at the earliest." She was scheduled to speak at a dinner hosted by a local association of small business owners.

"I'll contact Derek," Jeff said. "Rather than camp out at your place or wait for you to call us, why don't we meet at mine, say around eleven? You know where I live?"

"Yes," she said. "I'll be there."

CATHERINE HAD PLANNED to review the telephone records Risa had given her before the meeting with Jeff and Derek, but it was already after ten by the time she reached home. Feeling clammy, she decided on a quick shower and change of clothes before going to Jeff's house.

As tepid water sluiced down her sweaty skin, she recalled how she and Jeff had washed each other in the shower down the hall. A giggle bubbled through her as she reached for the soap. Better to think other thoughts, she decided, and tried to imagine what Jeff's house might be like. The typical pad of a confirmed bachelor? Something about him suggested otherwise. His office, for one. Neat. Uncluttered. And the way he'd handled himself in her kitchen. Methodical. Organized. No wasted motion. He hadn't dirtied every pan and bowl just to cook a few eggs. No, not typical.

It surprised her that they fit so well together, given their circumstances. He was still a young man, while she…was middle-aged, yet she couldn't imagine a more compatible match, not just in bed, but intellectually and emotionally.

How would she have reacted if a man had made love to her in a guest room of his house instead of in his own bed? Was his acceptance an indication that he didn't take their lovemaking seriously? That for him it had been a pleasant interlude but nothing that required commitment? His initial reaction had been to take offense. She'd seen that. He'd accepted her decision only after thinking about it. But wasn't that the point, that he had been willing to mull it over and consider her feelings?

What about her? Jordan was the only other man she'd ever made love with. She couldn't deny the purely sexual hunger that made Jeff attractive but that alone wouldn't have caused her to invite him to sleep with her. Other factors made her want to be with him, qualities beyond the physical. The security she felt in his company, for example.

Derek was already at Jeff's place when she arrived ten minutes after eleven. She handed Jeff the envelope with the stack of papers Risa had given her and explained what they were. "I'm sorry I didn't get a chance to run off copies."

"Not a problem. I have a copier here." He turned to Derek. "Would you mind getting the chief whatever she wants to drink?"

While Jeff crossed to a bedroom that served as his office, Derek rattled off a variety of beverage options and went to the kitchen.

She did a quick assessment of Jeff's living room and was impressed. The furniture was lean and clean. The graphics on the walls were numbered and signed originals. The bronze sculptures not exactly traditional in style, but there was an honesty about them that delighted her. His tastes were complex and sophisticated, something that pleased her more than she could explain.

She was sipping a can of diet cola and studying a

framed black-and-white lithograph of an old man and woman holding hands when Jeff reappeared with three stacks of papers. He kept one and distributed the others.

"I did a quick review of what you have here," he said to Catherine. "A lot of telephone calls between Tyrone Tanner and Buster Rialto."

Derek's brows narrowed as he flipped though his copy. "What does it mean?"

"That Tyrone may be involved in Rialto's gambling and prostitution businesses," Catherine said. "I doubt as a partner, more likely a paying customer."

Derek whistled. Catherine had never heard him express an opinion about Kelsey's uncle, but she had picked up enough vibes to know he didn't particularly like the man. Derek was inexperienced as a cop, but he could size up people quickly and accurately, an instinct that would serve him well on the force—if he chose to stay.

"That would give Rialto leverage over him," Jeff added. "It also explains why the *Sentinel* backed off on the missing yellowcake story."

She held up the thick sheaf of papers. "We don't know what was said in those conversations, so this is all speculation."

"Do you think Tyrone is being blackmailed?" Derek asked.

Catherine pinched the bridge of her nose to ward off the fatigue that was beginning to swamp her. "His father paid off a mountain of gambling debts several years ago. Tyrone swore he was finished, but—"

"Did he undergo formal counseling?" Jeff asked.

She snorted. "Ty? Does he strike you as the kind of

man who would take advice from a shrink? Counseling is for sissies."

"Then I doubt he's stopped. Gambling is as much an addiction as alcohol, drugs…or sex," Jeff said. "You don't get up one morning and decide you're not going to do it anymore. Just saying no is a great philosophy, and some people actually do it, but it takes will-power—"

"Something my brother-in-law is not famous for."

"A phone tap would answer our questions," Jeff said.

"Except we don't have enough evidence to get one from a judge, nor do we have the manpower for an illegal tap, which would be inadmissible in court and could poison a good case, if it were uncovered. No. A tap is out."

"So where do we go from here?" Derek asked.

"This only covers the last six months, and it's inconclusive."

Jeff picked up on where she was headed. "But it's enough to justify delving deeper." He turned to Derek. "Can you get the complete records of both Tyrone's and Buster's calls over, say, the past two years?"

"Sure," the cop replied. "There'll be a lot of them."

"Analysis will be easier if they're in an electronic format. We can sort for individual numbers, times of day, length of calls, that kind of thing."

"You got it," Derek said.

The rookie left a few minutes later, taking his copies of the logs with him.

"Where did you park your car?" Jeff asked Catherine.

"I brought Jordan's pickup. I use it when I don't want to be recognized."

"Can you stay the night?"

She smiled. "Is that an invitation?"

"I have only one bed...if you'd care to share it with me. It comes with breakfast in the morning."

Her response was a wide grin, then a chuckle. "Bed and breakfast. Sounds like an offer I can't refuse."

CHAPTER SIXTEEN

"YOU WERE MARRIED ONCE." Catherine's head lay in the crook of Jeff's arm, her hair flaring on his shoulder. "What happened?"

He had never tasted the warm afterglow of lovemaking he was experiencing with this woman, never comprehended that the pleasure didn't end when the last orgasm was complete. He wouldn't allow her question to alter that euphoria, though the subject wasn't one he liked to talk about.

"It was ten years ago."

She rested her hand on his chest. "How long did it last?"

"Less than twelve months." He shifted the hand he had on her back, enjoying the feel of her soft skin. "We met at a rock concert."

She raised her head and gazed at him, her lips bunched in a smile of amusement. "Rock and opera. You certainly have a broad range of musical tastes."

He laughed. "I was on duty in plain clothes. Sandy was a fan. We hit it off immediately." Had sex that same night, which should have been a clue that things were moving too fast. "Six months later we tied the knot."

"A whirlwind affair." Catherine was mocking him with humor. No matter. He deserved it. As for the humor, it had taken him a long time to laugh at himself for being so stupid.

"Unfortunately, we weren't compatible." He stroked her arm. He couldn't seem to get enough of touching her.

Her head was on his chest. "In what way?"

"We enjoyed being together, and we agreed on what we considered the basic essentials—music, food, cars, clothes, where we wanted to live. Externals."

"Sex."

He couldn't see her face, but he could feel her smiling. Why not? It was true. "Sex, too," he said. "We were in our twenties, immortal, hormone-crazed and impatient."

"I remember the feeling," she muttered and snuggled closer.

Their hormones had certainly been in an uproar a few minutes ago. That much hadn't changed. But neither of them were in their twenties anymore, and they both knew all too well they weren't immortal. Maybe that was why he could take so much pleasure in just lying here with her in his arms, preposterously happy with this little slice of time.

"So what went wrong?"

He stared up at the dark ceiling. "A few small details didn't become apparent until we returned from our honeymoon." He still caught himself resenting the way his wife had held back until after they were married, thinking she could change him once she had his ring on her finger.

"Sandy didn't like having guns in the house. I offered

to teach her how to handle them, but she refused. She'd seen me wearing a sidearm often enough, but I'd always left it behind when we went out on dates." It hadn't occurred to him that she might be afraid of it.

"Then there was my erratic work schedule," he continued. "My hours had been predictable enough when I was on patrol, but I was promoted to detective shortly after we were married. Not exactly a nine-to-five job."

"Didn't she work?" Catherine asked.

He toyed with the ends of her hair, while he watched the curve of her breast rise and subside with each breath. He remembered the thrill he'd felt with Sandy, but he had no recollection of this sense of contentment. Maybe it was his maturity, but he thought it had more to do with the woman.

"She was an insurance adjuster," he said.

Catherine stretched luxuriantly against him, then brought her leg up across his thigh, seriously threatening his contented repose. "She must have put in long hours, too."

He took a deep breath. "She argued that her hours were by appointment, and she didn't get called out in the middle of the night or during dinner in a restaurant."

Catherine's chuckle vibrated against his ribs, further accelerating his blood flow. "Right on both counts."

"Then there was the danger element," he went on. "She complained that when I went to work she never knew if she would see me alive or in one piece again."

"It is a risky job. So are a lot of others."

He felt the old arguments rising. "I tried to explain that to her, but I didn't help my case by pointing out that there was more chance of her getting breast cancer than me getting shot."

Catherine raised her head and gazed at him with a jaundiced eye. "That probably wasn't the most diplomatic comparison you could have made."

"I figured that out too late." He sighed. "What I didn't realize was how wide the gulf was between us, until she complained that my only friends were other cops. She associated with a variety of businesspeople, builders, bankers, lawyers..." He peered down at the woman nestled against him. "I didn't tell her what I thought of some of them."

"Very wise," she said, grinning.

"Sandy couldn't understand that police work is more than a job. She took offense at our politically incorrect conversations, our disrespectful slang and wisecracks. She couldn't see why humor, even the sick variety, is sometimes our only release from the ugly underside of humanity we see every day."

"We're not saints," Catherine admitted.

"How did Jordan cope with your job?"

She grew pensive. After a few seconds, she said, "We had our tense moments, especially in the beginning, but his family helped us get past them."

"They were okay with you being a cop?"

She laughed. "Just the opposite. They hated it." She smiled at the puzzled expression on his face.

"First of all, they didn't approve of me as a person." With her cheek resting again on his chest, he could feel her words as well as hear them. "A blond-haired, blue-eyed lower-middle-class girl didn't fit their image of a suitable daughter-in-law. They also had what they considered a healthy disrespect for the police. Given the times they grew up in, I can't say I blamed them. I still don't. Money allowed them to eat well and sleep in comfortable beds, but it didn't insulate them from prejudice and discrimination. They tolerated the police because they had to, not because they had any reason to consider them friends or allies."

"Two strikes against you."

She tightened her hold on him, her voice softening but not losing the edge that had crept into it.

"The third came when Kelsey was born a year after we were married. I took the usual maternity leave, then went back to work. They were furious, especially when the nanny we hired was a white woman. We hired her because she was the best qualified, not because of the color of her skin, but that didn't seem to make any difference."

"Why did it matter?" Jeff asked.

She didn't answer immediately. "It's complicated, but essentially they felt I was trying to deny Kelsey her heritage, and that I was setting her up for disappointment and failure."

He raised his head. "I don't get it."

"A white nanny would teach Kelsey white values and attitudes, alienating her from her true identity in society, which is black. In effect Kelsey wouldn't fit into either community. They had a valid concern."

"But Jordan didn't agree with them?"

"There was a time when their point of view had merit, but Jordan was able to see times were changing and that the only way to perpetuate that change was to embrace it. I understand where his parents were coming from. I respect their strength and courage in enduring what they did, but—"

"How does Kelsey feel about all this?"

Catherine smiled. "As far as racial issues are concerned, she's mature and well-adjusted."

"Thanks to you."

"Thanks to her father. He was the one who taught her to accept and be proud of who she is."

"Did you ever feel like an outsider?"

She shook her head. "With them? Never. With his family. Always. Except for Melissa, Ty's wife, and their kids."

Jeff noted she didn't include Tyrone in her comfort zone.

"You said Jordan's parents helped you," he reminded her. "How?"

"Their rudeness and hostility toward me forced him to choose between us. They miscalculated. He chose me, told them they either treated me with the respect and courtesy his wife deserved or he would cut them out of our lives altogether."

"Would he have followed through?"

"He did for almost two years. It was Melly who finally reconciled them."

"So you got along after that?"

Catherine shook her head without completely raising it. "They tolerated me…for Jordan's sake…especially after his father had his heart attack, and Jordan had to take over the paper."

"And since his death?"

"We don't see each other except in public, like the

other night at the concert. They're too proud to be impolite in front of strangers."

"How do they feel about Kelsey?"

Jeff couldn't see Catherine's face, but he sensed regret and maybe anger.

"They're ambivalent. She's their flesh and blood, but she's also mine, and even after all these years that doesn't sit well."

"I'm sorry." He tightened his hold on her, wishing he could hug away the pain. "She's innocent. They're being grossly unfair. They're also robbing themselves of a lot of happiness."

A moment passed. "I can forgive them for excluding me, but I can't forgive them for rejecting her. I wonder if they have any idea how much she's wanted their love."

Jeff considered changing subjects, but then decided it might be best to get these issues out of the way, so they could move on. He didn't ask himself where to. He wasn't sure yet, but the bond growing between them suggested something more than friendship.

"How do they feel about her becoming a nun?" he asked.

Catherine huffed, her breath warm against his bare skin. "They blame me, say she would have given up this crazy idea if Jordan had lived." She sighed. "On that I'm sure they're right. He had a way…" She trailed off, unwilling to finish the sentence.

He tilted her head toward him so he could see her eyes. He didn't like the heartbreak he saw there, the sense of failure and defeat.

"You're a good mother." He dragged his thumb down her cheek. "Seeing the two of you together I know that."

She rested her head on his chest and pressed her hand to his rib cage. "I wonder," she said forlornly.

"There's tension between you, but that's natural under the circumstances. You've both been through a lot. She loves you, Cate, that's also obvious."

Her smiling at his pet name for her made him feel good. "Give her time."

"Speaking of time," she said. "I ought to be getting home."

He wanted to tell her she was home, with him, where they both needed her to be. But he'd be rushing things. He didn't know where this was going; he only knew where he wanted her to be. Right here—in his arms.

He shifted, readjusting the way their bodies touched.

"I promised you breakfast."

"It's still dark outside," she said.

"I guess we'll have to find some way to kill time until the sun comes up."

"Time is a terrible thing to waste."

"It waits for no man," he murmured as he nuzzled her ear and the delicate skin beneath it.

She ran her hand down the length of his torso, past his navel, pausing only when she reached an obstacle. "It certainly doesn't seem to have waited for you."

"I'd say let's make hay while the sun shines," he replied. "Except, as you so wisely observed, it's dark outside."

She let out a giggle. "I don't think hay is what we're about to make."

They were both laughing when he flipped her onto her back. "How about making haste?"

"HOW BAD IS IT?" Catherine asked Saturday morning.

Paul Radke, the head of Internal Affairs, rested his elbows on the wooden arms of the chair across from her and laced his fingers in front of him. "Bad."

He'd just informed her the D.A. was initiating an investigation of the Houston medical examiner's office.

"Lost autopsy reports, some incomplete. A few appear to have been totally fabricated. Tissue samples stored for later DNA comparisons are also missing, and there's suspicion that those on hand may not have been properly labeled."

"This is a nightmare," Catherine said. "Any idea how many cases are affected?"

"As far as we know, the problem started about a year and a half ago when Cliburne Vale took over. He went into the job with a clean record and a good reputation as a pathologist. Unfortunately his management abilities don't seem to have matched his laboratory skills."

"An entire M.E. office doesn't become incompetent overnight," Catherine said. "There's more to this than sloppy bookkeeping. Who's heading the investigation?"

"Haven't got a name yet. The D.A. had to turn it over to the feds. He didn't have any choice in the matter."

"I'm sure that thrilled him."

Hollywood and the media exaggerated the animosity between law enforcement agencies, but there was no question it existed. They got along fine focused on an outside enemy. It was when one of them was placed in the role of investigating the other that pride entered the equation, tempers flared and the organization under scrutiny went into a full defense mode.

"I want a list of all the cases affected on my desk Monday morning."

"I'm not sure we'll have all the data by then."

"With computers it can't be that difficult, Paul. Monday," she said flatly.

Blowing out a breath, he climbed to his feet. "You'll have it."

The minute the door was closed behind him, Catherine took out her cell phone and poked in a number. She wasn't surprised when she got voice mail. Without identifying herself, she said simply, "Call me on my cell at twelve-thirty," and disconnected.

She was in her Lexus on her way to an appointment with the city council when the phone chirped. It was half past noon precisely.

"Thanks for getting back to me," she said. "I need a list of every case the medical examiner's office has dealt with since Cliburne Vale took over. Can you e-mail it to me by Monday morning?"

The pause was brief. "Yes, ma'am."

"Thanks. I appreciate this."

"Glad to help."

It would be interesting to see how Derek's case list compared with the one Radke produced.

CHAPTER SEVENTEEN

CATHERINE MANAGED to leave the office around three o'clock the following day. She didn't always come in on Sundays but with so much happening she needed the quiet time there to sort through the mountains of paper that had been accumulating on her desk all week.

She returned home just before three-thirty and went directly to her computer. Derek had called around one to say he'd sent her the telephone logs of Tyrone and Rialto's calls that Jeff had requested. She knew Jeff would analyze them in detail, but she wanted to examine them personally to see if she could discern any pattern.

While the files were downloading, she went to the kitchen, fixed herself sliced turkey on rye and carried it to her workstation.

The records, as Derek had predicted, were voluminous, stretching back two years since before Jordan's death. Was Tyrone already involved with Rialto then, or did the connection come after he'd taken over the newspaper? She scrolled back through the data. The association seemed to be long-standing. Had Jordan known about it? He hadn't said anything to her, and she felt sure he would have.

She zeroed in on the date of Jordan's death. That was curious. Rialto had phoned Tyrone right after the meeting in the mayor's office.

Why? To say his attempt to get Jordan to hold off on the yellowcake story had failed? Why would Tyrone care? Or had Rialto wanted Tyrone to convince his brother not to run the editorial?

Catherine noticed Rialto's next call…to someone identified as Calvin Griggs. She'd seen or heard the name before, but in what connection, she couldn't recall.

She'd just taken a bite out of the second half of her sandwich when the phone rang. She jumped, then picked up the receiver.

"Hello, Cate."

A warm feeling crept its way through her. She nearly sighed with pleasure at the sound of his voice, picturing his deep brownish-green eyes and the way he had looked at her when they'd made love the night before.

"Hi," she all but purred, "I was just thinking about you."

"Isn't that a coincidence? I've been thinking about you all day. I was wondering if I could see you. I may have found something."

"Now?"

A split second's pause. "Unless you have other plans?" He sounded disappointed, maybe even hurt.

"No." She laughed. "No other plans." The prospect of having him near her, by her side, lifted her spirits immeasurably. "Come on over. I'll fix coffee."

"You're good at that."

"My special talent."

"And not the only one. But I accept the offer. I'll see you in about twenty minutes."

She hung up, stared once again at the screen and shook her head. Had Jeff made the same discovery? Was he thinking what she was thinking? Picking up the uneaten portion of her sandwich, she padded out to the kitchen.

She turned on the coffeemaker and tried to concentrate on the implications of the information on her computer screen, but her mind kept flashing to images of Jeff reminding her of the comfortable feeling she had when she was around him.

Cheered by the prospect of being with him, she sauntered back to her bedroom, removed the clothes she'd worn to the office and slipped into a sky-blue cotton shirt and white twill slacks. She touched up her lips and ran a brush through her hair, then spied her cologne and put a dab behind each ear.

She was debating whether to open the second button on her shirt when the doorbell rang.

AN ALLURING FEMALE SCENT wafted to Jeff on the cool air coming through the open doorway. Catherine's blouse was form-fitting at the midriff, enhancing the generous swell of her breasts. Her white pants hugged the curve of her hips, her honey-blond hair pulled back in a manner that was both sophisticated and girlish. Not exactly the image of a hard-bitten police chief.

"Come in," she said.

He waited until the door was shut behind him before he sidled up, held her wrists at her sides and kissed her on the lips. Hot.

"I'm glad you're here."

"So am I." He followed her through the dining room, watching the gentle sway of her hips, remembering the feel of her legs curled around him. Definitely hot.

She went to the refrigerator and removed the carafe of coffee she'd put there to cool. "I thought with today's heat…" She trailed off and he knew the kind of heat she was talking about had nothing to do with the beverage.

"Can I help?"

At her direction he filled two oversized glasses with ice. The cubes crackled when she poured the still warm coffee over them.

"I made it extra strong so it won't dilute too much." She was babbling. He liked having that effect on her.

They wandered into her office. He stood behind her as she clicked the mouse, banishing the screensaver and revealing the data files Derek had sent.

"I was looking these over," she explained, "and no-ticed Rialto called Jordan's brother right after their meeting."

"I saw the same thing."

"Rialto made another call a minute later. I recognize the name but can't place it."

"Cal Griggs," he supplied.

She gazed up at him. "You know who he is?"

"The guy Tyrone played racquetball with that day."

She leaned back, her eyes fixed on the screen, her nerves tuned to the man who had just placed his hands on her shoulders. "Why would Rialto call him?"

"I did a quick search of his name." Jeff kneaded mus-cles that begged to be caressed. "Griggs works for Rialto as a consultant. He also has a criminal record. Arrested a couple of times a few years back on assault charges. Released on both occasions when the victims withdrew their complaints, saying it was all a misunderstanding."

"So he's an enforcer."

Jeff stroked the base of her neck. "Which means Tyrone's association with Rialto may not be altogether voluntary."

"I wish we had a transcript of their conversation."

"It would be interesting."

"I got a call from Risa Taylor today."

He released his hold on her, pulled over a rolling chair and sat down beside her. "Go on."

Her eyes feasted on him. The way his thick brown hair was mussed from his nervous habit of combing his fingers through it when he was deep in thought—or frustrated. The hint of five-o'clock shadow that she found sexy as hell. The way he laced his long fingers in front of his flat belly.

"I had her and several other people I trust keeping an eye out for Harvey Stuckey."

He folded her hand in his. "Why do I have the feeling this isn't good news?"

"Stuckey fell down a flight of steps yesterday and broke his neck."

"An accident?"

"They did a drug-alcohol screen on him. No narcotics, but he was definitely staggering drunk. It could have been an accident. Nobody saw him fall, but he had bruises on him that suggested he'd been roughed up before he died."

Catherine shifted in her seat and huffed out a disheartened breath. "So we no longer have a witness—"

"I'm sorry, Cate. I let you down. Promised to find him for you."

She rose and paced the oriental carpet. "You did the best you could. He wouldn't have been a very credible witness anyway."

"But his statement might have been enough for you to request an exhumation," Jeff pointed out.

She sucked in her breath. "It doesn't matter," she said.

"Of course it matters. He was our link to—"

"Tell me if you see anything wrong with this picture," she said. "Rialto had either tapped into the *Sentinel's* computer system or he had a spy at the newspaper who somehow got wind of Jordan's editorial exposing the missing uranium. He contacts the mayor and asks him to set up a meeting with Jordan."

"Okay," Jeff concurred, "but why didn't Rialto go to Jordan directly? It's not as if they don't know each other. Why involve a third party?"

"I can only speculate that the mayor was already involved in some way, or Rialto thought he might have a more compelling argument with Walbrun backing him, maybe even making threats of his own."

"What kind of threats?"

She pursed her lips. "The mayor is in a position to persuade certain businessmen to pull their advertising from the newspaper, even withdraw their support for me as police chief."

"That would get me pretty hot under the collar," Jeff insisted.

"It would Jordan, too, but he wasn't without weapons. My guess is that he countered with a threat to expose their cabal."

"The pen versus the sword. Okay, I'm with you so far," Jeff said. "Go on."

"Rialto would have been furious at Jordan, so he calls Tyrone and either asks or tells him he'd better convince his brother to back off. I imagine Rialto's leverage against Ty was gambling debts—or maybe an affair Ty couldn't afford to have exposed."

"Would he have gone along with Rialto's request?"

She shrugged. "No skin off his nose, and he'd have to protect himself. His father would have a stroke if Ty went to him with more gambling debts after swearing he was going straight. Ty might have talked to Jordan on their run, if the weather hadn't been so hot. He probably figured he'd get a chance to plead his case later."

"If Tyrone had leveled with him about what was at stake, would Jordan have backed off?"

She shook her head. "If we were talking about a social scandal or a human interest piece, he might have delayed publication for a day or two. But this story involved national security. Jordan would have felt he had no choice. And don't forget he was a newspaperman. Holding back on a story of this magnitude could give his competition a chance to scoop him."

"Would Tyrone have understood that?"

She paused to consider. "He's dishonest, but he's not stupid. He'd also know his brother would never compromise his principles. Ty's problems were of his own making. Jordan would have felt disgust for his brother and sympathy for his family, but that wouldn't have deterred him from doing what he felt he had to do."

"Okay, so where does that leave us?" Jeff asked.

"We know from the telephone records that Rialto talked to Ty for only a minute, then hung up and called Cal Griggs." She scrolled to those entries on the screen. "That conversation lasted more than two minutes. Since Cal and Ty played racquetball a few minutes later, it's fair to assume Griggs was already at the gym. But was he with Ty? Did Ty know Rialto and his racquetball partner were talking to each other?"

"This still doesn't answer the question about precisely how Jordan was murdered or by whom."

"I may have part of the answer," she said, but there was no satisfaction in the comment. "The medical examiner's office has come under state investigation for mishandling forensic evidence. I've asked my people in the department for a list of vulnerable cases. I've also asked Derek to compile the same list. Jordan's autopsy should be on both."

"You're not talking about just mishandling evidence, then," Jeff said. "You're talking about corruption and conspiracy."

"Jordan's drink bottle was poisoned, Jeff. I don't know with what, but I'm going to find out. Then the question will be who did it, Griggs or somebody else."

"Or Tyrone," Jeff added.

She released the mouse because her hand was shaking. She didn't want to think of Jordan being murdered by his own brother. It would be too much, maybe more than she could endure.

"I hope he wasn't involved in any of this." Her voice flattered. "Melissa has endured enough humiliation. Finding out her cheating husband is also a murderer, a fratricide, will be devastating. As for his parents—" she let out a ragged sigh "—I'm not sure how they'll cope with it. Marcus is in poor health already, and Amanda…she's strong, but this may be more than she can handle."

The afternoon sun, slicing through the blinds, cast the room in sober, prisonlike stripes. Jeff reached across the table. She placed her hands in his.

"We'll figure out who did it and how," he promised. "In the meantime, I'm here for as long as you want me."

Catherine studied the man leaning toward her. He was committing himself to her unconditionally. *For as long as you want me.*

She tried to imagine just how long that might be and realized she didn't want to see an end to their relationship, couldn't imagine watching him go out the door one day and not come back. She'd had one great love in her life, a man whose memory she would always treasure, but…

Her guilt for wanting Jeff had her doing mental gymnastics. She wasn't dishonoring the memory of the father of her child but honoring what they had together by pursuing it again.

Rationalizing, she decided. She was justifying what she would never have contemplated before, but time and circumstances had changed. She was alone, and she didn't want to be.

When Jeff's mouth found hers, she had no choice but to melt into the kiss. Thoughts and logic fled like seabirds in a storm. She was possessed now by sensations, by the magical feel of his body pressed against hers, by the taste of his mouth on hers and the giddy joy welling inside her.

Then he did something she hadn't anticipated. He picked her up in his arms, throwing her off balance, not just physically but emotionally, as well. She hooked her elbow around his neck.

"I think we'd better find that guest room."

"No," she said, so sternly he stopped and stared at her, misinterpreting her objection. In his eyes she saw disappointment, then acceptance. His muscles shifted in preparation for putting her down.

"Not the guest room," she murmured. "My room."

He studied her with longing. "Are you sure?"

"I'm sure," she whispered.

He turned down the hallway to the double doors at the end. He let her turn the knob when they got there, let her push the door open. He pressed his lips to her temple before crossing the threshold.

Afternoon light cast the spacious room in silver hues. The square-canopied king-sized bed dominated the far wall, the maple paneling behind it a golden reflection of the sun pouring in through the wide expanse of south-facing windows.

At the foot of the bed Jeff lowered her to the thick carpet, their arms still entwined. When they kissed this time, she threaded her fingers through his thick brown hair. Her breath caught as he began to undo the buttons of her blouse. In the process, his hands brushed the sides of her breasts. Her nipples hardened.

It took far too long for them to get out of their clothes, yet she treasured every slow, meandering sensation. She ached for release while savoring its anticipation. When the last garment had been kicked aside, they stood and stared at each other—and smiled.

She whipped back the decorative duvet, exposing satiny rose-hued sheets. He came up behind her, placed his hands on her bare shoulders and nipped at the base of her neck. She curled into his touch, shivered with delight as his hands cruised down her arms, then turned her to face him.

He cupped a loose fist under her chin. "Cate," he began in a seductive whisper.

She crossed his lips with a finger. "Shh. No words." No promises.

She stretched out on the bed and beckoned him to join her.

He lay beside her and began caressing her skin, the peaks and valleys of her body. She smiled as he held his breath, bit his lips and closed his eyes when her hands skimmed over his chest. She dragged her nails along his naked ribs, coursed down his stomach. Beneath her palm she felt his muscles constrict, tighten, throb.

Grinning, he rose to his knees and splayed his hands at her sides. She welcomed him when he lowered himself just enough for their bodies to make light contact. She accommodated him when he entered her and closed her eyes, enraptured by his torturously slow rhythm.

She cried out when the first wave hit her. Heard him suck air between his clenched teeth. She saw him grimace, suspended in the abyss between pleasure and pain. He captured her mouth with his. Hot, hungry and wet. Her pulse hammered.

Her hips rose to meet his. She felt a kind of giddy glee as she read the sweet agony she was meting out. Then she watched him turn inwards, and for a moment was jealous of his solitude, until his eyes shot open, reuniting them. This time when she went over the edge, she took him with her.

CHAPTER EIGHTEEN

THE ROOM WAS STILL filled with light when Catherine roused an hour later. She stirred, turned away from the window and was jolted wide awake. She was lying in her own bed, the one she had shared with her husband for most of their married life, with a man who was obviously not Jordan. Again a flicker of guilt raced through her, but when she put her hand out to touch Jeff's shoulder, she experienced another emotion. Hope.

A year ago she had tried to reconcile herself to a life alone. Her husband was dead. Her daughter had deserted her. Her parents had long ago abandoned her, and her in-laws despised her. She'd dedicated herself to her work, tried to take solace in it, but it was no substitute for having someone to touch, to talk to, to be with.

Then she found Jeff. Could there be a more unlikely partner, either as an investigator or a lover? She'd humiliated him, destroyed his career. He was six years younger than she, and yet somehow they connected. She stretched under the dark sheet covering them, aware of the heat of his body. Yes, they'd definitely connected.

He opened his eyes when she touched him. His lips curled in a playful smile. "Hi," he murmured.

"Hi, yourself." The temptation was too great. She gave in to the urge to snuggle up beside him, to place her leg over his and rest her forearm on his chest. She kissed his cheek, then luxuriated in his warmth.

"Are you hungry?" He brushed a strand of golden hair from her face.

"Ravenous." For him.

"I thought maybe I could fix you dinner."

"Where?"

"Here. Seems to me I saw a dead chicken in the freezer when I was getting ice."

She chuckled. "I hope it's dead. Hate to think of it shivering in there all this time."

"Do you have any Marsala wine?"

She raised herself on one elbow. "Marsala? You're talking serious cooking, aren't you?"

"Eating is one of the great pleasures of life. There are others, of course." He nibbled her ear, sending shock waves to places she had no idea were in direct communication with her ears.

"We could have our appetizer here in bed and adjourn to the kitchen for the rest of the meal."

"Hmm. Would that be the entrée or the dessert, do you think?"

She was on top of him when she became aware of a muffled voice. The door burst open.

"Mom?"

Catherine whipped around in a panic.

Wearing her gray-and-white nun's outfit, Kelsey stood in the doorway, one hand on the doorknob, the other over her mouth. She bolted down the hall.

CATHERINE LEAPED from the bed, dashed into the bathroom, grabbed blindly for her robe and shot out the door. This couldn't be happening. It couldn't.

"Kelsey," she called out. "Kelsey, wait."

Expecting to hear the sound of the front door slamming, she raced into the living room and was relieved to find her daughter still there.

"Wait, please, let me explain."

Kelsey spun around and glared through tear-flooded eyes. "There's nothing to explain, Mother. I know what sex is. Grandma was right. You are a slut."

Catherine's breath caught in her throat. Her heart stopped. Then, rage exploded in her with more violence than anything she had ever experienced. She'd been insulted many times over the years, called things designed to cut deep, and sometimes they had, but never had words inflicted pain this intense.

She began to shake. Had this person, standing within arm's reach, not been her daughter she would have slapped her across the face with all her might. Had Amanda been here, she might have throttled the woman.

Catherine knew she had to say something, but what? Any denial would ring hollow, any defense would sound like an excuse.

"When did she tell you that?" she asked, and wondered if her daughter could hear the anger in the question.

"Does it matter?"

"I guess not, if you believe her, which you obviously do. I'm just curious. Is that why you chose to become a nun, so you could atone for your mother's sins?"

This time Kelsey flinched. The two women glared at

each other, the chasm separating them for the moment unbridgeable.

Because her knees were wobbly, Catherine staggered to the chair by the telephone table.

"Answer my question. Just when did your grandmother inform you that I was a slut?"

Kelsey turned to the door. "I'm leaving."

Catherine shot out of her seat and blocked the door. "You're not going anywhere until you answer my question. When, Kelsey? It's important."

Kelsey worked her jaw. "Last week, when I went to see Grampa about the editorial in the paper. I wanted him to make Uncle Ty stop saying those things about you."

Catherine closed her eyes. Her daughter had tried to stand up for her and been rewarded with this slander. She gazed at the troubled girl, the child she had loved, still loved, without question.

"But he wouldn't, would he?"

Kelsey bit her lip. "No. He said they had a civic duty. I told him that was bullshit."

Catherine was shocked. Even before she'd taken the veil, Kelsey never used coarse language. Like her father, she considered it unnecessary.

"He said he knew things about you that I didn't, but he refused to tell me what they were."

"So your grandmother enlightened you." How generous of her. "What did she say?"

"That when you were dating Dad you came on to Uncle Ty, but he rejected you. She wondered how many other men you'd been screwing."

Catherine felt sick to her stomach. She'd always

known Amanda didn't like her, that she considered her something of a fortune hunter, but she had no idea her antipathy was so vicious. "And you believed her."

"Not then."

"But you do now."

"What am I supposed to think?" Kelsey cried.

Catherine drew close and put her arms around her daughter. Kelsey froze up, but didn't pull away. Grasping for the smallest straw of encouragement, Catherine took it as a positive sign.

"Listen to me, Kelsey. No matter what you think of me at this moment, I want you to know that I love you, and that I was never, ever unfaithful to your father. I loved him with all my heart, and I would never have done anything to hurt him."

"What about just now?"

"Kelsey, your father is dead—" She knew the instant the words tumbled from her mouth, they were a mistake.

Kelsey pushed away.

"Go home and pray, and think back on our life together," Catherine said, her tone defeated, filled with hurt. "All of us, you, your father and me. Think about us as a family. If in your heart you truly believe I was a bad mother and a bad wife, then maybe the convent is the right place for you. You'll never have to face the agony of being in love with a man and losing him. You'll never have to suffer the heartbreak of being hated by your own children for not being perfect."

The tears she had held back would no longer be contained. They rolled down her cheeks unchecked.

"I regret that you walked in on Jeff and me, but I

won't apologize for it. My conduct doesn't meet your moral standards, and for that I am truly sorry. I've never claimed to be a saint."

Compressing her lips, she turned and walked away.

AFTER CATHERINE HAD torn out of the master bedroom, Jeff threw on his shirt and pants and ventured cautiously after her. He stood behind the dining room door to eavesdrop on the conversation between mother and daughter. He'd caught only snatches of it, enough for him to realize neither woman was pleased with the responses of the other.

He retreated to the bedroom and was sitting on the edge of the easy chair by the window, tying his shoes, when Catherine came in.

"I'm sorry," he said, looking up. "I never meant to come between you and Kelsey." He'd never imagined a nun would walk in on his lovemaking, either. "I'll leave."

He wanted her to tell him to stay, but he wasn't surprised when she didn't. Regardless of what she might feel for him, her daughter came first. He had a few arguments he could use to persuade her otherwise. That her daughter was an adult, who should be able to respect other people's choices. That Catherine was a single woman, who had the right to live her own life. He could even point out that Kelsey had violated her mother's privacy. But he didn't raise any of them. They were all true and Catherine understood them without being told, yet they didn't matter.

He felt her watching him as he straightened his

clothes. He glanced at her several times. Her eyes were red, her cheeks damp with tears, but her expression remained fixed. Maybe in private she would break down into a sobbing cry, but not in front of him. He wondered what that stoicism was costing her.

"I'll call you as soon as I get any more information…about anything," he said at the door.

She walked toward him. He waited, not sure what to expect. She stopped in front of him, raised a hand, touched his cheek and closed her eyes for a moment.

He placed his hand on hers. "I'm sorry, Cate." The moment lingered. Finally he turned and made his way to the front of the house, painfully aware that she was following him. He reached for the doorknob.

"I'm sorry, too," she said to his back.

He didn't have to see her face to know she was saying goodbye. He heard the sadness in her voice, desolation that matched the ache in his heart.

His head bowed, he paused, then opened the door and left.

DEREK WAS PULLING INTO the police chief's driveway when Kelsey came racing out the door and ran to her car. One glance at her puffy, red-rimmed eyes was enough for him to see she was upset. Had something happened to her mother? Had she received bad news?

He drew to an abrupt halt, left the engine running, jumped out of his vehicle and sprinted to the Honda. Kelsey's face was contorted with anger, and her hand was shaking as she tried to jam her key into the ignition.

Fear replaced fury when he tapped on the window. Her head snapped up. He leaned over.

"What's the matter?" he shouted through the glass. "What's wrong?"

"Go away." She swiped at the tears with her wrist.

He tried the door, but it was locked. "Damn it, Kelsey, talk to me."

Her key went in. The engine roared to life. She rammed the transmission into gear and squealed out of the driveway, almost knocking him over.

The problem couldn't be Catherine, he concluded. If she was sick or injured, Kelsey wouldn't have reacted this way. Besides, there'd be an ambulance. Unless she'd already been taken away, but he would have heard about it on his police radio if something had happened to the chief.

He jumped back into his cruiser and shot down the driveway. The Honda was already out of sight. Calculating Kelsey was on her way back to the convent, he turned right at the end of the street and saw her car a block ahead. She didn't come to a full stop at the stop sign or signal her turn. He flipped on his overhead light bar and hit the siren for a moment, enough to get her attention. Kelsey swerved to the right side of the tree-lined street. Her car tilted forward and rocked back when she slammed on the brakes.

Derek exited his cruiser and strode up to the left side of the vehicle and faced the driver.

"Roll down your window," he instructed in cop mode. He didn't say please.

Jaw clenched, she glared up at him with venom in

her eyes. He stared back unflinching. Defeated, she lowered the power window. "What do you want?"

"You were driving erratically, exceeding the speed limit in a built-up area, disregarded a traffic sign, failed to signal a turn and had poor control of your vehicle when you stopped."

She inhaled and exhaled, her chest heaving.

"Get out of the car," he ordered.

"What?" She shot daggers of defiance at him, but being a cop's daughter she knew she had no choice. Resisting would only make matters worse.

"Get out of the car," he repeated. "Now."

If looks could kill... She opened the door and climbed out, her movements jerky, unsteady. Her hands were shaking. He reckoned her knees were weak, as well.

"I'm out. Now what, Officer?" she demanded. "Are you going to arrest me?"

"I don't know. Have you done something that warrants taking you into custody, something I should know about?"

She clamped her mouth tight.

He moderated his tone, labored to keep his voice even, sympathetic. "What's going on, Kelsey? Something's wrong. Maybe I can help."

"You can't."

"Then I can listen."

"I don't want to talk to you."

They used to spend hours with each other, chattering about anything, everything. He thought they had no secrets from each other. Obviously he was wrong.

He considered his options. He couldn't force her to

talk to him, but he couldn't let her go, either. Not in her present state. He'd never seen her so out of control. No telling what she might do to herself or someone else. She was an accident waiting to happen, and he refused to have that on his conscience.

"Then we'll just wait here until you calm down. You're too upset to drive. I have a duty to protect the public—"

His words incensed her anew. Her eyes were spanking fire.

"Don't you dare preach to me about civic duties and responsibilities."

Her outburst added further to his bewilderment, as if he'd just hit a hot button.

He said nothing for several seconds to give them both time to simmer down.

"I stopped by to see your mother," he said, almost conversationally. "To give her a report she asked for that might help us figure out what happened to your dad." The list of cases that might be affected by the debacle in the medical examiner's office. "Is she all right?"

For a moment he thought Kelsey was going to relent. But the thaw was fleeting.

"Oh, she's just fine," she said, her words dripping with sarcasm. "She was screwing that detective she hired when I walked in."

Derek's jaw dropped, not only at the unwanted picture that came to mind, but he'd never heard Kelsey speak this way.

"I thought it was guys who hired playmates," she said. "Of course, Rowan is younger. I guess that makes him a boy toy. I wonder if she pays him."

Derek's muscles tensed. "Shut up, Kelsey. Just shut up. You have no right to talk about your mother that way."

"My grandmother told me she was a tramp. I guess she was right."

He was having trouble getting all the words to connect. What did Amanda have to do with this? And why would she call Catherine a tramp? He'd met Kelsey's grandmother a few times and didn't like her. No matter how polite and well dressed he was, she always made him feel inferior, like the dirty slum kid he had once been.

"And you believed the old witch?" he asked.

"Don't refer to my grandmother that way."

He raised his eyebrows. "But it's all right for you to call your mom a tramp? What the hell's gotten into you, Kel?"

"I went home and found her in bed with him. You don't think I should be upset about that?"

He'd had a minute to let the concept sink in and now tried to assess his reaction. Surprise, certainly. Disappointment? Not really. He liked Catherine. He liked Jeff, too, for that matter.

"They're both mature adults," he said. He could understand Kelsey being upset, but he still had the feeling there was more to this raw anger than finding a man in her mother's bed.

She looked away, her expression one of disgust.

"She cares for him, Kel. I've spent more time with them than you have. I could see from the beginning they were attracted to each other." When she didn't respond, he asked, "Is the idea of sex so terrible? Is that why you don't want to marry me? Because you're afraid? There's no need to be, sweetheart." His voice softened to intimacy. Resisting the urge to reach out, to touch her was agony. "I promised you…the first time—"

"Well—" she held her head up "—somebody beat you to it."

He blinked. "What?" He must have misunderstood. "What did you say?"

She refused to make eye contact. "Can I go now?"

His blood was pounding in his ears. "No," he shouted. Now he was the one whose nerves were shattered. "Kelsey, you can't just make a statement like that and drive away." She'd told him she was a virgin, that she was saving herself for him. "Are you telling me you've had sex with someone else? Who?" he demanded. "Tell me."

"What happens in my life is none of your business." She turned around and gripped the door handle.

"Kelsey, please," he begged. His stomach knotted even as his muscles seemed to drain of strength. What did all of this mean? He put his hand on her shoulder to hold her, to steady himself. "If I've said or done anything—"

She shook loose. When she turned back to him this time, her soft eyes were brimming and filled with such wretchedness his heart ached for the anguish he found there. But he saw an emptiness, as well, as though she'd removed her soul and locked it away inside an impenetrable fortress.

His head still spinning, he dropped his hand, then stood and watched her climb back into her car and pull away.

"I'm sorry," he whispered.

CHAPTER NINETEEN

AFTER JEFF LEFT, Catherine returned to the master bedroom. She considered filling the tub with bubble bath and crawling into its soothing caress, but decided she needed the violence of a shower beating on her skin. She let the pinpricks of hot spray drum on the back of her neck and work the tight muscles while she hung her head and allowed tears to blend with the water sluicing down her chest, between her breasts.

She kept seeing the horror on Kelsey's face.

"Grandma was right. You are a slut."

So Tyrone had co-opted her from the beginning, poisoned the well by telling his parents she had come on to him. It explained the hostility the senior Tanners had always felt for Catherine. Obviously Tyrone had been very careful to advise them not to mention it to Jordan. Apparently, too, Tyrone hadn't told his wife, otherwise Melissa wouldn't have been her friend all these years. Why hadn't he told her? Because in spite of her devotion to him, Melissa had no illusions about the kind of man he was? Because, unlike his indulgent parents, she wouldn't have believed him?

Catherine had been able to avoid a head-on confrontation with her in-laws before Jordan's death, in part because she walked on eggshells around them, but mostly, she suspected, because they realized that through such a conflict they would lose their son again and the second breach would be permanent.

That Jordan was unconditionally on Catherine's side had always been a source of tremendous security for her, but being the cause of the deterioration of her husband's relationship with his parents had also been a burden. He wouldn't have held it against her if those ties had finally been broken, but awareness that she had the power to cause a rift in the family weighed heavily on her shoulders.

Jordan was gone. Catherine was alone, and as far as Tyrone and his parents were concerned, vulnerable. Whether Marcus had approved Tyrone's editorial attacks on her beforehand, she wasn't sure. She doubted it. She'd never sensed the same depth of animosity from him as she had from his wife. Catherine had often wondered why Amanda disliked her so fiercely. Now she knew.

"Grandma wonders how many other men you've been screwing."

Catherine's eyes were bloodshot when she stepped from the shower. Lethargically she donned clean but frayed loose-fitting jeans and an unpressed cotton T-shirt, the outfit she wore for working in the garden.

Dressing for her therapy, as she called it, conjured up another memory. Jeff.

She'd been so unfair to him, starting with dismissing him from the police force last year. It still amazed her that he was willing to forgive her. Finding common ground had been remarkable enough, but that they should become lovers was astounding. She'd all but written off sex after Jordan died. For months the idea itself had been banished from her consciousness.

As she ran a comb through her damp hair, she realized what most attracted her to him wasn't physical, though he was a turn-on, but the warmth of companionship she felt when she was with him. Long talks about architecture, interior design, music. Sharing the kitchen, lingering over a meal or a glass of wine. She'd missed those things even more than the sex, and Jeff had given her both.

Now they were gone again. But for the plea in the depths of his hazel eyes, he had left without protest, yet with a promise to be around if she wanted him.

"Oh, sweetheart, if only you knew how much I do."

Which brought her full circle to the loathing she'd seen on Kelsey's face when she'd confronted her in the foyer. Loathing and shame. Catherine had never imagined her daughter would feel that way about her. How had they ever come to this?

The old woman's accusation explained a lot, but not why Kelsey believed her. That was the biggest mystery of all.

The doorbell rang. Catherine's pulse quickened. Kelsey had come back to apologize, to explain. She raced through the house to the front door and swung it open. "Kel—"

Derek stood there, looking shaken. "Uh, Chief—"

Hope crumbled. "Come in," Catherine said, after her heart ceased its thumping. "I thought you were Kelsey."

"I saw her when she left," he said, stepping inside. "What happened…I mean she told me, but—"

"She told you?"

"I shouldn't have said anything." He refused to make eye contact. "It's none of my business. I swear I'll never—"

"I trust your discretion." She tried to reassure him with a tight smile. "Let's go sit down."

"I brought you the names of the medical examiner cases—"

"We'll get to them in a minute."

She led him into the living room and motioned him to the couch. She took the chair on the other side of the coffee table.

"Derek, I'm very concerned about Kelsey. What happened between you is none of my business, but I hope you know you can confide in me whenever you want."

"Yes, ma'am. Except nothing happened between us. I didn't know—" He dropped his gaze, folded and unfolded his hands in his lap, bit his lip. Catherine had never seen him so nervous, so unsure of himself.

"Didn't know what?" she prompted.

Silence lingered until he mumbled, "She said she wasn't a virgin anymore."

Catherine was stunned. She'd never inquired into her daughter's sex life. The two of them had had the appropriate discussions, about taking precautions, about being sure, but that had been a long time ago. Catherine had assumed Kelsey and Derek had at least experimented. And, Catherine hadn't been upset at the thought.

"Does that mean you and she—"

"No, ma'am." Again he refused to make eye contact.

"So she's been with someone else." Catherine muttered, more to herself than the young man sitting across from her. "Do you have any idea who…or when this happened?"

"No, ma'am." His voice shook as he gave the polite but terse reply. Catherine realized he was embarrassed to the point of humiliation, and if she continued to press she would make matters worse. She didn't want to alienate him.

"Thanks for being so honest."

After the briefest of pauses, she reached for the manila envelope he'd placed on the table. "And thank you for getting this to me so quickly."

"All the deaths that have gone through the M.E.'s office in the past eighteen months," he said, snapping out of his funk, "ever since Cliburne Vale took over."

She paged through till she came to the names beginning with T. There it was: Tanner, Jordan. Under the heading Manner of Death was the word: *Accidental*.

But was it?

JEFF'S NIGHT WAS restless. In his mind he kept seeing the transformation that came over Catherine when she realized Kelsey was standing in the bedroom doorway. The frolicking joy of uninhibited sex had shattered into embarrassment, then sheer terror.

He pictured the loneliness and despair in her eyes when she said goodbye. Perhaps Kelsey would never have approved of her mother remarrying, but Jeff also realized that even if Sister Kelsey gave her blessing, she wouldn't condone her mother sleeping with a man outside wedlock.

Marriage. After his experience with Sandy, he'd given up on connubial bliss. He must have been out of circulation too long, though, if he was fantasizing about cherishing till death us do part after just a couple of lovemaking sessions.

Except this was different. Making love to Catherine was the result of what he felt for her, not the cause. That had been the problem with Sandy. They'd jumped into bed, indulged in casual, randy sex too soon—before they really knew each other. It was different with Catherine. Even if he couldn't touch her again, he'd want to be with her. He'd still love her.

Maybe this was for the best. He had no right to be thinking of anything permanent with Catherine. There was the difference in their ages and social positions. He was the cop she'd fired from the force. That taint would be there forever. Hooking up with the chief of police would injure her reputation, and wouldn't improve his. He'd be the gold digger, the fortune hunter who married for money and status.

Unable to sleep, he climbed out of bed, trekked to his home office and dug out the financial records he'd earlier tapped into.

Tyrone paid his bills online, no doubt for convenience, perhaps also because that way he wouldn't leave a paper trail.

"Oh, but you're lazy," he muttered when the Web site accepted the password that had taken Derek just six minutes to recover from Tyrone's office computer. "Didn't anyone ever tell you to use different passwords and change them frequently?"

At this point, Jeff wasn't sure what he expected to find, but the mass of information was a challenge. Maybe somewhere in all the data was a clue to what had happened to Jordan Tanner.

"My, aren't you a busy boy—and not particularly discreet."

Tyrone spent lavish amounts at exclusive restaurants and high-priced nightclubs and sent flowers and chocolates to a host of women. Nothing to his wife.

The guy was a sleazebag of the first magnitude. Catherine said Melissa was aware of her husband's infidelities and tolerated them. But did she? Jeff had seen the former model at Jones Hall the night of the charity concert. The woman was a knockout. Men stared at her as she walked by. How long could such a beauty endure being scorned? How would she take her retribution? Death and mutilation were ancient remedies. Based on Tyrone's continued activity with women, he hadn't been gelded.

Gas credit cards showed Tyrone made periodic trips to the Lake Conroe district north of Houston, no doubt to the Tanner compound Derek had told him about. A pattern began to emerge. Using a calendar to check dates, Jeff realized Tyrone gassed up there every Wednesday.

"So that's how you spend your golf afternoons. But what's this?"

A year ago last April, at the end of the month, he'd

used his credit card at a convenience store on a Saturday afternoon.

"What were you doing up there that day? A family get-together?"

Something niggled at the back of his mind, something Derek had mentioned. The date fell on the weekend at the end of April. Wasn't that just before college exams? When Kelsey had used the place to study.

Jeff decided to drive to the lake the next morning, get the lay of the land firsthand and ask a few questions.

MONDAY MORNING WAS always hectic. Catherine reviewed the weekend blotter of arrests and incidents, met with various department heads and coordinated a week's worth of appointments. She was annoyed when Captain Paul Radke, head of Internal Affairs hadn't shown up by noon with the list of M.E. cases she'd asked for, but decided it was probably just as well. She had to speak at a Kiwanis luncheon, and by waiting until afterward she'd be better able to concentrate on the information he gave her.

When he finally showed up at two o'clock, his list was shorter than the one Derek had furnished.

"The M.E. has only handled three hundred cases in the past fifteen months?" she asked.

"These are the cases the medical examiner's office had to testify at."

"I asked for everything, Paul, not just those that went to trial. How many others are there?"

Radke sucked in his cheeks before answering. "About twice that number."

"I need all of them. These three hundred are ones the M.E. may have screwed up in court. We need to find out how many cases didn't get that far because the lab botched them."

"You're not considering reopening the whole lot?"

"Not officially. But we have to at least review them to determine if there might be justification for further investigation."

Forensic pathology was capable of things no one had even dreamed of a decade or two earlier, but it still started with careful initial observation and analysis. A gunshot wound was hard to miss, though there were documented cases of it happening. Bruises sustained in a fall might mask those resulting from a beating. Murder could be passed off as a drug overdose. Drowning could be seen as accidental or a suicide rather than homicide. And a man could die of an apparent heart attack, when he was actually poisoned.

"That'll take forever." Radke was shaking his head. "We haven't got the resources or the budget—"

"We'll have to get them." She shuffled through the papers, noted Jordan's name wasn't on the list, but decided not to mention it. "This is all on computer. It shouldn't be that difficult to expand the parameters of the search. I want a complete list by eight tomorrow morning."

Her deputy didn't appreciate being treated like a clerk. Until recently she'd considered him one of the good guys.

"Bring me the list personally, will you, Paul?" she said, when he turned and was moving toward the door. "I'd like to keep this under wraps for the time being."

He froze in mid-stride, then continued out the door.

THE FORTY-MILE TRIP to Lake Conroe took a little over an hour and a half with traffic moving at a steady clip, no accidents jamming things up or foul weather slowing them down. Assuming Tyrone had a heavy foot in his shiny black Lotus, he could make the trip in less than an hour under ideal conditions, assuming he wasn't stopped for speeding. Jeff would have Derek check to see if he had been issued any tickets.

The cozy town of Conroe was a favorite tourist spot, especially in the spring when bluebonnets were in bloom. Jeff found the gas station where Tyrone had filled up. It came as no surprise that the middle-aged woman who ran the place knew the six-foot-six black man or that she had only positive things to say about him. A true gentleman.

"We went to school together," Jeff lied. "I have a getaway place of my own just up the road in Willis, so he stops by sometimes on weekends when he's in this neck of the woods. Now that I think about it, the last time he dropped by must have been over a year ago—time sure flies—when his niece was at their cabin studying for her exams."

"Kelsey. Yeah, sweet girl. Pretty, too. Always fills up here on her way to the family compound. Too bad about that fall she had. Do you know if she recovered all right?"

"She's fine," Jeff said, and wondered what fall she was referring to. Neither Derek nor Catherine had mentioned her getting injured.

"I guess it turned her off of the place, though," the woman said. "I don't think I've seen her since."

"What exactly happened, anyway?" Jeff asked, as he

snagged a tin of mints from the wire rack by the cash register. "I never did get the full story."

"Tripped on a tree root while she was out hiking and took a tumble down an embankment. Got bruised real bad. Called her uncle who was visiting someone near here—" She looked up at Jeff. "I guess that was you."

He smiled without actually confirming her assumption.

"Mr. Tanner came right over and wanted to take her to the hospital, but she refused. I reckon she just needed someone to talk to. Poor dear. She sure was moving painful when she stopped by to get some Tylenol on her way home the next day."

"Did her uncle stay with her?"

"He was there a few hours is all, said she insisted on getting back to her books. As miserable as she was, though, I don't see how she could have concentrated."

Jeff thanked the woman, paid his bill and left.

He was home by midafternoon and found a message from Catherine inviting him to her house that evening at nine. Derek would also be there.

CHAPTER TWENTY

CATHERINE FELT a long-overdue jolt of confidence that she might be closing in on the ring of corruption that had plagued her administration and the one before it. She knew now Paul Radke was part of it, but she felt equally certain he wasn't the man in charge, the mastermind. In spite of the ambition that had gotten him to the position of deputy chief, he was essentially an unimaginative man, a person who took advantage of opportunities rather than someone who created them. A cog in the wheel, one Catherine could use to get to the hub and to the spider who was pulling all the strings.

She worked in her office till six, then drove straight home. She'd asked Jeff and Derek to meet her there at nine. After changing into more comfortable clothes, she made a couple of telephone calls, threw together a sandwich, though her mouth was watering for one of Jeff's omelets, and sat down with the phone logs Derek had given her. She focused on the dates surrounding Jordan's death. She already knew about Rialto's calls to Tyrone and his racquetball buddy the morning of Jordan's death. What else did these contacts tell her? Beyond the fact that Tyrone and Rialto were more than casual acquaintances, not much.

She expanded her review and checked out the most frequently called numbers, tracing their identities online. Mostly businesses and a few people associated with the newspaper.

Then she spied another pattern. Every Tuesday evening Tyrone called the same number in Houston. She traced it. A woman who ran an escort service. At eleven o'clock on Wednesday mornings he made another call, each week to a different, unlisted number. Catherine ran a trace on three of them. Two came up with only initials for first names. The third belonged to a woman. Using her special access, Catherine researched the name. It belonged to an eighteen-year-old who had been picked up half a dozen times for soliciting.

Catherine leaned back in her chair. Now she knew what her brother-in-law did on Wednesday afternoons. Jeff was reviewing Tyrone's credit card charges. Maybe they would tell her where he was taking his "escorts."

She copied down the dates and the telephone numbers of the women he called. There were over forty. If she could coax statements from a few of them, she would have leverage against Tyrone.

The doorbell rang.

Since it was ten minutes to nine, Catherine assumed it was Derek. Her heart did a somersault when she found Jeff standing on her doorstep. In his eyes she saw the desire she felt.

"You're early," she said, as he came in.

"I wanted to see you alone for a few minutes." When the door was closed, he asked, "Have you talked to Kelsey?"

Rather than give him the chance to touch her—she didn't think she'd be able to hold out against the emotional power of feeling his arms around her —Catherine started for the living room, then altered her course and went to the kitchen. Because of the time they'd spent there—quality time—it had become the focal point of her house. That and the bedroom.

"No." She opened the refrigerator, only to realize the pitcher of lemonade she'd planned to serve was nearly empty. Digging into the freezer, she removed a can. Jeff snagged a pot from the rack over the butcher block island and filled it with warm water. Catherine concentrated on his hands as he worked. Good hands. Awareness of what they were capable of prickled her skin.

"She hasn't called me and I haven't tried to call her," she said. "I need to give her time. I guess I need some, too."

He plunged the can into the pot in the sink to defrost it while she got out three glasses.

"I came across information today I need to talk to you about," he said. "In private."

Her movements slowed. Was this an excuse for him to be alone with her? No, he wouldn't play that kind of game. She just wished he'd take her in his arms and hold her. She needed to feel the warmth of human contact, have a shoulder to cry on. His shoulder. He'd promised she could use it whenever she wanted.

But she'd made up her mind. She couldn't keep him in her life—or bed. Regardless of what she felt for him, her first obligation was to her daughter. Kelsey was very fragile right now, and that was Catherine's fault. Her little girl was an adult. She had the right to make her own decisions, her own choices, but a mother has an obligation to guide by good example, and Catherine hadn't done that.

"Stay after Derek leaves." She began filling the glasses with ice from the freezer door. "We can talk then."

He pulled the tab on the lemonade can and squeezed the cardboard cylinder, forcing the still frosty contents into the glass pitcher she had given him. He added water. She stirred while he disposed of the empty container. The two of them sidestepped each other with the choreography of assembly line workers who'd been on the job for years.

Jeff was carrying the pitcher to the breakfast-nook table when Catherine went to answer the door a second time. She returned a minute later with Derek. He greeted Jeff with a silent nod. They all sat down.

Catherine explained that Captain Radke had given her a short list of M.E. cases that would need review, and that she had requested an expanded list for the morning. She turned to Derek.

"We have the legal right to monitor telephone calls and computer usage in the workplace. See who he's been contacting outside the department, either by phone or e-mail. If you come up with anyone suspicious, like Rialto, I can get a court order to put a tap on his office and home lines."

Derek nodded.

"You mean you never checked who in the department was talking to whom?" Jeff asked.

"Of course I did," she answered, more annoyed with herself than at his question. "My mistake was using in-house resources to do it. I made an assumption the people in Internal Affairs were clean. Radke and his people have been very supportive...or seemed to be until now."

"If he's your man, he's probably purged the files of incriminating evidence."

Derek spoke up. "That's not as easy as it sounds. When the new system was installed two years ago, a backup, read-only folder was created on a second, remote server. Data can be deleted from the working files, but not from the backup."

"How soon can you get me the logs?" Catherine asked.

"I'll have them here by six tomorrow morning."

"I don't need them that fast," she protested. "Get some sleep. You look bushed."

"There'll be plenty of time to sleep later."

Catherine sensed frustration in his reply. At her for overloading him? She didn't think so. More likely at his encounter the day before with Kelsey.

"Thanks for coming," she told him. "I know I'm putting a lot on you—"

"No problem, ma'am. Glad to do it. See you in the morning." He rose to leave.

Catherine was very conscious of Jeff watching her as she showed Derek out. They'd both agreed to end their personal relationship, but making the decision and living with it were two different matters. How could she be in his presence and not be affected by him?

"Now what it is you wanted to talk to me about?" she asked upon her return to the kitchen. She felt him start to put his arm around her, then pull back. She should have been pleased by his self-control. With a sigh she shook off her regret and disappointment.

"I was having trouble sleeping last night," he said, "and decided to go over Tyrone's personal bills. Among them were gasoline charges. I discovered he uses a filling station in Conroe every Wednesday. Why do you suppose he would go all the way to Conroe in the middle of the week?"

Catherine resumed her place across from him at the breakfast table. "That explains the telephone calls. Every Tuesday he calls an escort service here in town. On Wednesday at eleven, he phones another number, always a different one, probably to coordinate picking the women up. I was wondering where he took them. The cabin at the lake. Makes sense. The family only uses it on weekends."

"Seems like a long way to go just to get laid," Jeff commented.

"Think of it as a power trip," Catherine said. "The place is also private."

"What's wrong with the guy?" Jeff asked, not bothering to disguise his disdain. "He has a beautiful, intelligent wife. Why does he have to mess around with other women?"

Catherine gave him a wry smile. "You're a man. You tell me."

He shot her a wounded expression. "We're not all like that."

He was right. She'd been married to a good man. Without thinking, she reached out and put her hand on Jeff's. "I know that. But a lot of men are."

He studied her. "I discovered something else last night. Tyrone was up at Conroe on the Saturday of the weekend Kelsey was there studying for her finals."

It took a moment, then Catherine felt the blood drain from her face, from her heart.

"According to the woman at the gas station," Jeff continued, "Kelsey fell while out hiking and bruised herself, so she called her uncle. He drove up and wanted to take her to the hospital, but she refused to go. The clerk said Kelsey stopped by on her way out Sunday evening to get some Tylenol. She was moving very stiffly."

"No," Catherine mumbled. "He wouldn't...he couldn't—" She covered her face.

"Cate, what is it?" Jeff moved around the table and knelt at her side. Hot, scorching tears slipped out from between her fingers. She bit her lips.

"Sweetheart, what is it?"

Taking a deep gulp of air, Catherine straightened, reached for a paper napkin from the dispenser on the table and blotted her cheeks. Eyes still unfocused, she continued to take raking breaths for a long minute. Finally, she steeled herself.

"I'm going to tell you something, Jeff, I've never told another soul, not even Jordan. It's the one thing I held back from him. I need your word that you'll keep it to yourself, that you'll allow me to decide if and when it's ever disclosed to anyone else. Will you do that for me? I'm asking you to keep a secret without even knowing what it is."

"You can trust me, Cate. I give you my word."

She started to pour herself more lemonade, but her hand shook so badly, Jeff took the pitcher and refilled her glass for her.

She managed a tiny sip. "Jordan and I had been going together for about six months before I finally got to meet his brother. Tyrone was six years younger than Jordan, which made him three years younger than me. He was a sophomore at Notre Dame at the time, home for the summer. Drop-dead handsome in a boyish sort of way—and he knew it."

Catherine hadn't been unaware of his good looks or his charisma. Later she'd asked herself repeatedly if in some way she had led him on, given him the impression she was more fascinated with him than she was. Perhaps that guilty suspicion explained why she'd never told Jordan, or anyone else, about what happened.

"In those days the Tanners owned a thirty-five-foot cabin cruiser that slept six. For me, the notion of sailing in Galveston Bay on a private yacht was like something out of a fable. Jordan was supposed to pick me up at the apartment I shared with a girlfriend at two o'clock that Saturday, but when I opened the door I found Tyrone. Jordan had been sidetracked at the last minute, Ty explained, and had asked him to pick me up."

It had all seemed so innocent. She'd always felt safe with Jordan. How different could his kid brother be?

"I let him into the apartment while I got my stuff. My roommate had already left for the weekend. I was anxious to go, but Ty seemed intent on admiring a couple of watercolors I'd painted and had hung on the wall. I was standing beside him, apologizing for my genuine lack of real talent when he pulled me into his arms and kissed me hard on the mouth. The move was so quick and unexpected that for a moment I didn't react, didn't resist."

"Which he took for acquiescence," Jeff supplied.

She nodded. "As soon as the initial shock wore off, I fought him, but he just laughed, claimed he knew I wanted him, that I obviously liked black men, that he was black and all man."

In truth, his attitude, the gleam in his eyes, the almost sadistic curl of his mouth had frightened her more than anything else in her life.

"He pinned my arms to my sides and pressed himself against me so I could feel his erection. He tried to kiss me again, but this time I was prepared and resisted with all the force I could muster. He laughed and tore my blouse right down the middle. I wasn't wearing a bra. When he backed off to gape at my breasts, I yanked my knee up and kicked him between the legs as hard as I could. I was terrified. Adrenaline was pumping, and I guess that made me stronger than I realized, because the next thing I knew he was writhing on the floor in agony. He couldn't get his breath and for a minute I was afraid he was going to die. He lay doubled over for some minutes before he finally recovered. Then he did something I hadn't expected. He apologized."

"He apologized?"

"He said he was sorry. He sounded so genuinely regretful. He explained that he must have gotten his signals crossed and asked me to forgive him for being out of line. He promised it would never happen again. He insisted he didn't mean to hurt me, that he would never hurt a woman."

"And you believed him."

"He sounded so contrite, Jeff. So penitent and sincere. We drove to the harbor in silence in his Corvette. It wasn't until he was parking the car that he advised me not to say anything to anyone, especially Jordan. There was no sense stirring up a hornet's nest, he said. Besides, neither Jordan nor anybody else would believe me."

"Sneaky son of a—"

"He said it all very casually, not even bothering to make eye contact as he delivered his little speech. But he didn't have to. The implied threat came through loud and clear. That's when I realized the apology had been nothing but a tactic to get me into his car so he could deliver me to his brother, as promised."

"What did you do?" Jeff asked.

"I tried to put on a smiley face as we cruised around the bay. Tyrone devoted himself to his date, who'd shown up in her own car. He treated me with the kind of affable consideration you'd expect a guy to show his older brother's girlfriend."

Catherine cupped her hands in front of her mouth and rocked back and forth as she recalled the fear that had possessed her.

"Jordan had laid on an elaborate assortment of food for my first boat trip. He wanted to impress me. I ate almost nothing. I tried to fake enthusiasm for everything he was showing me, the fine appointments of the cabin, the sophisticated navigational equipment... He even let me take the wheel. But all the time my mind was frozen with conflicting anxieties. Should I tell him what Ty had tried to do, what I had done? What would be gained? I'd be pitting one brother against the other, and Ty was right, it would be my word against his. Even if Jordan believed me, no one else would. He could end up fighting with his family. Worse, Ty could twist things around and make Jordan look like a fool, a gullible black man who thought he could have a blond, blue-eyed, white girlfriend."

She sagged in her seat.

"I couldn't do that to him, Jeff. I couldn't hurt him that way. He was a good, decent man who didn't deserve to be shamed and humiliated like that, especially among his own people."

His own people. The term buzzed around in her head. What she and Jordan had felt for each other had nothing to do with race or color, wealth or class. They had moved past that in their first conversation, during which they'd come to see each other as two people who had so much in common. The differences in their skin tones or social status were irrelevant.

"I'm sorry you didn't have a good time today," she remembered him saying that evening when he took her home.

"I did," she'd protested.

He'd smiled sweetly. "You tried to, and I love you for that. The sea isn't for everyone."

"But I do like the water," she argued. "Let's go out again, and I'll prove it. I just wasn't feeling too good today."

"You were seasick? Why didn't you say so? I had some Dramamine you could have taken."

"It wasn't that," she'd said, and did something she'd

never done before or since. She'd told him she was suffering from menstrual cramps.

To her amazement he hadn't been spooked or embarrassed. Instead he showed genuine sympathy. "I wish you'd told me," he'd said. "We could have done something else, something that would have been less uncomfortable for you."

She'd kissed him then and had to fight to hold back tears. Yes, she'd decided, she'd made the right decision in not telling him about his brother.

Two weeks later, Jordan invited her to go out on the boat again, this time, just the two of them. But even as they climbed aboard, Catherine kept picturing Tyrone's face when he squeezed up against her, and the pure hatred in his eyes when she'd rejected him. His words, "No one will believe you," had echoed in her head. Her stomach had already been queasy when she'd stepped aboard.

Fifteen minutes after they'd left the dock in Galveston, she really did get seasick. She took the Dramamine Jordan offered and they'd stayed out a couple of hours before the weather turned sour and they were forced to return to shore. Convinced now that Catherine was not a good sailor and that she didn't enjoy boating, Jordan never again suggested they go out on the yacht. Which was a pity, because she would have enjoyed making love to him under the stars to the sway and pitch of the luxury craft on Galveston Bay.

During the intervening years, her relationship with Tyrone was cordial, if not completely relaxed. He must have known from the start that she hadn't told Jordan about the incident at her apartment, but it took some time for her to realize he wasn't sure she never would. If she ever did, Jordan would have believed her, which put Tyrone, who had developed a reputation for infidelity, at a distinct disadvantage.

Power shifted with Jordan's death. Tyrone was now in a position to avenge her rejection. His editorial attacks in the *Sentinel* weren't about the police department. Her job was just a convenient excuse for getting back at one of the few women who had ever refused him.

"Cate…"

Her head snapped up. Jeff was talking to her.

"Sorry. I was taking a tour down memory lane. Where was I?"

"You said you didn't tell Jordan about the incident."

"I knew if I did he would confront his brother and their relationship would be forever shattered. Their parents would blame me. I didn't want to come between him and the rest of his family. In fairness," she added with a sigh, "Tyrone never made a move on me again. We had an understanding that as long as he kept his distance, I would maintain my silence."

Her eyes pooled with tears. "I thought I was doing the right thing, Jeff. I didn't know it would come back to haunt me. And my daughter."

"Explain."

What she was about to say made her stomach heave. She tasted bile and jumped up, prepared to bolt into the washroom just past the pantry. Her heart pounded. She drew air into her lungs and sat back down. The sip of lemonade she took burned her throat.

"Kelsey told me the other day after she walked in on us that she'd gone to see her grandfather to ask him to make Ty stop writing those editorials against me. He refused. Then her grandmother accused me of being a tramp. It seems years ago Tyrone told her that I had tried to seduce him, and that he valiantly rejected my advances."

Jeff voiced his outrage with a few choice expletives.

"You said the woman in Conroe told you Kelsey had called Tyrone."

"Yes." He gaped at her. She could see he was beginning to put the pieces together. "But I was unable to find any record of him receiving a call from her or from the family compound that day or any other day."

Catherine again stood up and began pacing. "Kelsey wouldn't have called him, Jeff. If she was hurt and needed help, she would have dialed 911 or the local hospital. Otherwise she would have contacted her father or me. Not her uncle."

"You're saying—"

"I think Tyrone showed up at the cabin unannounced." She paused and squeezed her eyes shut, then opened them and stared straight at Jeff. "I think Tyrone raped my daughter."

CHAPTER TWENTY-ONE

JEFF STUDIED the woman whose hands he had taken between his. They were cold, she was shivering, while he was hot with rage. He didn't question her statement. It explained so much. The honors student who came back from a weekend of intense study, only to flub exams that should have been a snap. Her spurning Derek, the man she had been saving herself for. Her choosing to enter a convent, rather than embrace the life of wife and mother she had dreamed of. It also explained her cold attitude toward virtually everyone, including her mother.

He tried to imagine the agony Catherine was going through, all the second-guessing and self-blame. She'd withheld one thing from her husband, and that secret now appeared to have destroyed her family.

"What are you going to do?" he asked.

"I'll have to talk to Kelsey, find out from her if I'm right. If I am, I'll get her counseling." Her face collapsed. "My little girl—" she moaned.

Jeff gathered her in his arms. She dropped her head on his shoulder and cried the tears of a woman whose heart would never mend. He stroked her back, searching for words that would ease the pain. None came.

After several minutes, Catherine pulled away and wiped her eyes with her wrist. Jeff offered his handkerchief, then massaged the back of her neck. He could feel the tension there, the taut, trembling muscles.

"Kelsey takes after you," he said. "She's strong, Cate. She'll come through this, and she'll love you all the more for being there for her."

"She thinks I'm a—"

He touched a finger to her lips to silence her.

"You're her mother, Cate. She grew up with you as the center of her world, and she knows you too well to take notice of what others might say. She's confused and angry right now, and she has every right to be. What happened to her should never happen to any woman. Holding it in all this time, especially when her father died so soon afterward... A woman of lesser strength would have completely collapsed under those circumstances."

He rubbed her arms, trying to warm her cold skin. "It's a tribute to the goodness and character you and Jordan instilled in her that she's made the honorable decisions she has."

He tipped her chin up so he could peer into her eyes. "She could have channeled her rage into violence or abuse of drugs and alcohol, but she didn't. Instead, she chose a life dedicated to doing good, to helping others. That's one tough Sister."

Catherine tried to smile through her tears and almost succeeded.

"Even if Kelsey confirms what you suspect, there may be nothing you or she can do to Tyrone," he warned. "It's been too long. There's no evidence—"

"I don't care about the law," she said, the old defiance creeping back into her voice. "There are other ways to punish, and I swear by all that is sacred, Tyrone Tanner will pay for this."

"What can I do to help?"

CATHERINE REALIZED that for all Jeff knew she might have been planning mayhem and murder—they held a certain appeal—yet this man didn't flinch, didn't question or hesitate. His support was unconditional, and for this moment alone she would always love him. She hadn't said it to him, maybe she never could, but it was true. She did love him.

For Kelsey's sake, however, she had to keep her emotional distance from him. Until now she hadn't realized how painful that vow would be. She shoved her chair back, disengaging herself from Jeff in the process, and stood up. Marching to the end of the counter where there was a box of tissues, she grabbed a fistful and dried her eyes.

"I want you to compile a detailed report on Tyrone's activities." She was in police chief mode again. "The people he associates with, the women whose company he keeps, the way he spends his money."

"That won't be difficult," Jeff told her, accepting her switch in role from grieving mother to tough cop. "Most of the information is already on my computer. I can have a complete dossier for you in a matter of days."

"Let me know if you run into any problems."

He stepped toward her, his arms outstretched. She shifted away.

"You better get going," she said. "You have a lot of work to do."

"Cate…"

She turned away from him. "Thanks for your help. Now please go."

They stood staring at each other for what felt like an eternity.

"I'll call you as soon as it's ready," he said at last, paused a moment, walked to the front door and let himself out.

OVER THE NEXT HOURS Jeff worked at his home computer. A good deal of the effort was mechanical, which was just as well. What Tyrone Tanner had done to Catherine and to her daughter simmered and seethed inside Jeff so strongly he was having a difficult time concentrating. He had dealt with murderers and thieves, with violent felons and sophisticated con artists who bilked old people out of their life savings, but no crime called out for vengeance like rape, for no form of justice could restore innocence.

At 2:00 a.m. he finally shut down his program, not because he was finished but because fatigue and anger were increasing the likelihood of his making a serious mistake and screwing up the data he was trying to sort.

He had just put his head on the pillow, it seemed, when the phone rang.

"Can you be here in twenty minutes?"

He pinched the bridge of his nose and checked the bedside clock. Three-fifteen.

"Cate?" A call at this hour didn't bode well. "What's happened?"

"Can you come right over?"

"Yes—" The phone went dead.

No longer groggy, he sprang out of bed and ran to the bathroom. He took a minute to brush his teeth but didn't bother to shave, threw on a pair of casual slacks and a light knit shirt.

If what Catherine suspected was true, there was no telling what additional psychological trauma it might have caused when Kelsey found him with her mother. If only she hadn't walked in when she had. Now Jeff would forever be the man violating her father's bed. Kelsey might eventually have agreed to her mother dating, even remarrying. She might have come to accept Jeff, too, but not when every time she looked at him she'd see her mother having sex with him. Damn, damn, damn.

He set his security alarm and rushed out the door. When he arrived at Catherine's house ten minutes later, Derek's new black Isuzu Rodeo was parked in the driveway.

Jeff bounded out of his car. The front door opened before he got there, and Catherine stood before him in worn jeans and a clinging T-shirt. A sudden wave of lust careened through him. He wanted this woman, and judging from the way she avoided eye contact, she wanted him, too. But she'd made a vow, one he had to honor.

He followed her to the kitchen. Derek stood when they came into the room. Catherine had put on a pot of coffee and its rich aroma filled the air.

"Derek has found the yellowcake," she announced, as she poured the steaming brew into three mugs.

Jeff gaped at the young man. "You're serious?"

"I think I have," he amended.

"How?" Jeff asked, almost breathless. The three of them sat down.

"Without knowing when it went missing," Derek began, "I had to make a few assumptions. I worked backward from the date the Superfund inventoried the place. The barrels could have been moved one by one in the backs of small trucks, in which case we'd never find them, but I went on the premise that whoever took them wanted them gone fast. So I checked trucking companies making pickups in the area for delivery to the Ship Channel."

"Makes sense," Jeff agreed.

He'd been observing Catherine. The dark circles under her eyes told him she hadn't gotten much sleep. He saw more than exhaustion there, though; he saw hopelessness and defeat, too. He'd give anything to erase that bleak despair. Being dismissed from the job he loved hadn't made him feel nearly as helpless as he did now.

Shifting his attention to Derek, he asked, "So what did you come up with?"

"Alto Trucking, a subsidiary of Rialto Corp, was hired thirteen months ago by Nadir Enterprises, a Middle Eastern import-export company, to move twenty crates, weighing a thousand pounds apiece from a nonexistent address on Market Street to a wharf in the Ship Channel.

"Rialto's warehouse was on Market Street," Catherine pointed out.

"There's a cargo ship due to set sail next week for Pakistan."

"All of the pieces fit together, except for one thing,"

Jeff said. "Why has it taken this long to get them out of the country?"

Catherine stopped blowing her steaming coffee. "Jordan gave a lot of publicity to the yellowcake being found in the Rialto warehouse. If it had only recently disappeared, it might have become too hot to handle at the time. After 9/11, cargoes were subject to a lot more scrutiny."

"So what do we do now?" Jeff asked. "Turn this info over to the feds?"

Catherine rotated her cup. "It's too early. The feds aren't very happy with me at the moment because I publicized the missing barrels. If I tell them we've found the yellowcake, and they raid the wharf only to find...toothpaste, my credibility will be further shot—and so will theirs."

"What do you propose?" Jeff asked.

"A special task force. Tomorrow morning I'd like you to call me from a public phone, identify yourself as a former employee of Alto Trucking, and say you think you know what happened to the missing yellowcake."

Jeff sat back and grinned.

"Refuse to give your name," Catherine went on, "but say you helped load barrels at the Rialto warehouse before the cleanup began and that they were taken to a wharf in the Ship Channel."

Jeff rubbed his forehead. "Yes, I remember now. The pickup address on the shipping order was wrong, and when I brought it to my supervisor's attention, he told me to shut up and get back to work. I figured whatever it was had to be hot, but I needed the job, so I did what I was told."

"Good," Catherine said, her eyes twinkling at him across the table.

"I don't care about any reward," Jeff added, "because I'm a patriot and believe in protecting America. But I would like to know who my family should sue if I die of radiation sickness."

Catherine chuckled. "Just don't overdo it."

"Who, me?"

"That'll give me an excuse to convene the task force," she said.

"Do you think we'll find anything?" Derek asked.

She shrugged. "We'll at least spook Buster Rialto, into maybe making a mistake."

"Or into trying to kill you," Jeff added seriously.

FOREMOST IN CATHERINE'S MIND when she dragged herself out of bed at six o'clock after a sleepless night was to see Kelsey. She would give anything to learn her suspicions were wrong, that her daughter hadn't been violated, but the weight on her heart and the circumstantial evidence—even now she thought like a cop—told her she already knew the truth. What she had to do was confirm it.

After showering and dressing, she nibbled on a bagel while she drank her coffee and paged through Radke's telephone logs Derek had e-mailed her only minutes earlier. She didn't know when the young man slept.

Her deputy chief had been calling Rialto or members of his staff several times a month for the past year. Most recently there had been a flurry of calls immediately after her announcement that she'd turned over evidence of twenty missing barrels of yellowcake to federal authorities. She wondered how deeply involved Radke was in Rialto's organization. As a deputy chief and the head of IA, he had access to virtually everything going on in the department. Was this a new development? How had Rialto convinced the thirty-year veteran to betray his allegiance?

Derek answered the first question by producing logs that showed the captain had been in Rialto's pocket several years.

Catherine shook her head sadly.

She arrived at police headquarters at seven. At eight Jeff played his informant role and Catherine set the wheels in motion to follow up on the fantastic story about transporting a hot shipment of unknown goods to a wharf on the Ship Channel. Her task force was made up of twenty experienced officers and included all the remaining women from Catherine's police academy days, because she knew she could count on them. Risa Taylor, Lucy Montalvo, Crista Santiago. She put Lt. Mei Lu Ling in charge of the operation.

At nine Radke stalked into her office without knocking and slammed down a thick stack of papers in the middle of her desk.

She scowled. Did he think his belligerence would intimidate her into backing off? He ought to know better.

"Close the door," she said.

He worked his jaw, spun around and came close to slamming it.

She didn't invite him to sit while she flipped through the additional M.E. files he had brought. When she found Jordan's name where it should be, she knew this time she had it all, though she would do a page-by-page comparison later just to be sure. What Radke had left out might be more significant than what had been put in.

She moved the stack aside, opened her middle drawer and withdrew the logs of his telephone calls. She passed the papers across the desk to him. "I'd like an explanation."

"What's this?" His defiance faltered when he saw the data she'd highlighted in green.

"You tell me," she said.

"Where did you get this?"

"Why have you been calling Buster Rialto?"

Reverting to rebelliousness, he pointed out that he had a right to talk to anyone he damn well pleased. "This is an invasion of my privacy."

Her hand sliced through the air. "Cut the attitude, Paul. It's over. I want to know how involved you are with Rialto."

He collapsed in the chair and raked a hand through his hair. "I...I pass on information...about things of interest to him. That's all. Look, I've got three kids in college. My wife is suffering from chronic depression, and insurance doesn't pay a quarter of the bills for her treatment. I need the money."

"Do you get involved in planning any of his operations?"

"Absolutely not. I would never—"

She huffed out a breath. "I'll make a deal with you. Give me a detailed, sworn statement about your role in feeding information to Rialto, and tender your resignation. In exchange, I'll talk with the D.A. about not prosecuting you on corruption charges, provided there's no evidence to indicate you actively participated in any of Rialto's illegal activities."

He started to object.

"Or—" she held up her hand "—I will relieve you of duty right now and place you on indefinite suspension. I'm sure the FBI will want to delve more closely into your activities and those of the rest of your family. Either way, Paul, your career is at an end. Cooperate with me and you might be able to hold on to your pension. Don't, and you'll go to prison. I don't think I have to remind you that cops don't fare very well in penitentiaries. Which will it be?"

He took a barrelful of air into his lungs and slumped deeper into his seat.

"Catherine, I never—"

"I need your answer now."

He closed his eyes, wheezed out a breath, then studied her only a second before averting his gaze. "I'll tell you what I know. But you're going to be disappointed," he added. "I'm a very minor element in his organization. When word gets out, I'm a dead man. You'd better cover your back, too, Catherine, because you're not going to be safe. Neither will your daughter."

CHAPTER TWENTY-TWO

THE CONVENT OF the School Sisters of Our Lady could have been mistaken for any other house on the east side of town, except it was bigger than most. The two-story, yellow-brick, fifty-year-old residence was unremarkable. The lawns that flanked the cracked concrete path leading to the front door were raggedly trimmed and not weed-free. The shrubbery under the windows could have used fertilizing and pruning.

Catherine pressed the doorbell. She jumped when the door opened.

"My name is Catherine Tanner," she said to the thirtyish woman wearing a blue shirt dress and a wooden cross around her neck. "I'd like to see my daughter, Kelsey."

"I'm Sister Karla," the woman said. "Please come in."

Catherine stepped inside. "I apologize for coming here unannounced, but it is important I see her."

Sister Karla's smile was kind and understanding. "You can wait in the parlor while I get her."

"Thank you."

The room was medium-sized, plainly furnished, and felt unlived in. Catherine was staring out the lace-draped window, watching a cardinal in its bright red plumage peck at something on the ground, when she heard footsteps behind her.

She had met Sister Cornella last year when Kelsey had joined the order. In her late fifties or early sixties, the mother superior was polite but somewhat remote, a woman who projected competence and efficiency, rather than warmth.

"Mrs. Tanner, or should I say Chief Tanner—" she approached with outstretched hand "—good afternoon."

"Catherine, please. I've come to see Kelsey."

"Yes, I know." Her gray eyes were piercing and unflinching. "She asked me to convey her apologies, but she doesn't want to see you right now."

For a moment, Catherine panicked. She wasn't surprised that Kelsey was reluctant to talk to her, but she hadn't considered the possibility that she would refuse, or that the mother superior might stand in the way of their meeting.

Catherine's first impulse was to insist, to remind Sister Cornella that Kelsey was her daughter and that…what? She had the right to make demands, to violate this house of refuge? Perhaps Kelsey had told her about walking in and finding her mother in bed with a man.

An aggressive approach would accomplish nothing with this woman except put her back up. Catherine was there on sufferance. While she hesitated to tell this stranger why she needed to see Kelsey, there seemed no alternative.

"May we sit down?" Catherine asked. "I owe you

an explanation. Perhaps then you will understand why I'm here."

Waving her to a stiff-backed armchair, Sister Cornella took the one at ninety degrees to it and waited for her visitor to begin.

Catherine told her story concisely, that many years ago her brother-in-law molested her, and she now had reason to believe the same man, her late husband's brother, may have raped Kelsey.

Cornella didn't recoil at the accusation.

"I know I can't force Kelsey to talk about it," Catherine concluded. "My hope is to convince her she's not at fault and that the only way to get past this is to acknowledge it happened and to help me make sure it doesn't happen again. Her uncle has a young daughter and other nieces. If he can force himself on his brother's daughter, what's to keep him from attacking other young girls?"

Cornella remained silent. The woman would make a damn good interrogator, Catherine reflected. It took willpower not to squirm under her piercing gaze.

"I'd like to talk to Kelsey alone," Catherine said, "but if the only way I can get to see her is with you present, I'm willing to accept that condition. She needs help, Reverend Mother. I can't do it all, but talking to me is a necessary first step."

"I agree." Cornella rose to her feet. "I'll get her. You may speak to her privately, but I'll be right down the hall in case I'm needed."

Catherine sighed. "Thank you."

She didn't know what to expect from her daughter.

More than a year had passed since that terrible week-end, enough time to recover from physical wounds, but the damage wrought by rape to a young woman's pride, her confidence and self-esteem, her hopes and dreams, didn't heal on a time schedule. Catherine had compounded the problem by her indiscretion with Jeff, especially in light of her grandmother's vicious slander.

Minutes passed. Catherine was beginning to wonder if even the good offices of the older nun were inadequate to bring Kelsey to face her own mother.

Then the door opened.

Catherine was shocked at Kelsey's appearance. Dark brown smudges hollowed her amber eyes. The corners of her mouth were drawn down, and the air of hopelessness in her stiff posture made Catherine's heart ache. She ran up to her daughter and hugged her, but Kelsey was unresponsive.

What have I done? Catherine cried to herself. *Dear God, what have I done?*

"Sister Cornella insisted I see you."

"Oh, honey. Please sit down." Catherine waved to the chair she had vacated and took the one the older nun had used. "I know you are very angry with me, and you have every right to be. But I'm not here to make excuses or to beg for your forgiveness. That's something I'll have to earn, and frankly, I'm not sure I ever will."

"Why are you here?" Kelsey asked.

"To tell you something and to ask you something in return."

Kelsey remained silent.

"My story starts before you were born," she said. "Before your father and I were even engaged."

She recounted the summer day when Jordan invited her to go boating for the first time. She told Kelsey about her initial encounter with Tyrone, about the disgust she felt for herself that day and the days that followed. About the terror that surged through her whenever she saw him. And above all about the unbearable fear that if she said anything she would lose Jordan.

"We weren't engaged yet. We hadn't had sex. But I knew I loved him, loved being with him, loved the feeling I got whenever I thought about him, which was all the time." She smiled ruefully at the fond memories. "He was so handsome, so smart, so much fun to be with, and he made me feel special. I knew I was safe when I was with him, safe and treasured. And then Tyrone tried to rape me."

"Why are you telling me this?" Kelsey asked.

"Because you need to know. Because I should have warned you about your uncle a long time ago."

"Did you tell Dad?"

Catherine shook her head. "I should have, but I was afraid. Afraid he might not believe me, but most of all I was ashamed. I blamed myself, thought it was my fault, that I had somehow encouraged Tyrone, sent him the wrong signals. I thought I was responsible for what he had tried to do.

"I wasn't, of course. But I was young and insecure. Suppose word got out? My parents hadn't met Jordan yet, and I knew they wouldn't approve of him. I was hoping to convince them he was a good man, but if his brother stood accused of attempting to rape me, what chance did I have of changing their minds, or anyone else's?

"So I kept quiet. I thought I had made the right decision. Ty never bothered me again. Neither of us ever mentioned the incident, at least not to each other. I had no idea he'd poisoned his parents against me, and ultimately against you. All because I kept quiet, because I wanted to protect myself. In the end I sacrificed you."

Kelsey had been listening with quiet respect. Now she became agitated. "I don't know what you're talking about."

Catherine wished she didn't have to go on, but she'd come this far. She plunged ahead.

"Ever since you told me about Bill Summers and the yellowcake in the warehouse, I've been investigating your uncle because of his close ties to Buster Rialto. As a result, I know Tyrone was up at the family compound on the Saturday you were there studying for your finals."

Kelsey shot out of her seat. "No," she snapped, her voice raised in panic.

For a moment Catherine feared Sister Cornella would storm in and end the visit, but the door remained closed.

"I have a credit card receipt showing he gassed up in Conroe that day. A witness talked to him at the convenience store there after he left you. Tyrone claimed you'd called him after you fell while hiking. On your way home on Sunday, you bought Tylenol at that same store because you were still in pain."

Catherine regarded her daughter with concern and love. "He was there, honey. There's no point in denying it. Don't try to shield him."

Kelsey started breathing through her mouth, the first stage of hyperventilating. Then she collapsed into her chair, buried her face in her hands and began weeping.

Feeling utterly helpless, Catherine knelt in front of her daughter. She clasped Kelsey by the shoulders and drew her forward into her arms. Together they rocked to and fro. Catherine didn't try to still her, didn't urge her to stop crying, or tell her everything was going to be all right. Only time would bring a kind of peace.

Gradually Kelsey's sobs receded.

"Can you tell me what happened?" her mother asked.

More pain. I'm bringing my little girl more pain.

But it was necessary if Kelsey was to come to terms with what had happened—and for Catherine to get the information she needed to hang the son of a bitch who had done this. Tyrone would pay, she vowed. She would make him pay.

"It was my fault, Mom. I shouldn't have provoked him."

Catherine bracketed her daughter's face and raised her head. "Listen to me, Kelsey. You are not responsible for what he did to you. He is. He alone. No one else. You are not to blame for what *he* did. Do you understand?"

As tears continued to stream down her face, Kelsey nodded, but Catherine knew the wounded young woman didn't believe her, no matter how much she wanted to.

"Now, tell me what happened."

Kelsey closed her eyes and took a shuddering breath. "I was studying." She opened her eyes, though they were focused on another time and place. "It was close to one o'clock. I was thinking about fixing myself a sandwich when Uncle Ty showed up. I was surprised to see him and a little annoyed. I didn't want any interruptions. That was why I'd gone there in the first place."

She sank back in the chair. Catherine sat in the other one, reached out and held Kelsey's hand to let her know she wasn't alone.

"He asked if I'd been out on the lake. I told him no, that I was busy studying. He said you used to like to go sailing, which surprised me, because I'd always had the impression you didn't care for boats."

"Now you know why."

"He said you used to go out on the family cruiser off Galveston with him. Just the two of you, and that you liked…to have sex with him there. I couldn't believe what I was hearing. It didn't make sense, but he insisted it was true. I called him a liar, then…" She stopped and hung her head.

"What happened then?" Catherine prompted.

"I did something I shouldn't have, Mom. I reached up and slapped him. I knew I shouldn't, but he made me so mad. I slapped him, and he laughed. He said he was glad to see I liked it rough, too, because that was his favorite."

Catherine clamped her jaw, as rage burned through her.

"He grabbed me and put his arms around me. I struggled to get away, but the more I did, the more he seemed to enjoy it. I didn't know what to do. Fighting him made him more aggressive, but I couldn't not fight. I was scared. I could feel him getting—" she blew out a breath "—aroused. I'd never—" She broke off and started crying again.

Catherine swept her into her arms. "I know, honey," she murmured. "I know."

"I was saving myself, Mom. For Derek. Now—"

"Shh. We'll talk about that later. Tell me what happened next."

"I tried to kick him, but he was holding me from behind. I managed to get him once in the shin, but it didn't make any difference. He dragged me into the small bedroom, to the closet and got out some leather belts I didn't even know were there. I tried to fight him, Mom. I really did, but he's so big. He bound my arms to the brass headboard. I bucked and cried. He laughed at me. Then he pulled off my pants and tied my legs…apart."

Tears spilled down her face from bloodshot eyes. "I screamed when he did it, Mom," she said, almost as if she were in a trance. "It hurt so much. I screamed as loud as I could. But there was nobody around. No one heard me. I screamed and I cried and all the time he kept laughing, said I was even better than you were."

Catherine's heart slammed against her rib cage. Everything went white as pain racked her. Hot tears burned her eyes, congested her nose, clogged her throat. In spite of her determination to be strong for her daughter, she was crying now, too. The rage inside her was so fierce, that if Tyrone had materialized at that moment, she could have killed him with her bare hands. She had listened to rape victims tell their stories before and couldn't help being moved by them, but those women had been strangers and so had the rapists. She wasn't listening to a stranger this time, but to her own flesh and blood, the child she had borne, the best part of the love she had shared with Jordan. As terrible as it sounded, she was glad he was no longer here. This would have destroyed him.

"It's over now," she assured Kelsey. "He'll never hurt you again, and I'm going to make sure he doesn't hurt anybody else."

In the course of the next hour Catherine had to walk the fine line between being a sympathetic mother trying to console an injured child, and a police investigator collecting evidence of a heinous crime. Since Tyrone went to the cabin with a different woman almost every week for rough sex, it seemed reasonable to assume that not all his partners were pleased with the way he treated them. Of thirty or forty women there had to be a few who were willing to talk. Catherine was determined to find them.

When the opportunity presented itself, Catherine steered the conversation to Derek. Kelsey insisted she could never face him again.

"You don't believe me now," Catherine said, positive and upbeat, "but you will be able to face him, and you'll be able to tell him what happened—"

"No. I couldn't."

"He loves you, Kelsey. He's been walking around in a trance since you left him. His first question when he sees me is about you, how you are, whether you're all right. He loves you, and that's why you'll be able to tell him what happened. He deserves to know. He'll be furious, of course. At Tyrone. And I have to warn you, he'll be a little angry at you, too, for not trusting him with the truth. But he'll understand, and he'll still love you. If he doesn't, then he's not the man I think he is, and he's unworthy of you."

Catherine tipped up her daughter's tear-wracked face. "You promised him he'd be the first man to make love to you. He still will be. What Tyrone did wasn't love. In a perverted way it wasn't even sex. It was a vicious exercise of power. It will take time, and it'll take a patient and loving man to help you recover from what Ty did to you, but you can still be the wife and mother you've always wanted to be."

She could see her daughter ached for what she heard to be true, but it would take weeks, maybe months of therapy for her to believe and embrace it.

"You need professional counseling, honey, and I'm going to see to it that you get the best."

She hugged her daughter and kissed her on the cheek. "Now I need to talk to Mother Superior, because we have some other issues that have to be dealt with."

As if on cue, and confirming Catherine's suspicion that Sister Cornella had been listening in the next room, the door from the hallway opened and the elder nun entered.

"I require your help, Sister," Catherine said without preamble. "My daughter needs counseling, which of course I will pay for."

She didn't want to say in front of Kelsey that she might also be in physical danger. Catherine had to take seriously Radke's warning that Rialto wouldn't accept being cornered without putting up a fight. Considering the severity of the offenses he was likely to be charged with, kidnapping wasn't out of the question.

Sister Cornella nodded. "We have a retreat house devoted to situations like this, a place where she can get spiritual and psychological help." Then, with a knowing glance to Catherine, she added, "She'll be perfectly safe there."

Catherine's parting with Kelsey a little while later was tearful for both of them, yet she left with a renewed sense of confidence that her daughter was going to come through her ordeal.

But Catherine's work was not yet done. She still had to deal with Tyrone and his family, corruption in the police department, Derek Pager and Jeff Rowan.

CHAPTER TWENTY-THREE

JEFF WAS STARTLED when he looked up from his computer screen and found Catherine walking through his office door. She strode toward him, her expression resolute, fuming.

He jumped to his feet.

She ignored his outstretched arms and plopped down in the visitor's chair. "I just saw Kelsey." She didn't have to elaborate.

"I'm sorry." He could see she had been crying, but she wasn't now.

"I need you to do something for me," she said.

"Anything."

"Kelsey told me Tyrone keeps leathers in a closet in the small bedroom at the cabin." She dug into her purse and handed him a set of keys. "These were given to Jordan and me for our use. I want you to go there and poke around. Stop by the sheriff's office in Conroe. Bud Cleveland knows me. I'll call ahead and tell him you have my authorization to search the place and remove anything you feel is appropriate. Find the leathers, Jeff. The son of a bitch strapped her down to rape her."

Jeff's chest tightened at the thought of what the

young woman must have endured. His immediate concern, however, was for her mother. "Are you all right?"

"I'm fine."

He knew she wasn't. How could she be? What she meant was she wouldn't stop or allow herself to be sidetracked.

"And Kelsey?"

"She's going away for counseling. She'll be safe."

"Good." He nodded by way of encouragement. "She'll come through this, Cate."

Her jaw quivered. "A quarter of a century on the police force and I've never wanted to hurt anyone. But I want to kill Tyrone Tanner. I want him to suffer."

"We'll get him." Jeff hoped it was true. He'd promised to locate Stuckey and failed.

"Find his playthings," she ordered. "I just hope he hasn't removed them. When you do, turn them over to the sheriff for DNA testing to determine who's handled them. I know we'll find Tyrone's DNA all over them. If we're lucky, we'll find Kelsey's, as well as some of his other victims."

"I'll leave now." He studied her. She was tough, but she was also human. He stepped around the corner of his desk and pulled her to her feet, then wrapped his arms around her. He didn't say anything, he just hugged her.

She rested her head against his shoulder. "I failed her, Jeff. I didn't mean to, but I failed to protect her."

"That's not true, and you know it." He held her at arm's length so he could gaze into her eyes. They were dry, but just barely. The desolation in them wrenched his heart. "You love her, and that love is going to help her get through this. She loves you, and that's what's going to keep you both sane. You'll see."

"I hope you're right." But she didn't sound very convinced. "Call me and let me know what you find." She slipped her hand out of his.

"I will."

"And thank you," she said.

"No need to thank me, Cate—"

She picked up the handbag she'd dropped on the desk and started for the door.

"Cate," he called out. She turned. "Can I see you tonight?"

She paused, uncertainty in her watery blue eyes. "I don't think that would be a good idea," she said, and walked out.

"I disagree," he muttered, as she disappeared from sight. But he'd made a promise, and he would keep it.

ONCE OUTSIDE CITY LIMITS, the drive to the lake was a clear shot, and Jeff was able to make up for the time he had lost in Houston traffic. Forty-five minutes later he pulled into the parking lot beside the sheriff's department in Conroe.

The office was quiet. Not much happened on a midweek afternoon. The man with the star was at a desk behind a high counter. Stocky, but fit, he had a full head of gray hair and a ready smile.

"You must be Rowan." He rose from his seat and came forward with an outstretched hand. He was taller than Jeff had realized, close to six-four. His handshake was firm. "Catherine told me what we'll be looking for."

"Did she tell you why?"

"Unfortunately, yes." Disgust tightened his mouth. "I have latex gloves and evidence bags outside. We'll take my car so there won't be any question that this is official business. Since Catherine was given a key by the family for her personal use, and we've been designated her representatives, there is no need for a search warrant."

Jeff had gone as far as the property gate the first time he'd been here. The ranch-style house was barely visible through the dense pines. He unlocked the gate, and they drove up to the bungalow on top of a wooded hill. Bud parked under the three-car carport. Off to the right was a metal outbuilding, big enough to be a workshop. He would check it out later. For now, he was more interested in the house.

The door from the carport led through a cozy kitchen to a great room. A picture window offered a magnificent view of the lake. To one side of it was a fieldstone fireplace, on the other a built-in entertainment center featuring a four-feet-wide plasma screen. It looked like *House Beautiful,* but there was something about the place that made Jeff's skin crawl.

Bud rubbed his hands along his upper arms, as if he were cold, yet the room was stifling, since the air-conditioning wasn't on. "I don't like the feel of this place."

"I thought it was just me," Jeff said.

Some experienced cops claimed they could feel evil at crime scenes. Jeff had encountered the sensation on a few occasions. This was one of them. That Bud reacted the same way was reassuring—and unnerving.

Across the room, a hallway gave access to a master suite and two smaller bedrooms that shared a bath. Following Catherine's directions he went to the bedroom on the right, the one Kelsey said she'd been dragged into. The room was very feminine, almost childlike, with lace curtains, a frilly floral spread on the shiny brass bed and delicate gold-on-white furniture.

"Kelsey told her mother," Jeff said, "that her uncle reached into the closet and removed some leather straps."

He walked to the far side of the room and slid open a pocket door. The storage area behind it was long and shallow. A few metal hangers hung from the clothes bar, and a pair of flip-flops sat on the shoe shelf just above the floor. Otherwise the closet appeared to be empty.

Jeff stepped inside and scanned from right to left. Nothing. He was turning around when he realized there was a shelf over the door. Much too high for an average-sized person to use. But Tyrone was exceptionally tall. It wouldn't be inconvenient for him.

Jeff dragged over a chair, stood on it and, with his gloved hands, reached up and felt something in back. He pulled out leather belts with buckled loops at both ends. His stomach did a sickening somersault.

"Brazen," Bud said a minute later, as they stuffed them into paper evidence bags and labeled them. "Leaving them here for anyone to find…I guess he thought no one ever would."

"If they did," Jeff said, "he'd claim utter mystification about what they were, maybe suggest vandals were breaking in and using the place for orgies."

"Let's check out the rest of the house," the sheriff said. "No telling what else we'll find."

But they uncovered nothing.

"How about the linens?" Jeff asked.

"In the year since Kelsey was here, I'm sure they've been laundered several times," Bud observed.

"But Tyrone and his girlfriends have been here since then," Jeff pointed out. "It won't hurt to be thorough."

The sheriff fetched several collapsed cardboard boxes from the back of his vehicle. They filled them with all the bed linens they could find, labeling each with where they had been found.

Jeff locked up; the lawman hung yellow crime-scene tape across the doors and windows.

Jeff walked over to the outbuilding and punched in Catherine's number on his cell phone. It rang four times before she answered.

"We found them," he said. "Right where Kelsey said they would be."

He heard a groan on the other end.

"We've also taken the bed linens."

"I should have thought of that. Good."

"What about the metal building?"

"That's where they used to store the lake boat," she said, "but they sold it years ago. Just junk there now. Did you find anything in it?"

"It's locked."

"Hmm. Didn't used to be, but then I haven't been up there in a couple of years."

"It has a combination lock. Do you know the number?"

"No idea."

"What do you want us to do?"

"Cut it off."

She sounded as if she was about to say something else. When she didn't, he said, "I'll see you in a few hours."

After a brief pause, she disconnected.

"Have you got bolt cutters in the trunk?" Jeff asked the sheriff.

"You bet."

THERE WAS NO public announcement that the chief of police had obtained a court order for the exhumation of the body of Jordan Tanner, but Catherine wasn't surprised when she received an irate telephone call from Marcus, protesting the desecration of his son's remains.

"I have reason to believe Jordan was murdered."

"Murdered?" Hesitation. "That's ridiculous. He died of a heart attack."

"Jordan was an experienced athlete in perfect health, who dropped dead at the age of forty-seven. Don't you care that he might have met with foul play?"

"How dare you question my love for my children. He was my son, my firstborn."

"And he loved you, in spite of the way you disappointed him."

She heard a sharply indrawn breath at the other end of the line. Marcus Tanner wasn't used to being talked back to.

"Why are you doing this?" he snarled.

Annette appeared in her doorway. "Chief, you have a call from Jeff Rowan. He says it's urgent."

Apprehension whipped down Catherine's spine.

"On line two," Annette said.

"I'll call you back, Marcus." She cut him off and stabbed the button for the blinking outside line. "Jeff?"

"Better call the feds, Cate. We just found twenty barrels of yellowcake in the boathouse."

THE NEXT FIVE HOURS WERE as chaotic as any Catherine had ever experienced. She had just called the federal authorities and relayed Jeff's message, giving them detailed instructions on how to get to the Tanner compound, when her task force team chief called from the wharf on the Ship Channel.

"You won't believe what we just found," Lt. Mei Lu Ling said, in her usual businesslike manner.

"It isn't yellowcake."

"No, but how about twenty-five crates of assault rifles, hand grenades and shoulder-launched antiaircraft missiles, all marked as oil-drilling supplies, bound for the Middle East?"

"Have you notified anyone yet?" Catherine asked.

"No, I wanted to call you first."

"Good. Have you secured the area?"

"For now. The place is deserted. We have all the doors guarded, but if anyone shows up in numbers we'll need help."

"Backup's on its way. In the meantime, take whatever steps you deem necessary, including the use of deadly force to protect the site until the feds get there. I promise you they won't be long."

"Will do," the lieutenant said, then added, "Sorry it wasn't the uranium you're looking for."

Catherine chuckled. "That's quite all right." She could picture the quizzical expression on the face of her protégée. "Keep me posted as things develop."

She broke the connection and immediately dialed her contact at the FBI. Her pulse was thrumming with excitement. Finding terrorists' weapons at one of Rialto's warehouses established sufficient cause for a warrant to search all of his properties and to confiscate his business and personal records.

Two hours later, the results of fingerprint checks on both the illegal weapons and the yellowcake barrels had come in. Among the confirmed matches were those of Calvin Griggs, Tyrone's racquetball partner, and Eddie Fontanero. An hour later Griggs remained at large, but the police sergeant was picked up at the airport, getting ready to board a plane to Mexico City. Catherine was hanging up the phone, when she saw Jeff standing in her doorway, a satisfied smile on his face.

"The feds are tripping all over themselves at Conroe," he said.

"Any idea how long the barrels had been there?" she asked.

"The sheriff found several people in town who saw a moving van driving up to the compound a week ago. They figured the Tanners were getting new furniture. Since the property is secluded, no one saw what was unloaded. Your announcement that the feds were searching for the missing uranium must have panicked the bad guys. What better place to hide the stuff than under the nose of the chief of police."

"There's something I have to do before the feds close

in down here." She picked up the phone and dialed a number by heart.

"Marcus, this is Catherine. I'll be over within the hour. I want Tyrone and Melissa there when I arrive...I'm not asking you, Marcus. I'm telling you. If they're not there, I'll issue an all-points-bulletin and have them arrested wherever we find them, in public or private.... Yes, you have every right to get your lawyer and impede me any way you can, but I strongly advise you to hear me out first. You're not going to like what I have to say or do, but I'm willing to handle this as discreetly as I can. Fight me and you'll lose."

She listened for a moment, then said, "I'm also grateful Jordan isn't here. Within an hour." She hung up and fell back against the leather of her chair. To Jeff she asked, "Would you be willing to do me one more favor?"

"Name it."

"Come with me to the Tanners. You won't have to say a word. Just be there."

"I'll go through the fires of hell for you, Cate. Don't you know that yet?"

"The fires of hell," she repeated and forced a thin smile. "This may come pretty close."

CHAPTER TWENTY-FOUR

CATHERINE PRESSED the button on the brick pillar. Before she had a chance to identify herself, the gates of the Tanner estate swung open. She proceeded up the driveway. The house became visible after the first bend in the road. Even in the dark Jeff could see it was an imposing mansion, the kind that bespoke old money and refined tastes. Lights blazed on the lower floor. Exiting his side of the car, Jeff peered up at the dormers. They were dark and forbidding against the star-studded sky.

Catherine said nothing as three police cars pulled up behind her, their light bars turned off. While the occupants got out and dispersed around the house, Jeff followed her to the front door. It opened before she had a chance to reach for the bell.

"Good evening, Mrs. Tanner," said a short, compact black woman in a maid's uniform. "The family is waiting for you in the study."

"I'm sorry to keep you up so late, Ophelia. This is Mr. Rowan."

"Good evening, sir." She turned back to Catherine. "Please come this way."

Jeff had no doubt Catherine could have found the

study by herself, but this formality established distance, made it clear she wasn't a guest but an intruder.

The large room to which they were brought reminded Jeff of a set from a 1940s movie. The ceiling was high and crossed with dark wooden beams. Bookcases covered one wall. The carpet on the shiny parquet floor was rich and oriental. The oversized and overstuffed furniture also harked back to another era. Floor and table lamps provided the only sources of light, giving the chamber an almost Gothic atmosphere.

A man sat behind the massive, deeply carved desk in front of a row of French windows. Marcus Tanner was a large, broad-shouldered man with mocha-toned skin that, even in this artificial light, suggested he didn't spend enough time in the sun. His dark eyes were piercing, his white hair short-cropped. He was a distinguished-looking man with a hard mouth and large hands, which he kept folded on the oxblood leather desktop. He didn't rise when Catherine entered the room.

Sitting beside the desk in a brocade upholstered armchair, facing the room was a small, birdlike woman, whom Jeff assumed to be Amanda, Marcus's wife of fifty years. Her hostile stare matched her husband's.

To her left Tyrone lounged in a leather wingback, his long legs crossed. His wife, Melissa, rose nervously from the couch across from him, came forward and pressed her cheek to Catherine's. The young man who'd been sitting next to her also approached.

"Aunt Catherine," he mumbled, and kissed her on the cheek.

Like his father and grandfather, he was tall, lean and

square-shouldered. He shared their features, too, but there was a gentleness in his eyes that contrasted with the older men's.

"Dante, I didn't expect to see you here."

"I wanted to be," he said. "Did you find out who killed Uncle Jordan?"

"Yes," she told him, her reply filled with regret.

He bit his lip, resumed the seat next to his mother and took her hand.

"Who is this man?" Marcus demanded of Catherine.

"The private investigator I hired to look into Jordan's death. His name is Jeff Rowan."

"The disgraced cop." The old man huffed with disdain.

"And your lover," Tyrone added.

Catherine refused to be riled. "Would you bring me that chair?" she asked Jeff, while pointing to an armchair by the doorway through which they'd entered.

He set it in the middle of the room, facing the desk, far enough back that she could take in the others with a turn of her head. He settled into the other one against the wall.

"I have several announcements to make," Catherine began. "First, I received the pathologist's report late this afternoon. A second autopsy has confirmed that Jordan did not die of a heart attack as originally reported. He was poisoned with cyanide."

Amanda sucked in an audible breath. Catherine saw Melissa stiffen. The men remained less demonstrative, but she could see Marcus's eyes soften. Tyrone remained unmoved. Dante clasped his mother's hand more tightly.

"How?" Melissa asked in a small voice.

"His Gatorade bottle was contaminated."

"Can you prove that?" Tyrone asked.

"We have a witness who saw him drinking from his bottle just before he went into convulsions and died." She didn't mention that the witness was dead.

She stared at her brother-in-law. "I find it interesting that you don't seem troubled by the fact that he was murdered. You're only interested in whether we can prove it. Why is that?"

When he failed to reply, she asked, "Could it be that you already knew he'd been murdered, that you had foreknowledge of it, that you could have prevented it but chose not to?"

"That's preposterous," he said.

"Are you accusing my son of being an accessory to murder?" Marcus asked.

"I haven't made any accusations. Yet. Did you know your son was murdered?"

He drew back. "Of course not. The coroner said he died of a heart attack."

"And of course you didn't question that."

He started to object, but she went on, cutting him off.

"My second announcement is that we have recovered the yellowcake that was missing from the warehouse owned by Buster Rialto. Anyone care to speculate where it was found?"

This time Tyrone did react, staring at her openmouthed.

"I see you know," she said to him.

"What…what are you talking about?"

She had never heard him stammer before. Even his mother glanced at him in surprise.

Catherine addressed Marcus. "It was found today in the boathouse at the family compound at Lake Conroe."

"What?" the old man and his wife said together.

"Who discovered it?" Tyrone demanded.

"I did," Jeff said from behind Catherine.

"What the hell were you doing there? That's private property."

"I sent him," Catherine said.

Marcus glowered at her. "I think you had better explain. What would yellowcake be doing in our boathouse?"

"You had no right to search our property," Amanda blurted, her words angry, haughty, but also apprehensive.

"I had a key, which you provided. That gave me the legal right. At my request, Sheriff Cleveland also participated in the search. It was all done by the book."

"Why would you be looking for this…yellowcake up there?" Melissa asked.

"We weren't. We were looking for something else."

"What?"

Catherine paused. She wished it hadn't been Melissa who had asked the question, but it had to be answered.

"The leather straps Tyrone used when he tied Kelsey to the bed in the small bedroom and raped her."

The room exploded. Tyrone, Melissa and Dante jumped to their feet. Everyone was talking at once, except Marcus.

"Sit down. All of you," he finally bellowed. When they'd complied, he addressed his daughter-in-law, in a voice brittle with rage.

"I have powerful friends in this state. You won't be

police chief much longer. I'll take you to court and see to it you pay for this outrageous slander."

"How dare you," Amanda sputtered. She was wringing a lace handkerchief to the point of shredding it. "This is disgraceful."

"You're finished," Tyrone said in a menacing voice.

Catherine's attention, however, was on Melissa. She said nothing, just stared with hurt eyes at the man she had been sleeping with for over twenty years. Tears trickled down her face.

Catherine had let in the whirlwind. Now she had to contain it. She held up her hands for silence.

"You won't get away with this," Tyrone shouted.

Catherine ignored him. "For years I wondered why you hated me," she said to his parents. "From the very beginning, you rejected me without a word of explanation. You even extended that coldness, that hostility to your own granddaughter, though Kelsey has never done anything to deserve it."

She crossed her hands in front of her. "I have to admit that for some time I thought you might be prejudiced against me. Jordan and I certainly felt various levels of social ostracism over the years, but it didn't take me long to realize that you're race conscious, not racists."

Amanda's lips tightened into a thin line. This was a subject they didn't talk about, a taboo each side seemed to respect.

"Last week Kelsey came here to protest the treatment I was receiving in the *Sentinel*." She turned to Amanda. "You told her something you didn't have the guts to say to my face, that you considered me a slut because I supposedly tried to seduce Tyrone when I was dating Jordan."

"You did," Tyrone insisted.

Catherine peered at him, shook her head with disgust and again addressed the older couple. "While Jordan and I were dating, before we became engaged, Ty came to my apartment to pick me up for my first cruise on your boat. You had a thirty-five-footer back then."

Marcus barely nodded.

"Ty tried to force himself on me. The only way I was able to save myself from being raped was by connecting my knee with his private parts."

"That's a damn lie," Tyrone shouted and sprang once more to his feet. "You came on to me, but I refused to participate."

She ignored his clenched fists, aware that Jeff was now standing behind her, protecting her. "Afterward," she continued, "he apologized and kept his distance, so I didn't tell Jordan what had happened. I didn't realize Ty had lied to you about it and poisoned your mind against me."

"This is sick," Tyrone said with a snarl and flopped down into the chair. Folding his arms, he glowered at her.

"What I find curious," Catherine said to Marcus and Amanda, "is that neither of you spoke to Jordan about it. I know that, because if you had, he would have told me, and he would have confronted his brother. Instead you let him marry a woman you had reason to believe was a sexual predator. Why?"

"Tyrone didn't tell me until after you were married," Amanda muttered. "By then it was too late."

Catherine wasn't sure she bought it. The strain between them had existed before then. Either way, the subject wasn't worth pursuing.

"The point of all this," she said, "is that Ty had demonstrated all those years ago that he was capable of aggressive sexual behavior. That he backed off me was due only to the fact that I was successful in fighting him. I made the mistake of assuming he had learned his lesson, a mistake I will regret for the rest of my life."

"I don't rape women," Tyrone declared in self-righteous indignation.

"That's not true, and I can prove it," Catherine countered with more heat than she had intended.

"You're bluffing," he said with contempt and stormed over to the wet bar on the other side of the room. Catherine didn't bother turning to watch him. With Jeff there, she felt safe from attack, though without his presence she wasn't sure she would have been.

"What kind of proof?" Marcus demanded.

"Kelsey told me Ty came to the cabin the weekend she was trying to study for her final exams. He overpowered her and grabbed some straps from inside a closet, straps she hadn't noticed, because they were in the back of a high shelf most people don't even bother with. He used them to tie her down on the bed while he raped her."

"This is nothing but a pack of lies," Tyrone fumed.

"I sent Mr. Rowan and the sheriff to search that room today," Catherine went on. "They found the leather straps exactly where she said they would be. They have buckles on both ends."

"I don't know a damn thing about any straps, leather or otherwise, in closets up there."

"I'm sure the DNA testing they're undergoing right now will prove you a liar. I suspect they will also show you used them on other victims."

His eyes went wide as he glared at her, but the bravado was slipping. He had the look of a scared rat.

"Ty, how could you?" Melissa cried out.

"I didn't," he insisted.

"In your arrogance, you've been careless," Catherine told him. "When Mr. Rowan was talking to the operator of the convenience store in Conroe he learned you were up there last Wednesday."

"Rowan's making that up," Tyrone insisted. "Probably bribing the woman to say she saw me there."

His hand shook as he poured himself another drink.

"I didn't say the clerk was a woman," Catherine said. "We're subpoenaing your cell phone and credit card records. I'm sure they'll show you were there that day."

Amanda groaned, slumped in her chair and covered her face.

"It's all lies." But Tyrone was beginning to sweat.

"Mr. Rowan and the sheriff checked the hamper in the laundry room at the cabin. He found sheets that had not yet been washed. I'm pretty sure we'll recover both your DNA and that of the woman you took there with you last Wednesday."

"What's last Wednesday got to do with any of this?" Melissa asked.

"He takes a different woman up there every Wednesday afternoon for kinky sex."

"Oh, God." Melissa stared at her husband.

"Shut up," he snarled at her.

"You disgust me. All these years—"

Dante put his arm around his mother's shoulders and held her.

"Just shut up, Melly. Shut the hell up."

"Don't talk to her that way," his son shouted at him. "You're the one who was supposed to die. Not Uncle Jordan. The poison was for you."

CHAPTER TWENTY-FIVE

THE ROOM WENT SILENT as everyone stared at the young man.

"What do you mean, Dante?" Catherine asked as dread shivered through her.

He separated himself from his mother and sat up straight. "I knew all about Dad's women." He gazed at Melissa. "You always defended him, said he was work-ing late or was out of town, but I heard you crying at night. I knew what he was really doing."

"How did you know?" Catherine asked.

"Because I followed him one day when he took a girl up to the lake."

"Oh, honey." Melissa reached over and placed her hand on his cheek. "You shouldn't have done that."

"I wanted to kill him, Mom," Dante said, "for the way he was treating you."

"What happened that day at the health club?" Cath-erine asked.

"I'd taken some cyanide from one of the chemistry labs at school and had been carrying it around for a while, trying to work up the courage to use it. I knew Dad and Uncle Jordan went running on Wednesdays, but I didn't want Uncle Jordan to be around when Dad died. Then, that day Dad decided to play racquetball instead, so I figured it was time to do it. I poured it into his Gatorade bottle in the locker room while he was changing. He was alone, so I was sure no one else would pick it up by mistake."

He stared down at his hands. "What I didn't know was that on his way out to the running trail Uncle Jordan stopped by the racquetball court to talk to Dad. He must have picked up the wrong bottle when he left. Half an hour later I went by the racquetball court and saw Dad finish up the drink and toss the empty bottle away. He was joking around with one of the women on the next court."

Dante stared at his father with hate-filled eyes, drew air into his lungs, let it out and continued.

"I was terrified. I ran after Uncle Jordan, praying he hadn't touched his Gatorade, or that he hadn't drunk enough to hurt him. But I was too late. He was on the ground. Some guy was bent over him, shaking him. Then the guy raced off. I couldn't tell if he was just scared, or if he was going for help. I ran up to Uncle Jordan, but he was already dead." Dante's voice dropped to a near whisper. "He wasn't breathing. I checked his pulse, his eyes."

The young man wrung his hands and flexed his jaw.

"I didn't know what to do. I'd killed the one man I admired most." His voice broke, and he bit his lips trying to regain composure. "I looked around for the bottle. I was hoping there was still something in it. I wanted to die, too. I found it under a shrub, but it was empty. I sat there for a while, begging Uncle Jordan to forgive me. Then I heard people coming, so I grabbed the bottle and ran."

"What did you do with it?" Catherine asked.

He gazed blindly at her, as if the question didn't register. Then he seemed to realize why she was asking.

"It's gone," he said. "I brought it back to the club and washed it over and over in the janitor's sink, then crushed it so no one could use it again and tossed it in a trash can. I was just finishing when people started shouting that Uncle Jordan had collapsed and was being taken to a hospital. For a minute I prayed I'd been wrong, that he hadn't really been dead, that the doctors would be able to save his life."

The room fell silent again until Tyrone finally broke in. "You wanted to kill me?" His eyes were cold and hard, but his voice was filled with incredulity and fear.

Dante glared at him. "I hate you. If it wasn't for you Uncle Jordan would still be alive."

Catherine intercepted the violence she could feel building between the two men by asking Tyrone a question. "What did Rialto want when he called you that morning?"

He regarded her with a blank expression.

"Right after his meeting with Jordan in the mayor's office," Catherine elaborated, "he called you on your cell phone. What did he want?"

Tyrone's eyes flew back to his son, then resettled on Catherine. "He said Jordan had turned down his request to quash the uranium story and asked me if I would talk to him."

"What did you say?"

"That I would, but I didn't think it would do any good. Once Jordan made up his mind about something, he didn't change it, certainly not for me."

"Rialto called Griggs, too. What about?"

Tyrone shook his head. "I don't know, except that it had something to do with a job Cal had already done for Buster. Cal said everything had been taken care of."

Catherine realized she'd been wrong in assuming the calls were connected to Jordan's death. She wished now they had been. Knowing her nineteen-year-old nephew was a murderer was almost as painful as the death he had caused. She couldn't directly blame Tyrone for his brother's death, not under the law, but morally he had the lives of Jordan and Harvey Stuckey to answer for.

"You don't know what he was referring to?" she asked.

"No, and I didn't care." He kept staring at his son, transfixed by the depth of the hatred he saw there. This man who had been pampered by his parents, forgiven so many times by his wife, respected by friends and strangers, and fawned over by women was at last the subject of a loathing so deep it had provoked murder.

"Why did you let Rialto use the compound at Conroe?"

He seemed more annoyed than intimidated by the question. "He'd moved as much of the yellowcake as he could to the Ship Channel before the Superfund came in. He was trying to sell it, but twice the deal fell through because the buyers couldn't come up with the million dollars in cash he was demanding. When you announced you were looking for the missing uranium, he knew it wouldn't be long before his other warehouses were searched. He needed to hide it in a place nobody would think of looking."

Marcus made a growling sound, but said nothing. His son would have shrunk from the old man's glare, had he had the courage to meet his father's eyes.

"So you knew what he wanted to store at the boathouse? Why did you let him?"

"I had no choice. He threatened to go to Pop with my gambling debts if I didn't."

Marcus hung his head, then raised it. "You let that man store terrorist weapons of mass destruction on our property?" he asked his son. "You were willing to commit treason over gambling debts?"

"He also had a list of all the women I'd taken up there."

The old man squeezed his eyes shut. When he reopened them, they were glassy. He focused not on his son but on Catherine.

"I won't ask you to forgive me for what I have done to you and your daughter…our granddaughter." Amanda sniffled at his side. "My failings, my blindness and vanity don't deserve pardon. But I do want you to know that I am sorry for failing you and the rest of the family. I take full responsibility for what this man—he is no longer my son—has done. Had I been a good father we would never have reached this point, Jordan would still be alive, Kelsey would be unharmed and my grandson would have a bright, healthy future ahead of him."

Amanda stretched her hand across the desktop. He took it and swallowed it in his own.

As the two clung to each other, Catherine felt her animosity for them dissipate. They alone had created the hell they would have to live with for the rest of their lives. Nothing she did or said could add to or alleviate their suffering. She could have loved them once, if only for Jordan's sake, and maybe in a way, she did even now.

Melissa had moved closer to Dante and was clinging to him, as if she could shield him from what was to come. They were Tyrone's true victims. Two caring people, who would never recover from the evil of the man they had tried to love.

Catherine rose. "Tyrone Tanner, I am placing you under arrest for the rape of Kelsey Tanner—" Amanda began to sob "—and for violations of the Patriot Act—"

"The hell you are." Tyrone pulled open a drawer of the wet bar and produced a revolver. With outstretched arms, he pointed it directly at Catherine's head.

JEFF WAS ON HIS FEET, facing Tyrone and the other members of the family. Catherine's back was to him, a distinct disadvantage, since she was the one person he needed to act in concert with. Her gun was in the handbag at her feet. His was strapped to his ankle, equally inaccessible. At least for the moment.

"You're making a bad situation worse," she said, her voice calm.

The others in the room were a tableau of shock, horror and fear. Amanda, still sitting near the desk, was blinking slowly, as though unable to comprehend what was happening. Her husband was ramrod straight in his high-backed chair, his jaw working from side to side. Melissa's breathing was audible, her lips turned inward, as she stared at her husband.

Only Dante seemed unintimidated by his father's desperate move.

"The house is surrounded by police," Jeff told the man with the gun. "You won't get out of here alive."

"With her I will," he said, lowering the pistol to aim it at Catherine's chest rather than her head. A smart move, since the torso was a bigger target, easier to hit in a crisis.

Jeff wished he could make eye contact with her, signal a plan. They worked so well together.

"Dad," Dante said calmly from his father's right.

He received no response.

"Dad." The young man's tone was unconcerned, almost friendly, as if he were about to ask him for the car keys to go on a date.

"Shut up," Tyrone shouted to his son.

Melissa sucked in her breath when Dante took a step toward his father. Everyone's eyes were pinned on him.

"Stay back," Tyrone said in a tense voice, "or I'll shoot her."

Dante ignored him and moved directly into the path between his father and aunt. "You'll have to shoot me first."

"Get out of the way," Tyrone shrieked, frightened now, rather than belligerent.

Jeff watched Catherine. She was still in a difficult position. If she stepped out from behind Dante, she would make herself a target again, yet using her nephew as a shield was unacceptable.

Father and son stared at each other.

"Shoot me," Dante said. "I have nothing to live for. Shoot me. Then they'll arrest you for killing me, and I can die knowing I accomplished something positive with my life."

"Nooo," Melissa cried.

"Son," Marcus pleaded just above a whisper.

"Go on, Dad. Shoot," Dante insisted.

"Drop the gun, Ty," Catherine urged him. "Let's end this without anyone else getting hurt."

Jeff could see Tyrone was uncertain. Still, he clutched the revolver in his hand securely, unwilling to let it go. But the standoff wasn't to last.

Dante took the final step toward his father, reached out and grabbed the weapon by the barrel. Tyrone's finger tightened on the trigger. Neither man said a word. Their eyes locked, Dante twisted the gun and wrenched it from his father's hand. Lightning fast, he reversed the weapon and pointed it at his father's heart.

He was about to pull the trigger, when Catherine bolted from behind him, and in one swift motion, forced Dante's arm up. The gun went off.

Tyrone's face was a mask of stunned horror. The bullet had embedded itself in the ceiling, but not before it snipped off the tip of his left ear, confirming that his son had had every intention of killing him. In an uncharacteristic move, the big man covered his face with his hands and staggered to the couch.

Melissa dashed past him and threw her arms around her son. Dante stroked his mother's back. Dry-eyed, he assured her he was okay, and that everything was going to be all right.

Which, of course, it wasn't.

The shot had brought uniformed cops into the room, their guns drawn. Catherine kicked Tyrone's revolver under a chair where it was not accessible, then instructed her officers to holster their weapons. She ordered the arrest of Tyrone Tanner for rape and for violations of the Patriot Act. With an aching heart, she then arrested his son, Dante, for the murder of Jordan Tanner.

Melissa screamed when her son was handcuffed. She clung to him as he was being led away. Jeff restrained her while Catherine attended to formal police details.

Within a matter of minutes, the last siren had faded into the night and the stately mansion was quiet again.

With Jeff standing behind her, his hands resting on her shoulders, she addressed her in-laws.

Marcus looked defeated, wrung-out, Amanda numb.

"I'm sorry it came to this," Catherine said. "I truly am. In spite of everything, Jordan loved you both very much. I wish you could have let me love you, too."

Amanda's eyes blazed at her. "Get out," she said in a low growl. "Get out of our house."

Catherine nodded, her heart filled with sadness for these people who had closed their eyes to the wrongs they had spawned. She gazed at Melissa, who sat on the couch, her arms clutched across her slender waist. With bowed head, she rocked back and forth, sobbing inconsolably. Maybe in the months and years to come she'd be able to take some comfort in her other children. Catherine went over to the weeping woman and rested a hand on her thin shoulder. When Melissa looked up, Catherine expected to see reproach. What she found was a plea for forgiveness.

Catherine walked through the door to the hallway, then turned back one last time to behold a family destroyed.

CHAPTER TWENTY-SIX

JEFF ACCOMPANIED CATHERINE back downtown. The people on the force who had hesitated to greet him the first time he'd appeared there were eager to shake his hand and slap him on the back, now that they knew the role he'd played in bringing down Rialto and finding the missing uranium.

His former partner in homicide even suggested Jeff's firing last year had been a ruse, that the chief had had him undercover all that time. With a wink toward Catherine, Jeff skirted the issue, thereby enhancing the rumor. Perhaps the termination hadn't ruined his reputation after all.

It was nearly four o'clock in the morning by the time he and Catherine entered the parking garage adjoining the headquarters building. As they approached her Lexus, Jeff stopped short.

"What's the matter?" she asked.

"My car. It's gone."

"Where did you leave it?"

He pointed to the zebra-striped no-parking zone.

Catherine nearly doubled over laughing. "You can get it out of the impound lot tomorrow—for a price."

"I can't believe they towed it."

She kept laughing. "Come on. I'll drive you home."

By the time she had her engine started, he was laughing, too.

"Tired?" she asked, as she pulled out of the garage and turned south.

"I should be," he admitted. "But I'm not."

"Me, neither."

He gazed over at the woman behind the wheel. She was still in her professional role, the one that coped with death and disaster and kept a cool head. But this case hadn't been someone else's disaster. It had been hers. She'd invested more than half her life in the Tanner family. She bore their name. She'd offered them her loyalty and friendship, and they'd rejected both. More than that, they'd rejected her.

"Where do we go from here?" he asked.

"It's not over," she said. "Rialto will be denied bail on the terrorist charge, but that doesn't mean—"

He covered her hand on the steering wheel with his own. "I meant where do *we* go from here. You and me?"

Biting her lip, she checked her rearview mirror. "I don't know," she murmured.

He saw the beginning of a chink in her cool demeanor. She was conflicted in a way he no longer was. He'd promised to separate himself from her for Kelsey's sake, but now with the young woman getting professional help, his promise to Catherine seemed less relevant.

"I want you," he said. "I want you in my life, Cate. And I think you want me."

She drove on. "It's more than that," she acknowledged. "I need you. I shouldn't, but I do. And that scares me."

She turned off the loop onto a secondary road.

"And I need you as I've never needed another person," he said, "You complete me, Cate. You make me…feel…like I'm just waking up. I love you."

Her lips quivered, but she continued to drive in silence.

"I made a promise that I would not come between you and Kelsey," he said, "and I intend to honor it, but—"

"I made a vow, too," she said. "I'm her mother. She has to be my first responsibility. I failed her—"

"You didn't fail her, Cate. There was no way you could have foreseen what Tyrone was going to do. He'd behaved for twenty-five years—"

"But that's just the point," she argued. "He wasn't behaving. I knew he was playing around, being unfaithful—"

"And so did his wife."

"But she had no idea he was capable of rape. I did, and I kept quiet about it. I endangered other people by my silence."

"He was aggressive with you, and he deserved what he got from you. But how do you know he wouldn't have stopped on his own, that he wouldn't have pulled back at the last minute?"

She glared over at him. "You mean I should have let him rape me so I could be sure he would?"

He shook his head in frustration. "Pull over, Cate."

"What?" She tightened her grip on the steering wheel.

"Pull over. Stop the car. Turn off the engine."

Annoyed and angry, she complied.

"Look at me," he said.

She swiveled to face him, her expression one of irritation and confusion, and a little girl lost.

"Don't you see what you're doing to yourself?" he asked, a note of censure in his voice. "You've backed yourself into a no-win corner. You blame yourself for Tyrone coming on to you. You blame yourself for kicking him in the balls too early or too late. You blame yourself for not telling Jordan at the time or later. No matter what the alternative is, you insist on beating yourself up for making the wrong choice."

He reached out and ran a knuckle along the line of her jaw.

"You did exactly the right thing twenty-five years ago. You handled a tough situation with strength and wisdom. You were right not to tell Jordan. As a result you had a beautiful marriage, one that brought you happiness and made his life a joy."

A tear spilled down her cheek. Jeff gently brushed it away with his forefinger.

"What happened to Kelsey is not your fault. It's not Kelsey's fault. It's not even the fault of Ty's narrow-minded parents or his too-tolerant wife. It's the exclusive fault of Tyrone Tanner, a man who knew what was right and chose to do the opposite." He lifted her chin and softened his voice. "Stop killing yourself for it. You won't help Kelsey that way, and you'll never be happy yourself."

She lowered her gaze.

He leaned forward and kissed her on the lips. "I want you to be happy, Cate. I hope you'll let me be a part of your life. I'll be disappointed—" miserable "—if I can't be, but as long as you're happy, I will be, too, even if it has to be at a distance."

She sniffled a sigh, reached up and clasped his wrist with her hand. "I love you," she murmured.

"Then," he responded, unable to suppress the joy her words ignited, "I suggest you start this car and drive to my place. There are no ghosts there, and no one is going to walk in on us."

She chuckled, brushed back the last vagrant tear, turned the key in the ignition and was about to put the car in gear, when Jeff said, "Don't forget your seat belt."

"Oh," she said, laughing as she buckled up, "you're the one who's going to need a seat belt tonight."

EPILOGUE

Three months later

"I OFFER A TOAST TO OUR CHIEF," Mei Lu sang out to the room full of women.

Catherine was standing in front of the picture window in her living room, feeling thoroughly and delightedly embarrassed. She tried to wave away the attention.

"Hey, it isn't every day the President of the United States personally bestows a medal on a cop," Crista reminded her.

"Especially a female cop," Lucy added.

"To Catherine," Risa said. "Who brought us all together again."

While everyone drank, Catherine considered the five women gathered around her. They'd graduated from the same police academy class six years ago. United, out to conquer the world, or at least the streets of Houston. Then Risa Taylor was accused of killing her partner and the spirit of sorority they'd enjoyed had evaporated.

If this recent operation had accomplished nothing but reuniting them, Catherine would have been content. Instead it had done so much more.

She'd arrested her husband's murderer, put her daughter on the road to recovery from the worst possible trauma, uncovered an international band of terrorists, and found love in a most unlikely man.

"I couldn't have done any of it without the help and support of each of you," she said. "Thank you for being my friends." If she didn't watch out she'd start blubbering. She drank a toast to them, and settled into her favorite chair between the couches.

"This whole turn of events has been incredible, bizarre," Abby Carlton said. "I know what the newspapers and media in North Carolina have been saying, but what have they been leaving out?"

Crista laughed and snagged a cheese-filled mushroom cap from the platter on the coffee table. "All I know is that once Rialto realized he was cornered, the rat, he sang like a bird to save his sorry hide. Is that a mixed metaphor?"

"Who cares?" Lucy dipped a corn chip into salsa and sprawled out on the couch.

Everyone was relaxed and that made Catherine feel good. It had been too long since they'd all been together, too long since she could just unwind with good friends.

"The names Rialto gave us cascaded into a list of contacts and operatives in a network of terrorists that span four continents," she said.

"Wow," Abby exclaimed. "I didn't know it was that widespread."

"Thus far," Risa noted, "more than a hundred Al Qaeda terrorist-cell leaders have been apprehended in Europe and the U.S."

"They've also confiscated large caches of illegal weapons, explosives and chemical agents," Mei Lu added.

Abby smiled at Catherine in admiration. "No wonder the president wanted to give you that medal personally."

The object in question was displayed on top of the piano on a satin pillow she'd pinched from Kelsey's old room.

"What about the M.E.?" Abby asked. "Was he involved?"

Catherine shook her head. "Cliburne Vale didn't have a clue. Poor guy was in over his head. The Peter Principle at work—promoted to his level of incompetence. One of the guys in his office was on Rialto's payroll. He resigned last week."

"And William Summers? Did you ever figure out what happened to him?"

Catherine nodded. "Eddie Fontanero visited him on Rialto's orders, forced him to climb the ladder, then pushed him off the roof. It was just bad luck that the old guy didn't die instantly."

The room went silent for a moment.

"How's your nephew?" Crista asked, before popping a chocolate-dipped strawberry into her mouth.

"His grandfather is assembling a dream team to represent him in court. When I spoke to Dante a few days ago, though, he was still adamant about pleading guilty."

Crista touched Catherine's hand. "I'm so sorry."

"I am, too. I talked to the D.A. yesterday. He's willing to lower the charges to manslaughter. With luck and good behavior, Dante could be out of prison in seven to ten years."

"Are you all right with that?" Abby asked. "After all, he did kill your husband."

Catherine nodded. "And he'll have to live with that for the rest of his life." She took a sip of wine. "For someone with a conscience that can be worse than a death sentence. The real villain is his father. I suppose I should take some consolation in knowing Tyrone will never see the outside of a prison again."

Eager to change the conversation to a more pleasant subject, she turned to Abby. "I understand you and Thomas want to come back here after he retires in a few years."

"I'm not so sure now." The former cop sipped her juice. "Those mountains and forests back East are awfully alluring."

"How far along are you?" Mei Lu asked.

Abby rubbed her belly. "Four more months. I can't wait."

Catherine chuckled, remembering with fondness the joy of young motherhood. "Remember that at your 2:00 a.m. feedings. You've been given a miraculous gift. Safeguard it with every ounce of your energy."

"Speaking of kids," Risa said, "how are Kelsey and her boyfriend getting on?"

The night of Tyrone's arrest, Catherine had taken Derek aside and explained to him what Tyrone had done. Tears spilled down his cheeks, then he flew into a rage. Finally he reined himself in and focused exclusively on Kelsey's well-being. It was then Catherine knew he was the man she'd thought he was, and that Kelsey was in safe hands.

"She's still in therapy. Probably will be for some time, but she's making progress."

The morning after Dante's arrest, Catherine had phoned her. They'd cried over her cousin's guilt. She'd also relayed Derek's request to see her. Kelsey had been hesitant, but a week later they'd visited in the garden of her retreat house in Louisiana. Kelsey had called her mother that evening to tell her Derek still loved her and wanted to marry her. They'd both cried again.

"Is she still in the convent?" Crista asked.

"For now, but I have a feeling that may change."

They continued to munch on finger foods while she got up and refilled the champagne glasses.

"I'm glad they finally cleared Jeff Rowan," Risa said, "and restored his good name." Having been a pariah, she understood better than the others what he had experienced.

Catherine smiled. Throughout the entire ordeal he'd been there. A friend. An advisor. A lover to cuddle her in the still moments of the night when doubts and demons haunted her, when what she needed most was to be held.

"At the reception for the president, Grady told me Jeff was offered his old job in homicide," Lucy said. "Is he going to take it?"

"He chose early retirement instead," Catherine explained. "He's doing well as a P.I., and he enjoys the independence it gives him."

Mei Lu had a gleam in her eye. "And if the two of you get married, his being in your chain of command could raise questions of conflict of interest."

The other women gaped at the chief with twinkling eyes.

"Has he asked you to marry him?" Crista asked.

"We've talked about it," Catherine admitted, "but he agrees with me that we shouldn't do anything until we know Kelsey is all right with it."

Jeff had promised to wait—a lifetime, if necessary. Catherine hoped it wouldn't take quite that long. Her daughter would never be the same innocent she had been before her uncle raped her, but Jeff was right. She was strong, and she would come out of this horrible experience stronger, especially with Derek by her side.

The front door burst open to the sound of boisterous male voices.

"I hope you're better in the Army than you are on the golf course—" Jeff razzed.

"If it hadn't been for that sudden gust of wind—" another man said.

"Are you kidding? That wind sheer is what saved your butt," a third party chimed in.

"That slice of yours was headed for the hole behind you," Jeff noted.

"No appreciation of finesse."

"You boys have a good time?" Catherine asked, as the men slipped into the living room.

Jeff gave her a kiss on the cheek. "We're taking you all out to dinner."

"Are you asking us or telling us?" Catherine winked at the other women.

"We're inviting you, sweetheart," he told her.

"In that case, we accept."

"Aren't you going to check with the others first?" he asked.

"No need," she explained. "We'd already decided you were taking us out."

He laughed. "I told you they'd be ahead of us."

Ten minutes later when the others had left for the restaurant, Catherine emerged from her bedroom where she'd applied fresh makeup and the cologne she wore just for Jeff. She collected her purse from the hall table and spun around to see him leaning against the door frame, his arms crossed, a smile playing on his lips. "What?"

"I just like watching you."

A warm feeling flooded through her. She walked up to him and planted a soft kiss on his lips, then ducked away when he tried to pull her into his arms. "Ready?"

His eyes gleamed. "What do you think?"

She grinned. "I think we'd better go, or we'll never make it to dinner, and after such a vigorous day on the links, you must be hungry."

"Ravenous."

Still laughing, she patted his cheek.

Ten minutes later, they arrived at the seafood and steak house. As he was escorting her to the front door, Jeff pointed to the headline on the *Houston Sentinel* displayed in a newspaper box. "City Proudly Honors Police Chief."

A happy ending of sorts, but one that was bittersweet.

She loved the man holding her hand, loved him in a way she couldn't have imagined six months ago. She would never forget Jordan, nor did she want to. He'd given her a child, nearly twenty-five years of happiness and much, much more. He'd given her the strength to go on without him.

And Jeff? He made her feel things she thought she'd lost forever, made her want things she still wasn't sure she deserved. He didn't just satisfy needs, he filled her with a sense of power and joy.

As he opened the door and allowed her to pass in front of him, she made a vow. She'd do her best to make him happy, to be worthy of the gift of love he'd given her.

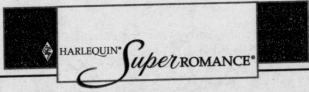

If you enjoyed what you just read,
then we've got an offer you can't resist!

Take 2 bestselling
love stories FREE!

Plus get a FREE surprise gift!

Clip this page and mail it to Harlequin Reader Service®

IN U.S.A.	IN CANADA
3010 Walden Ave.	P.O. Box 609
P.O. Box 1867	Fort Erie, Ontario
Buffalo, N.Y. 14240-1867	L2A 5X3

YES! Please send me 2 free Harlequin Superromance® novels and my free surprise gift. After receiving them, if I don't wish to receive anymore, I can return the shipping statement marked cancel. If I don't cancel, I will receive 6 brand-new novels every month, before they're available in stores. In the U.S.A., bill me at the bargain price of $4.69 plus 25¢ shipping and handling per book and applicable sales tax, if any*. In Canada, bill me at the bargain price of $5.24 plus 25¢ shipping and handling per book and applicable taxes**. That's the complete price, and a savings of at least 10% off the cover prices—what a great deal! I understand that accepting the 2 free books and gift places me under no obligation ever to buy any books. I can always return a shipment and cancel at any time. Even if I never buy another book from Harlequin, the 2 free books and gift are mine to keep forever.

135 HDN DZ7W
336 HDN DZ7X

Name	(PLEASE PRINT)	
Address	Apt.#	
City	State/Prov.	Zip/Postal Code

Not valid to current Harlequin Superromance® subscribers.

Want to try two free books from another series?
Call 1-800-873-8635 or visit www.morefreebooks.com.

* Terms and prices subject to change without notice. Sales tax applicable in N.Y.
** Canadian residents will be charged applicable provincial taxes and GST.
All orders subject to approval. Offer limited to one per household.
® are registered trademarks owned and used by the trademark owner and or its licensee.

SUP04R   ©2004 Harlequin Enterprises Limited

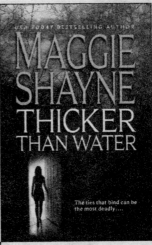

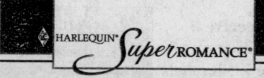